Praise for *365 Days*

"YA novel or not, *365 Days* absofreakinlutely blew me away. The writing is crisp and clever; the characters are simple yet multi-dimensional; and the storyline is fresh but familiar. Ms. Payne artfully captures the confusion and concerns of a young woman coming to terms with her lesbian libido, as well as life with her family, the inconvenience of schoolwork, morphing dynamics with friends, the torment of waiting for a text, an email, or a call, and the near-consuming fear of losing it all. I don't know how she did it, but KE Payne delivered a remarkable debut in the simple form of a teenage lesbian's diary. It's all the things I hoped it would be, and none of the things I feared. I'm giving this sweet, little gem a 5.0 out of 6 on the Rainbow Scale, and encouraging everyone to give it a read – it really is that good."—*Rainbow Reader*

"This hilarious novel consists of a series of daily diary entries by Clementine, an English teenager who's funny in the style of Adrian Mole and Georgia Nicolson. Why do the British do teen diaries so much better than Americans? I mean, I love *The Princess Diaries* as much as anyone, but Clem is just funnier than Mia….Please, KE Payne, write a sequel, would you?" —*Queer YA*

"Payne capture's Clemmie's voice—an engaging blend of teenage angst and saucy self-assurance—with full-throated style."—Richard Labonté, *Book Marks*

By the Author

365 Days

me@you.com

me@you.com

by

KE Payne

A Division of Bold Strokes Books

2012

ME@YOU.COM
© 2012 BY KE PAYNE. ALL RIGHTS RESERVED.

ISBN 13: 978-1-60282-592-5

THIS TRADE PAPERBACK ORIGINAL IS PUBLISHED BY
BOLD STROKES BOOKS, INC.
P.O. BOX 249
VALLEY FALLS, NY 12185

FIRST EDITION: JANUARY 2012

CREDITS
EDITORS: LYNDA SANDOVAL AND STACIA SEAMAN
PRODUCTION DESIGN: STACIA SEAMAN
COVER DESIGN BY SHERI (GRAPHICARTIST2020@HOTMAIL.COM)

Acknowledgments

My thanks to everyone at Bold Strokes Books for their continued help and support, especially Lynda Sandoval for her kind words, encouragement, and constant invaluable advice.

I'm also grateful to Chris for enlightening me on what "bat-shit crazy" means (who knew?!) and to my "CC friends" for their constant interest and enthusiasm in what I do.

Thanks to my family for always supporting me, and last but not least, to BJ for always having the knack of saying just the right things to me at the right time. Thank you.

To anyone who's ever been misled…

CHAPTER ONE

I don't know what it was that made me log onto the website that first time. Boredom? No, not boredom. An unknown curiosity, maybe? A curiosity, yes, but unknown? C'mon, who was I kidding? I mean, why else would I have gone out of my way to search for a website about a popular TV programme that absolutely fascinated me and where the two central characters just happened to be gay?

I'd been hooked by this show, a drama kinda unimaginatively called *Lovers and Sinners*, and I mean proper hooked. From the moment I'd seen the trailer for it, squeezed innocuously in between a wildlife documentary and the news, I'd known I had to watch it. Something about it, about the two female lead characters—Jess and Ali—was mesmerising. They were both gorgeous, and, I dunno, the fact they played a gay couple in it just seemed to pique my interest even more. It added an extra verve to it, and as much as I kept denying it to myself, I eventually had to admit that I had a walloping great big crush on the pair of them, and from what I'd read on the Internet and in the press, half of the country did too. It was that popular a programme, the type that everyone talked about the night after it aired, the type that everyone discussed who they fancied on it and what they thought should happen to their particular favourite characters each week.

So after I'd found myself at a loose end one evening before dinner and after I'd bored of Facebook and Twitter, I decided to Google *Lovers and Sinners*. The programme's official website had a message board attached to it, this kinda open forum thing where fans of the show could talk about it and all the characters' relationships with each other, plus a whole load of other things, like advice pages, general chat pages, stuff like that. It was brilliant! Intrigued, I'd read some of the messages on the general forum and thought the fans writing on it sounded a great bunch, so I registered my name and started posting.

The other people on the message board appealed to me. From what I read on there, they all seemed to watch it for the same reason I did. Interestingly, although there were a few stray guys posting on there, the majority of the people posting on the message board seemed to be youngish women. I was hooked right away.

I loved everything about the message board and felt right at home there from the first. The only thing I didn't particularly like was the way the other women on there all talked with such authority about what Jess and Ali were going through. Reading their messages, it was clear probably over half of them were gay, and I didn't particularly feel comfortable with some of the things they wrote, mainly because it made me feel really naïve and, well, a bit dumb.

But that was my problem, not theirs, right?

Aside from that, the message board felt like one big family, certainly to me, anyway. We were all joined in our love of the programme, our affection towards Jess and Ali, and our fascination of the story of their relationship being played out on our TV screens each week. I felt an affinity with the pair of them and really liked how their love story made me feel; I lived and breathed every argument they had, every breakup and every make-up. I felt their pain and loved their happiness, but I still told myself I had no *specific* interest in the lead women at all. All I was interested in was the story, the drama, and the unfolding sweet tale of love.

I made some good friends on the message board too. On that first night alone I'd made friends with, amongst others, a "Twiggy", a "Joey", a "Lone Star", and a "Betty Blue Rinse". Now here I was, a week after registering as one "Barnaby Rudge", slumped up in my room playing virtual karate and talking about football with one of the people on there, the first girl I'd chatted to on that first night, Twiggy, who was twenty-four and from Manchester.

Twiggy had been the first person to answer me on the message board, about ten minutes after I'd introduced myself to everyone. We'd had a bizarre first conversation about our favourite breakfast cereals and had kind of struck up a friendship based not only on the fact we both loved *Lovers and Sinners*, but that we were also nuts about football.

Our conversation, during a virtual karate match, went something like this:

He'll never get picked. Twanged his hamstring against City last week. Jab to your lower left side, Twiggy wrote.

I replied straight away. *Your move blocked*, I wrote. *But who else they got??? Milton's outta form, Bellamy couldn't score in a brothel! Coming atcha...high roundhouse kickin'.*

Ouch! That hurt!

S'meant to, stoopid! I grinned at the screen, imagining Twiggy rubbing her arm and mock grimacing.

Nah, but it means the manager'll have to play 3 up front instead. She was still banging on about the football.

A voice hollering up the stairs made me jump and swing round in my chair, stopping me in mid-type. It was Mum.

"Imogen! Tea!"

I sighed, not really wanting to leave my conversation with Twiggy, but kinda not wanting to miss my tea either. You know how it is!

GTG Twigs, 'rents calling me for tea.

Be back laters?

I looked at the yellow clock on my wall.

Dunno. Got this 2,000 word assignment to get finished for college tomorrow.

"IMOGEN! Last warning. If you're not down in five your dinner's going in the dog."

Mum again. Why did she have to shout at me like I was down the street or something?

GTG.

Wait! You on MSN? Twiggy asked me.

MSN? I pulled a face at the screen.

I had no idea what MSN was, but then I'd not heard of many things like that before I'd joined this message board. I was always shy. I was…what was it my mum called it? "A bit gauche."

I suppose I was a bit of a loner too, never making friends that easily, for whatever reason, and even though I'd had a few friends at school, a lot of us had kind of drifted apart after our final exams. A few of us went to college together, but as my friends eventually found other friends I suppose I got left behind. I had a couple of close friends at college, Beth and Emily, who I'd known since school, but I'm not really what you'd call gregarious, more happy in my own company, if not happy in my own skin—but I'll get to that later.

Yeah, MSN, dope. I could feel Twiggy's scorn coming through the screen. *You never heard of MSN Messenger?*

Nuh-uh, I typed and shook my head at no one in particular.

"Immy! Two minutes. We've already started."

"FFS!"

I looked frantically round at the door then back to the computer screen, willing Twiggy to answer—and fast.

'K, I'll add ya while you're having tea, Twiggy wrote at last. *I can find your e-mail details on your personal profile on the message board. Download MSN Messenger, then we can talk there, rather than on this shit-slow board. It's much quicker. And private. We can talk footy without the bloody Liverpool fans giving us grief!!!*

I left my PC downloading MSN Messenger and slumped down the stairs to the dining room where my mum, dad, and fifteen-year-old sister Sophie were already halfway through a plate of what looked like baby food, but which I was to find out later was actually cottage pie.

"You been on that computer again?" Dad said to me through a mouthful of mashed potato.

"For college, yeah," I lied.

Dad nodded and looked at me, fork poised en route to his mouth.

"Make sure it is for college and nothing else, understood?" he said, waving the fork at me, making a small gloop of potato fall onto the table.

"She's eighteen, for God's sake," Sophie muttered under her breath.

Dad flashed her a look.

"I've read about people on the Internet." He forked up some more potato and slotted the fork into his mouth. "Undesirables and all that," he mumbled, his mouth full of mash.

I chose to ignore his comments and instead ate my tea in silence. By the time I'd taken myself upstairs to my PC again half an hour later, Twiggy had gone, but I saw that MSN had downloaded and that she'd sent me an invitation to become one of her "buddies". I accepted. I wished she was online, though; I wanted to tell her about my dad jabbing his fork at me and telling me not to talk to any "undesirables". I wondered if Twiggy considered herself to be an undesirable…

There was just Joey online, but she seemed to be deep in conversation on the message board with someone called Totalitarian Rule about civil partnerships, which I didn't feel able to contribute towards. I checked my e-mails a few times, deleting all the junk that offered me Viagra and an enormous dick and shit like that, then drifted back to the message board again just to see who was around. I was bored; I wanted to chat to someone, and something kept drawing me towards the message board. Anything was better than that two-thousand-word essay waiting for me to finish it.

I posted a message.

Hiya, I wrote. *Anyone around?*

It was brief but asked all I needed it to ask.

I flicked screens and started Googling some stuff about the rise of Nazism for the assignment that I'd been putting off for weeks. I checked the message board again. No reply yet.

I went back to Google and made some notes, copying and pasting large chunks of text, hoping I could mould it into something resembling a half-decent, non-plagiaristic essay. After ten minutes I checked back again on the message board.

Hiya.

A reply! The message was from someone called Fickle, who I'd never spoken to before.

I typed out my reply, hoping that "Fickle" hadn't logged off.

Hey! How're you? I wrote, kinda wanting to write something else, but not knowing what.

I pressed the Refresh button once or twice, but whoever Fickle was, they'd obviously gone.

Until…

I'm good, ta. You?

And that was the start of our conversation.

We chatted for the next three hours that evening, my assignment well and truly forgotten. I immediately liked Fickle; she seemed so expressive and confident and had a wicked sense of humour that made me laugh out loud. In that first conversation alone, I found out more about her than I ever had about Twiggy, even after a whole week of chatting.

Twiggy was great, but she'd always managed to keep this barrier up when she was talking to me. Fickle was so different, so much more open and, I suppose, so much easier to talk to. I liked Fickle from the moment I first started talking to her, much more so than Twiggy. I couldn't tell you why, though, it was like something clicked with us that first night, something that clicked and then stayed.

We messaged each other again the next night too, our messages to each other slotting in between greetings and chats to other people on the message board. On the third night, rather than talking about *Lovers and Sinners*, Fickle told me some more stuff about herself. She'd already told me a few nights before that she was eighteen and lived up near Leeds with her mum. But on this night she told me that she was at college and she started telling me about the subjects she was doing—English, French, History, and Geography—and how much work she was being given now she was in her final year. I told her I was at sixth form college, doing English, History, Maths, and Economics. She liked that. She thought I was clever for taking Maths at A level, but I told her I thought she was cleverer, taking French.

I never got all the accents and stuff, I joked to her.

I never got past my two times table, Fickle replied. She added a *LMAO* and a winking-face sign. The winking sign made me feel a bit funny inside, I dunno why.

You on MSN? Fickle suddenly asked me.

Yeah, I am! I replied, trying to make it sound enthusiastic. After all, I was enthusiastic, I mean, how cool was that? So two nights ago I'd never even heard of MSN and now two people wanted to add me to it. God bless Twiggy, hey?

I gave Fickle my e-mail address and waited for her to add me.

Kewl, Fickle wrote back. *Now we can have private conversations on MSN. I'd prefer that, wouldn't you?*

I supposed I would prefer private conversations. Message boards are all okay but it's always a bit public, the things you say on there, aren't they? Everyone reading everyone else's messages. I wanted to keep some things private and I suppose if I was honest, there was a small part of me that worried that someone I knew might find out that I was posting stuff on a predominantly gay website. Private messaging would be perfect.

A message flashed up telling me that Fickle had added me to her MSN list. I accepted straight away.

I waited for Fickle to make the first move, so to speak. I felt excited at the prospect of having a private chat with her, but just as I was getting ready to talk to her on there, reality arrived to bite me well and truly on the bum with a text from Matt.

That would be the Matt who was my boyfriend, or was supposed to be.

Matt. We'd met at college through another girl in my class, a girl called Lyndsay who'd gone out with him before me and who said he would be perfect for me. Part of me questioned, if he was so perfect, then why wasn't she still going out with him? But never mind. Me and Matt had been dating for around six weeks, driving my two friends, Emily and Beth, insane with jealousy, but, I don't know, nothing was really happening for me with him. Still, I went out with him, more out of habit I suppose, and I was due to meet him later.

Still on for tonight? his text said.

I stared at it, then back up at the screen. I saw that Fickle had messaged me and now here it was, flashing irritably away at me.

Fickle: You there?

Dilemma time.

Fickle: You there? It's getting kinda cold out here on my
   own.

I grinned at the screen, imagining Fickle, whatever she looked like, wherever she might be, shivering like mad in front of her screen.

I started typing.

Barnaby Rudge: I'm here.

Fickle: Where you been?

I started typing again but saw Fickle's message flashing up at me.

Fickle: Aaaaand, I've been meaning to ask you. Barnaby
   Rudge?? WTF? What kind of name is that?!

That made me laugh.

Barnaby Rudge: LMAO, yeah I know. It's a Dickens thing.
   Blame my English teachers!

I looked back at my phone, waiting for me to text Matt back.

Matt was what everyone at college called "a catch". He was the same age as me—eighteen—and, yeah, good-looking I suppose, if you're into that sort of thing. He was cool too, in an Emo band called Anathema at college with his mates. He sang lead vocals and played guitar and they'd gig at places all over the city, and sometimes further away too. I'd gone along to some of his gigs but felt kind of out of place in amongst all the groupies all vying for his attention. Sometimes I thought, if they wanted him that badly, so bad they'd practically throw themselves at him, then they could have him. Perhaps I was being unfair.

He was a good guy, Matt, attentive and very into me, it seemed. I remember our first date. We'd met in town, down by Pizza Hut. I always get the impression other girls are looking at him, and our first date wasn't an exception because he was getting hot looks from all the girls inside Pizza Hut when we went in. I kinda thought they were all wondering what someone like me was doing with someone like him but tried to push that thought from my head, because I knew it would drive me crazy or something.

Anyway, that was then. For the now, his text was still looking up at me and I kinda figured I needed to answer him. And yet…here was Fickle waiting for me to talk to her.

Fickle: A Dickens thing? Like those times tables, just never got the Dickens thing either! More of a JK Rowling fan.

She did the winky face again. I looked at my phone, flipped it open, and texted Matt back.

Course. See you at eight.

Brief, yeah, but it said everything it needed to. I snapped it closed and looked back at my computer screen.

Barnaby Rudge: Fickle, I gotta go.

Fickle: Oh, okay.

Barnaby Rudge: Soz.

Fickle: No worries. Off anywhere nice?

Barnaby Rudge: Just out. Will you be here later?

Fickle: Maybe.

Barnaby Rudge: Or maybe I'll speak to you tomorrow?

Fickle: Yeah, that'd be good. Have a good evening, BR.

Barnaby Rudge: You too.

Nothing inside me wanted to leave my PC and go out into the cold night to see Matt. Nevertheless, I logged off and stared at the blank screen in front of me for a while before grabbing my coat and heading out of the house to meet him. I figured he was my boyfriend, after all, and I supposed I should give him the attention he deserved, whether I wanted to or not.

CHAPTER TWO

"You're quiet." Matt wiped his mouth and put his paper napkin down on the table in front of him.

"Am I?" I asked, smiling tightly.

"Yeah. Long day?"

"Not especially."

There was a silence, only punctuated by the sound of us both chewing our food, the wet, smacking sound seeming to echo loudly around the pizza place despite the god-awful piped music around us.

"We're doing a gig at the Metro tomorrow night." Matt licked a blob of tomato sauce from the side of his mouth. "Wanna come?"

I immediately thought about the prospect of an evening away from the message board. Boy, was I getting hooked! I smiled wryly to myself. Without me really realising it, that message board was slowly becoming my life. I made a mental note to have a laugh about it later with the others on there.

I looked at Matt blankly, almost resenting him for asking me to come out twice in as many nights.

"Well?" he opened his mouth wide and crammed in a piece of pappy pizza dough, chomping and studying me quizzically, head to one side.

"Sure," I said, not really knowing why.

"Cool!" Matt seemed pleased.

"What time?" I mentally calculated in my head. If he didn't want to meet until later, then I figured I could get in a few hours on the message board before I had to leave.

"I thought we'd go straight from college." Matt swirled his Coke round, the ice clattering against the sides of the glass. "It's gonna take, like, an hour to set up all the gear anyway so there's not much point in me going home first."

My mood got heavy. Going to the Metro straight from college meant meeting around five. Matt's gigs never finished much before midnight, so that meant over six hours out with him. I frowned.

"Problem?" Matt slurped on his Coke.

"Nah," I lied. I smiled, but it felt forced.

We walked home from Pizza Hut in near silence, primarily because I felt in a rotten mood. Matt tried striking up a conversation with me, but as much as I tried to make my voice sound light, I was aware—as I'm sure he was—that my answers to his questions and observations were abrupt. He had his arm round my shoulders as we walked down through the centre of town and headed up towards my house, and it felt heavy, leaden, like it didn't belong there, but there was nothing I could do about it, so I just let him leave it there.

We walked towards the little bridge that goes over the canal that runs just down from my house, and Matt slowed down. I knew what he wanted to do because he'd done it there before. Matt's kinda old-fashioned when it comes to dating, a rarity some would say in the twenty-first century. He feels awkward about kissing me outside our house, probably just in case either my mum or dad happened to look out of the window at the very moment he was going in for the kill. The bridge is, like, a thirty-second walk from my house. Matt always walked me to the bridge, kissed me, then watched as I headed to my front door, waiting until he saw I'd opened it. Then he'd wave, turn away, and disappear into the darkness. The same routine every time he walked me home, but it never felt normal. Certainly not the kissing bit, anyway.

"You sure you're okay?" Matt looked concerned. "You're very quiet."

I nodded, then stared down into the murky, dark water of the canal beneath us. A barge was parked up alongside the canal's edge, the lights inside it glowing cosily, and I wondered for a minute who was inside it and what were they doing? I was aware of Matt's arm still round my shoulder and my stomach knotted.

"So, tomorrow, yeah?" Matt said, turning me round to look at him. "It'll be cool you coming. I always play better when you're there." He smiled down at me and looped his arms loosely round my waist. I was suddenly conscious of my arms hanging limply by my sides so put them round his waist too, instantly pulling him closer to me. He looked at me a bit more, then bent his head to kiss me, his lips feeling cold and wet against mine. I think I made a fair show of kissing him back, even though I didn't feel particularly comfortable.

You see, I never felt comfortable kissing him. It was like it was expected of me, like it was something I ought to do, rather than something I wanted to do. I suppose part of me thought that if I didn't kiss him back then he'd think something was wrong, and then we'd have this whole, deep conversation about what was wrong, and I didn't want that. I just wanted to get the kissing over and done with so I could get back home again.

I guess that made me some sort of fraud, didn't it?

Anyway, we stood there in the darkness on the bridge kissing a bit longer and I grew tenser and tenser until, at last, he pulled away. He rested his forehead on mine and breathed out long and slow through his nose, so I could smell stale pizza and Coke.

"I better go. I've got lessons at nine tomorrow," I said, kinda lamely.

Matt pulled his head back away from mine and smiled at me again, kissing me briefly on my forehead and removing his arms from my waist.

"I'll wait here till I see you've gone in, okay?" he said, nodding his head in the direction of my house.

"Thanks," I said, unlooping my arms from his waist and turning to go. I turned to face him again. "See you tomorrow at lunch?" It was a bit halfhearted, but I was trying to make an effort.

"Can't, sorry." Matt shrugged. "Got to see Mr Parker about my coursework."

A sense of relief washed over me. "No worries." I turned towards home again, waving as I went.

"See you at five, though," he called out. Then, "I'll text you."

I reached my front door and turned back to see him still standing there on the bridge, illuminated under the moonlight, watching me. I waved again, fished my keys from my pocket and let myself in, poking my head back round the door just in time to see him disappearing into the darkness.

I breathed out slowly, feeling as I always did when a date with Matt was over, both a sense of relief and a sense of emptiness. I leant against the closed door and began to wonder what excuse I could come up with to cancel our date the next night, but before I had time to begin thinking, a voice from inside the lounge called to me.

"Immy! That you?"

Mum.

"Yup."

"Good. S'long as we're not being burgled."

I heard Dad give a sort of snorting guffaw before calling out to me too.

"How was your evening?"

I rolled my eyes to heaven in the gloom of our hallway as I took off my coat and flung it onto the stairs. I wandered into the front room to find my mum, dad, and Sophie watching some programme on the telly which appeared to be showing a bunch of mean-looking big cats eating something red, bloody, and very, very dead.

"Cheetahs in Africa." Dad jerked his head towards the telly as if by way of explanation. "Very interesting."

"How's Matt?" Mum asked, not moving her eyes from the screen.

"Yeah, good," I said, perching on the edge of the sofa. My phone beeped from somewhere deep in my jeans pocket and I saw Mum and Dad look at each other in amusement.

"Ahh, he only left you five minutes ago and he's missing you already." Sophie pulled a soppy face at me.

"Shut it." I glared at her, feeling myself reddening.

"He's keen, isn't he?" Mum kept her eyes fixed on the TV but there was a look of mischief on her face.

"Hmm." I fixed my eyes resolutely down on my trainers. "Right, I'm off to bed."

"To text Matt, more like." Sophie giggled.

I glared at her again and, without another word, left the room, secretly cursing Matt for making my phone beep and for making my stupid family feel the need to make even more stupid comments. That was, assuming it was Matt that texted me, of course, but I instinctively knew it had to be him.

Sure enough, up in my room I flipped open my phone to see his name flashing up at me. I read his message.

Thanx 4 this evening, blondie, it said. *It was wkd.*

I looked at the message and felt a sudden annoyance at the "blondie" comment. I knew that Matt loved my blonde hair, but I always grimaced when he called me that, and it irritated the hell out of me, I dunno why. Probably because most things Matt did irritated me. I guess that's what happens when you're not totally into someone, right?

I thought about Matt and our date, and rather than feeling irritation this time, I felt, well, nothing really. I typed out some lame message back to him, telling him I'd had a nice evening too and that I'd see him tomorrow, and then I hit the Send button, watching as my message disappeared and headed over to Matt's phone. I looked over to my computer, waiting patiently for me in the corner of my room, and wondered briefly if anyone would be around. Fickle? Joey? Twiggy? God, I needed to talk to someone, but something held me back from logging on.

I rubbed at my eyes grouchily and tossed my mobile down next to me on the bed.

You know when something niggles away at you but you just can't put your finger on it? That was what I was feeling right now—a sense of worry that just refused to leave me, no matter what I did or thought.

I looked at my phone again and sighed. I had an inkling of what was troubling me and made up my mind there and then that I would have to do something about it. I knew that if I wanted the worry to go away, I had to do something to make it go away, because that's the way it works, right?

If only it was that simple.

CHAPTER THREE

I had a crap night's sleep that night, punctuated by dreams of Matt, the images of which just refused to leave me all day. After giving up any hope of more sleep by six a.m., I decided to get up and arrived at college just after eight in a foul mood that kept getting darker every time I remembered I was having another date with Matt that night.

I'd lain in bed the previous night mulling things over and over in my head and had finally come to the conclusion that the root of my worry was that I wasn't into Matt as much as he was into me. But believe me, that wasn't really any surprise revelation, so I didn't know why it had taken me so long to realise it.

Here's what I *had* realised, though. I decided that I *had* been kinda into Matt when we first started dating, but I sure as hell didn't have feelings for him anymore. You know how exciting it is when you first start seeing someone? I had a piddling little bit of that, a kinda excitement of the newness of it all, of the attention he heaped on me, but the excitement never turned into the exhilaration, the goose bumps, or the mushy tummy that I thought it should. After all, you should have all that when you're first dating, shouldn't you? And then it turns into something deeper, more intense, if you're both really into each other. If you're not, then…well, I knew what happened when you weren't into someone because it was happening to me. I'd been with Matt for six weeks and I hadn't even got to the mushy tummy stage once, let alone any of the intense shit. Matt was bending over backwards to make things good with us, so I figured it had to be me.

I decided, at four in the morning—ha!—that it was time I made more of an effort to be into him as much as he seemed to be into me, then the worry would go away. It's a two-way thing, after all, isn't it?

So, despite arriving at college the next morning in a foul mood that I knew would most definitely be lifted by talking to the guys on the message board the minute I got home, I concentrated instead on that night's date with Matt and tried to feel positive about it, hoping that I might find some spark inside me that would make me give a damn about him. And besides, I figured it was better to be with someone in person than a group of anonymous people on the Internet.

The day at college seemed to go on forever, though. Even sneaking out to the pub with Emily and Beth at lunchtime didn't seem to break it up too much, and I ended up kinda wishing I'd never gone out with them in the end anyway, because they spent the whole hour and a half quizzing me about Matt, which was definitely not what I wanted or needed at that moment.

"He's a catch, Immy." Emily shook her head and sighed in mock exasperation.

"You think?" I looked at her over my glass.

"And what he's doing with you is anyone's guess!" Beth poked her tongue out at me.

"Thanks!" I threw my beer mat across the table at her. Why couldn't they change the record? Why did everyone have to keep telling me what a catch he was?

"So you guys serious, then?" Beth looked at me as she took a sip of her drink.

"Define serious," I answered, knowing I was sounding unhelpful but not really caring.

"Well, you know." Beth raised her eyebrows.

"Dunno," I said, sounding more sullen than I wanted to.

"You've been going out for ages," Emily said. "So you've gotta know whether it's getting serious or not, surely?"

"You slept together yet? That's what she really wants to know!" Beth leant back in her chair and grinned widely.

"Well, firstly that's none of your business." I grinned back at her. "Secondly, it's not been ages, we've only been dating, like, for, God I dunno, about six weeks, and thirdly," I laughed, "thirdly, I'm far too much of a lady to divulge such a thing."

"Yeah, right!" Beth snorted.

"That means they have." Emily nodded to Beth, who looked back at her with a smirk. "She's teasing us."

I could feel myself reddening, as I always did when the subject of me and Matt came up.

"So is he the stud we think he is?" Beth sipped at her drink again.

"I wouldn't know," I replied truthfully, trying not to sound coy.

"And you wouldn't tell us anyway, would you?" Emily laughed, apparently ignoring my comment.

I looked at Emily.

"He's cute, though, don't you think?" Emily turned and wrinkled her nose at Beth.

"I'd have him." Beth looked back at Emily and wrinkled her nose too.

"C'mon, so how is he in the sack, then?" Emily raised her eyebrows at me.

"I told you, I wouldn't know, and I wouldn't know 'cos we haven't done anything yet." I dropped my eyes before I could have the chance to see the look on her face and picked up Beth's beer mat, turning it over and over in my hand.

"Let me get this right." Beth put her elbows on the table and leaned closer. "You're going out with the fittest guy at college and you've not...you know...yet?"

I wondered why she thought that was so beyond the realm of possibility but said nothing; instead I carried on turning the beer mat over in my hands and stared down at the table.

"Aren't you gagging to, though?" Emily blew out her cheeks. "How can you keep your hands off him?"

"I know I bloody well wouldn't be able to." Beth grinned. "Love that Emo thing he's got going on, don't you, Em?"

I shrugged. "I dunno." I started ripping the corners off the beer mat. "It's just not something we've done yet."

"But you've been seeing him for long enough, though, haven't you?" Emily looked at Beth, then back to me.

"Yeah, but...it's just not happened yet, okay?"

FFS! I was aware I was sounding sullen, so I stopped ripping at my beer mat and took a large gulp from my drink, wiping droplets of beer from both corners of my mouth with my finger and thumb.

"Besides, we're not all slappers like you." I laughed at Emily, trying to sound as casual as I could, like it was no big deal to me that Matt and I hadn't slept with each other yet.

The truth was, it wasn't a big deal to me, but I sure as hell didn't want Emily and Beth to know that. I sat and looked at them exchanging sly glances between each other and wanted to tell them both the truth; that I'd done everything in my power to avoid being alone with Matt, anything to avoid what I knew would be the inevitable. I didn't want to sleep with him, simple as that.

He obviously wanted to take our relationship to the next stage, but for me, just dating and kissing were enough. I had begun lately to wonder if I was frigid, because of the whole "not feeling anything" when we kissed, and that worry was compounded by my lack of any interest in him. Because I wasn't into him, my not wanting to have sex with him was hardly surprising, was it? How could I tell my two closest friends that, though? The same two friends who thought Matt was the catch of the century, and two friends who I knew, if they were dating him, would jump at the chance to sleep with him.

I was different.

"You do fancy him, don't you?" Beth persisted.

I paused before I answered her.

"Yeah, 'course," I lied, picking up the tattered beer mat again. "We just haven't found the right time to, you know, do anything. It's no big deal."

"Well, all I'll say is that you'd better not let the grass grow and all that." Beth winked.

"Why?"

"Why?" Beth snorted. "Guy like that? You kidding me?"

I shook my head, fully understanding what she was saying, of course, but playing dumb for the hell of it.

"Guys like Matt have women swarming round them like bees round a honey-pot." Emily drained her glass and bent down to gather her bag from the floor by her feet. "If you hold back then he'll start looking elsewhere, is all we're saying."

"Blimey, Em!" I whistled impatiently. "I've told you, the moment hasn't been right yet, thassall!"

"Really? From what I heard he was banging his last girlfriend within a week of meeting her." Emily looked at her watch. "Ah shit it. Gotta go, next lesson's in five."

She rose from her chair.

"I'm not having a go, Immy. I'm just saying. Guys like Matt don't grow on trees."

I stared moodily into my beer glass as Emily hooked her bag over her shoulder and left the pub.

"She's only thinking about you," Beth said after Emily had gone. "You just don't show much interest in him, that's all."

"I do," I said defensively.

"You don't," Beth said gently. "You never talk about him. Every time we ask you about him you go real moody and won't tell us anything."

"I don't," I said, even more defensively this time.

"You so do! You should be bubbling about the fact you're with him, but you don't seem that bothered. Every time we ask you about him, you don't show much, I dunno, much enthusiasm."

"Maybe that's just the way I am," I said, draining the last of my beer.

"Maybe." Beth smiled.

"Anyway, I'm going to one of his gigs tonight," I said, scraping my chair back and heading for the door. "At the Metro in town," I added, by way of explanation.

"Then at least try and look happy about it," Beth replied, following me out of the door and back to college.

❖

College dragged all that afternoon, as I kinda knew it would. I spent most of my lessons alternating between thinking about what Emily and Beth had said to me at lunchtime and looking at my watch, waiting for five o'clock, but for whatever reason dreading it.

During my particularly dull English lesson that afternoon, I tried to figure out exactly why I wasn't looking forward to going to the gig that night. I'd forget about it, then as soon as I remembered that Matt would be coming for me after college, I'd get this pit-of-the-stomach feeling that I just couldn't fathom.

I didn't want to go; that much was obvious. But why? Other girls my age would give their right arms to get free tickets to a gig, even more so if they knew they'd be going with the coolest guy in the college. Perhaps I was hesitant because I knew something would be expected of me that night; that I'd have to play the doting girlfriend, lovingly gazing up at her hot boyfriend in his hot Emo gear, playing in his hot band.

It wasn't me, though. The doting girlfriend bit, I mean. It felt fake, like an act, like it always did when I went to see Matt play. I've never been a fan of the mosh pit, preferring to avoid being jumped on and flattened by some hairy seventeen-year-old tattooed kid, so I'd stand to the side and watch Anathema perform from there. I was always happy doing that. The band was wicked, and I did love the music they played, but I was always just happy watching from the sides while what seemed like hundreds of other teenagers went bat-shit crazy at the sight of Matt doing his thing. The fact it was my boyfriend playing up there on the stage was neither here nor there for me. Evidently I just don't do the gazing up stuff so well.

It's like, when I went to see his band play at the Cellar a few weeks back, I could see this girl standing in the pit shouting out his name, trying to reach out to him, telling him she loved him. You know, she was practically crying 'cos she was so overwhelmed by him. He was totally on fire that night, I'll grant you, but I remember just looking at her and thinking—*really?*

I could have told her I was his girlfriend. Hell, I *ought* to have told her I was his girlfriend, maybe I should even have thumped her for flirting with him, but what did I do? I just ignored her, never said a word to her. I just carried on moshing to the music at my safe position at the side of the pit, watching this sea of heads, happy to take a back seat from it all.

I thought when I got home that night that I should have felt jealous that this girl was practically throwing herself at my boyfriend, but all I'd thought at the time was, yeah, good band, good singer, good music. Nothing more. I didn't think about the lead singer being my boyfriend, I didn't care that this girl would have had him there and then if she'd had the chance. Then of course I worried that there was something wrong with me, like I was missing an envy gene or something, as well as being bloody frigid.

Now I knew that tonight was going to be the same as before: girls throwing themselves at Matt, and girls crying over Matt. I was dreading it.

When five o'clock eventually came and my lesson was over, I found Matt waiting for me outside my classroom, sitting a little way down the corridor with his back against the wall. He had a pencil tucked behind his ear and was busy writing something down on a piece of paper with another pencil—lyrics, probably—occasionally staring up at the ceiling before hastily scribbling something down again.

Two girls in front of me from my class spotted him and nudged each other, giggling between themselves, and not for the first time in my lifetime, I thought about just how shallow some girls could be.

"Hey, Matt." One of the girls stood in front of him, holding her folder tight against her chest, and looked down at him.

I saw Matt look up from his paper and watched as a wide grin spread across his face.

"All right?" He looked at the other girl and nodded an acknowledgment to her too.

I looked at Matt from over the girls' shoulders and tried to feel some spark of something—*anything.* Okay, so he looked good, even I had to admit that, with his hair swept over just so, his skinny black jeans and scuffed Airwalks on, slumped on the floor like he didn't have a care in the world. But that's really all I thought—*"nice Airwalks, Matt!"*

"You're playing Metro tonight, aren't you?" The first girl was still looking coquettishly down at him.

"You coming?" Matt looked up at her, still grinning.

"You're kidding me!" The second girl spoke now. "Tickets sold out, like, weeks ago for it."

"That right?" Matt chewed on his pencil as he carried on looking at them both.

The two girls looked at each other, the first girl trying and failing to hide a grin. All the time I watched them all from the doorway of my classroom, curiosity making me stay there rather than go out and speak to them.

Suddenly Matt flipped open his bag, which had been on the floor next to him, and put the piece of paper he'd been writing on inside it. He then rooted around inside the bag, evidently looking for something, finally bringing out two tickets. He hauled himself to his feet and handed the tickets to the first girl, who squealed and flung her arms round his neck.

"There's no such thing as sold out." Matt bent down and picked his bag up, putting it over his shoulders. "Not in my book, anyway."

"Wicked, Matt!" The girl looked at the tickets as if they were gold-leaf.

"I'll see you girls later, then?" Matt stuffed his hands in his pockets and leant against the wall. He turned his head and suddenly spotted me, still lurking by the classroom doorway, and a huge grin spread across his face.

"Hey, blondie!" he called over to me, lifting himself away from the wall and sauntering over, bending his head to kiss me when we were close enough.

I could sense the two girls, still behind him, and could imagine their reactions, their faces, like—*what's he doing with HER?*—but maybe I was being paranoid as usual.

He slung his arm casually over my shoulder and jerked his chin in recognition to the two girls as we walked past them, me shutting out their lowered voices as we walked down the corridor and out into the bright sunshine outside.

"We'll go and eat before we head over there, yeah?" Matt said, more as a statement than a question.

"Sure." I just kinda wanted to go home, but how could I tell him that? Without even realising it, I'd conceded defeat.

"Ryan texted me this afternoon. He's bringing the gear in the van later." Matt smiled down. "Means we can have longer together to eat."

Ryan was the band's drummer, a stocky guy of about twenty with a large tattoo on the back of his neck, and the only one in the band who could drive. More importantly, the only one with access to a van. He had a stunning girlfriend, some girl called Lou who he'd been seeing for over three years. He doted on her and she doted on him too; I often found myself wondering how it would feel to have such a level of unconditional love.

❖

The gig was, well, just as a gig should be. Matt was good, I'll give him that, but instead of listening to them perform from the mosh pit, I hung around in the wings, watching them from the sides. Perhaps seeing those two girls earlier that day had unsettled me; perhaps I didn't want to be seen as just another groupie. Perhaps I wanted to distance myself. Who the hell knows?

After they'd finished performing and loaded up the van, Matt talked Ryan into driving me home, something I was grateful for, because I just wanted the night to be over and to be back home, away from it all. Away from the pretence, I supposed.

Matt and I ended up being squashed up in the back of the van with the drum kit as Ryan took corners too fast, taking racing lines on the short journey out of town and back up to my house. I stared out of the window at the streetlights zipping past us and listened idly to the drone of Ryan and Lou's voices in the front of the van, talking over the sound of the engine.

"Man, you're so fickle! Do you know that?" Lou was joking with Ryan about something.

Fickle.

The sound of the word made me instantly think about Fickle and I wondered what she was doing right at that moment, and whether she would still be online by the time I got back. I thought about the conversations we'd had over the past few nights, smiling to myself as I remembered some of the stuff she'd said that had made me laugh out loud.

Fickle.

"So how was it?" Matt leant over and whispered in my ear, jerking me back to reality. "You enjoy it?" His voice was hoarse from the singing, giving it a husky edge.

I nodded. "It was good, yeah."

"Just good?" Matt gasped, pulling a pretend hurt face. "I thought we rocked."

"Well, you rocked good, yeah." I laughed.

"I'm glad you came, babe." Matt leant his head towards me, putting his arm round my shoulder, and kissed my hair.

I nodded.

After what seemed like the longest journey ever, Ryan finally turned the corner into our street and pulled up outside my front door, turning his head and grinning at me.

"Taxi for Miss Summers. That'll be ten quid please, love."

I grinned back at him, then turned my head and kissed Matt briefly on his cheek, then gathered up my bag.

"See you, Immy. Take care, yeah?" Ryan rammed the gearstick into reverse.

"Give us a minute, man!" Matt playfully cuffed Ryan's head, then reached over to grasp my hand, which was on the door handle. He tucked a stray bit of my hair behind my ear with his other hand.

"Your parents in?" Matt jerked his head towards our front door.

"Yeah," I replied. I tried to make a joke. "Probs watching some documentary about Marxism or dancing dogs or something."

"Shame." Matt winked at me.

I felt myself tensing, just wanting to get out of the van and into the house.

"You'll text me later, yeah?" Matt ran his hand up and down my thigh and looked at me intently.

"'Course." I smiled tightly, trying to make myself feel less tense.

Matt leant his head closer and, with his hand still moving up and down my thigh, kissed me. I surreptitiously tried not to make my head jerk back, instead I made an effort to kiss him back, jumping slightly as I felt his tongue slip into my mouth at the very same moment that his hand stroked my inner thigh, making me instinctively press my legs closer together.

"Get a room, guys, puh-lease." Ryan puffed out his cheeks in mock exasperation as he watched us from his rearview mirror.

"Young love, Ryan." Lou poked her tongue out at him. "You surely remember what that felt like!"

Ryan laughed, drawing Lou towards him and kissing her.

I pulled my head away from Matt and felt the urge to wipe my mouth, but knowing that I couldn't, instead smiled at him and pulled my bag up close to my chest.

"Thanks for the lift, Ryan." I grabbed at the door handle again, this time successfully managing to open the door without Matt intervening.

"No probs, babe." Ryan winked at me.

I turned to look back at Matt.

"See you soon," I said, getting out of the van before he had a chance to kiss me again.

"I'll ring you later, yeah?" Matt grinned up at me.

I nodded, shutting the van door a little harder than was necessary and walked to my front door. I stood there a while, feeling an overwhelming feeling of misery, coupled with the palpable relief I felt as I heard the van reverse slightly, then move off back down the road.

CHAPTER FOUR

I couldn't wait to get inside the house that night and log on. I was dying to talk to someone—anything to take me away from the reality that was my shit-confused life, if only for an hour. The rest of the family were already in bed, not ensconced in front of any Marxism documentary, of course, although the chink of light from under my parents' bedroom door told me that Mum, in all probability, was still propped up in bed with her nose in the latest Danielle Steel while Dad slept on, oblivious to the light.

I looked at my PC, sitting patiently waiting for me, and wondered how a machine could have this apparently innocent little message board inside it that was making me question everything about my life. It had become my lifeline, that message board; I was certain about that. Was that normal? Was it right? It was turning into an obsession. Was that healthy?

Maybe it was the anonymity of the board I liked, or maybe it was because the friends I had made on there listened without judging. What I did know was, lately, they were always there, at the end of the computer, waiting for me, ready to talk and listen, ready to laugh and joke. I liked that. I needed that.

I looked at the computer again.

Blast it. I logged on and saw that both Twiggy and Joey were on MSN, Joey having just added me the night before. I breathed a sigh of relief. Thank God! The voices of reason!

Twiggy: Hey you!

Barnaby Rudge: Hey, yourself! How you doing?

Twiggy: Crap day at work. Knackered! You?

Barnaby Rudge: All right. You work???!

Twiggy: Yeah, for my sins. In a supermarket. I'm one of those annoying checkout girls you're always served by!

This was progress. Now at least I knew what Twiggy did for a living.

Another box flashed up:

Joey: Hey chickeroo!

Barnaby Rudge: Hey, Joey!

I giggled. I'd been talking to Joey on the board for over a week now and already knew that she was eighteen, like me, and at college, doing Biology and something else I couldn't quite remember. I also knew that she called everyone, without exception, either chickeroo or kiddo. I liked that.

Joey: You been up to mischief?

Barnaby Rudge: Why you say that?

Joey: Well, it's a conversation starter, isn't it? Tell Joey all about it.

God, if only!

Twiggy: I'm logging off, BR. I'm on the early shift tomorrow.

Barnaby Rudge: No worries. You back tomorrow?

Twiggy: Yeah, of course! Cya!

I looked back at Joey's message.

Barnaby Rudge: I wish I could tell you about it, Joe, I really do!

Joey: I got all evening, kiddo. Well, not all evening 'cos it's like nearly midnight already, but y'know!

Barnaby Rudge: Nearly midnight? Whoa! How'd that happen? Good job it's Friday, hey?

Joey: Aye, indeed. No sodding college tomorrow, thank feck!

My eye was caught by Fickle logging on, just after Twiggy had logged off. I chuckled, knowing that the two voices of reason were about to change to one voice of reason and one voice of lunacy!

I grinned as a message flashed up for me.

Fickle: Hey!

Barnaby Rudge: Hey!

The minute I saw Fickle's name flash up in front of me, all the tension of the last few hours gradually left me and I began to relax for the first time that night.

Fickle: How was your evening?

Barnaby Rudge: Yeah, okay.

Fickle: Enthusiasm, I love it!

Barnaby Rudge: Sometimes I don't feel so enthusiastic!

Fickle: Oh. Everyone's gotta have enthusiasm! Wanna talk about it?

Did I?

Barnaby Rudge: I guess.

Fickle: Go ahead. I'm listening.

Barnaby Rudge: Gah, I dunno! I just worry sometimes that I'm not as into my boyfriend as he's into me.

Fickle: Goes like that sometimes.

Barnaby Rudge: Really?

Fickle: Hell yeah! I've been in relationships where it's been one-way traffic.

Barnaby Rudge: What did you do about it?

Fickle: Well, to be honest, it was usually me that wasn't as
    into the other person, so…

Barnaby Rudge: Ah! Heartbreaker, are you?!

Fickle: Something like that.

She added one of those poked-out-tongue icons, so I wasn't
sure if she was being serious or not.

I looked back at my screen and remembered Joey had told me
a few days before that she was doing assignments at her college that
week. Realising I'd been ignoring her while I'd been speaking with
Fickle, I hastily switched back to my conversation with Joey, and
asked her:

Barnaby Rudge: So how did your assignments go, Joe?

Joey: Ah, not bad. Get the results next week, so, fingers
    crossed, hey?

Barnaby Rudge: I'll keep em crossed for ya!

Joey: Thank you! LOL. So, how was your evening?

Barnaby Rudge: Yeah, okay. Went to a gig in town.

Joey: Wicked! Who'd you see?

Barnaby Rudge: Ah, local band. Anathema they're called.

Joey: Kewl name. Any good?

Barnaby Rudge: Yeah, not bad. My boyfriend's the lead
    singer.

Joey: So you gotta say they're good, right?!

Barnaby Rudge: ! Something like that, yeah.

Joey: How long you been seeing him?

Barnaby Rudge: Not long.

I briefly wondered if Joey might be interested in listening to me
about Matt, but before I could figure out what to say to her about it,
Fickle had messaged me again.

Fickle: Hey, I just had a thought. You got a picture of
    yourself? Be good to see who I've been talking to all
    this time.

A photo? Me and Fickle had only just started talking to each other—it hadn't even crossed my mind to send her my photo just yet. I frowned. I had some photos on the computer that I'd uploaded ages ago; they were taken about a year ago, so I guessed they'd be okay.

Barnaby Rudge: I'll send you one if you send me one!
Fickle: Sure! Wait there!

While I waited, I searched my computer for something half-decent, finally settling on a photo of me taken by Dad during our holiday in Scotland back in August. I peered at it, screwing up my face, wondering if it was suitable to send. Was it a good likeness? I had my hair up in the picture, but you could still clearly see that it was long and blonde. I wanted her to see that, I dunno why.

I wanted her to be able to see my eyes as well 'cos I've always kinda liked the way they are—blue, but with nice, long, dark lashes that never need touching up. Matt always said other girls would give anything to have eyes like mine...

Just then, Fickle flashed me another message.

Fickle: K, just sent one to your in-box.

I grinned, switching screens to bring up Hotmail, and found Fickle's e-mail.

Fickle: You got it? Now you gotta send me one!
Barnaby Rudge: Give me a chance! Just uploading it now.

Her picture appeared to me on my screen and I felt my breath quicken. I don't really know what I'd expected, but the person appearing in front of me wasn't at all what I expected, but I really liked what I saw. I mean, I *really* liked it.

I shook my head, as if to try and shake a thought that had just entered back out again.

Fickle was cute. Not beautiful, but cute, you know? Elfin, almost. Small face, freckles, and a cheeky, mischievous grin.

And pretty. So damn pretty.

You know how you can talk to an anonymous voice and build up a picture of that person in your head? Maybe you don't, but that's what I'd done with everyone I spoke to on the message board; Twiggy, Fickle, Joey, Betty Blue Rinse (God only knows what she really looked like!!), and Fickle definitely wasn't what I'd expected.

Fickle: You got it yet, slowcoach?!

Barnaby Rudge: Yeah, just looking at it now.

Fickle: So where's my picture?

Barnaby Rudge: Ahh, just sending it to you. Patience, woman!

Fickle: I'm not known for my patience...

I attached the Scotland photo to my e-mail and pressed the Send button, then looked back at Fickle's picture.

Fickle: At last! Got it now, just downloading it.

Barnaby Rudge: K, it was a windy day, so ignore my crazy hair!

Fickle: Coo! Nice! You look like you were having fun.

Barnaby Rudge: I was.

Fickle: You're right about your hair, BR! It's wicked. I like blonde hair...

I stared at her picture again, barely registering her comment about my hair, and tried to take in every detail of her face; her dark brown eyes, her skin, slightly tanned, her highlighted hair, tucked neatly behind her ears. I looked at her impish grin, the look of mischief in her eyes, then I looked at her perfect nose and nice lips.

My heart beat faster just looking at her lips. Lips I could imagine myself...

Jesus! Where the flip did THAT come from? Suddenly I felt a wave of sickness. I could feel my heart pounding in my head, so I got up from my chair and walked over to my bed, sitting down heavily on it. I puffed out my cheeks, trying to quell the feeling of nausea, and looked back over at my computer, where Fickle's photo was still smiling out at me. I saw she'd messaged me again, her name flashing on and off on the screen.

Fickle: You still there? Or has my picture frightened you off? LOL!

Now I'd seen her picture I could imagine her sitting at her computer, probably looking at my photo and wondering why she was even bothering to talk to me still, now she knew what I looked like. I wandered back over to the computer.

Barnaby Rudge: Soz! Hey, you're pretty, you know!

Fickle: Yeah, right! Shame you can't see my tongue piercing on it, though. Everyone always seems to like that...

Barnaby Rudge: You have your tongue pierced? Whoa!

Why did the thought of that suddenly make me feel weird? Good-weird, I mean!

Fickle: Sure do! You like?

Barnaby Rudge: Uh, yeah, I do.

Fickle: Good! That's what I like to hear. Hey, I like your picture too! Where was it taken?

Barnaby Rudge: Erm, Scotland. Some place near Edinburgh.

Fickle: Mmm, niiiice!

Nice? Why did she keep saying that?

My head was spinning and I suddenly knew that I needed some time out, time away from Fickle and her picture.

Barnaby Rudge: Hey, Fickle, I've gotta go.

Fickle: Oh, okay. Everything good?

Barnaby Rudge: Yeah, just don't feel too great so I'm going to go to bed.

Fickle: K. You sure you're okay?

Barnaby Rudge: Yeah.

I said my good-byes to her and logged off quickly before she could say anything else to me, suddenly needing to be in my bed, away from the computer, away from her, away from thoughts of Matt and the evening I'd just had.

Kicking off my shoes but not bothering to remove my clothes, I crawled into bed and pulled the duvet up over my head, wanting to block out the feeling of nausea and anxiety that threatened to overwhelm me. Every time I closed my eyes, images of Fickle swam in front of them, as if her picture was burned onto the inside of my eyelids or something, images that were interrupted by flashbacks of Matt kissing me and shoving his tongue in my mouth.

I tried to breathe more regularly and slow my heartbeat, but panic engulfed me and I couldn't do a thing about it.

Just what the hell was going on?

Chapter Five

What makes one person's features more attractive to you than another person's? What is it in someone's face that you can be instantly drawn to, that straight away makes your heartbeat quicken, your palms clammy? Is it their eyes? The smoothness of their skin? The way they look at the camera?

I didn't know. All I knew was that the second Fickle had sent me her picture and I'd seen her brilliant, expressive, cheeky, animated face smiling out at me, I'd been smitten. But why her? Why Fickle? I wasn't gay, was I? I was dating a guy, for God's sake—how could I be? But there was something about Fickle that sent shivers down my spine every time I looked at her photo.

I chose to stay away from the computer for a few days after that night, opting to use the equipment at college for work rather than logging on at home and risk seeing Fickle on MSN. The abrupt disconnect was total agony, though; everything inside me yearned to go online and talk to her, but I figured a few days away might sort my head out. I was obsessing…over her, over her picture. I'd spoken to her for hours on end for the last few nights but I could already feel an addiction towards her—an addiction that was out of control. I needed a few days' breathing space, and then I'd look back and laugh at just how stupid I'd been about it all, right?

I mean, it's not as if I'd ever fancied girls before. Okay, so

I'd take the odd sneaky look if I ever saw a fit girl when I was out and about in town. God knows, I'd even found myself on occasions looking at girls when I was out with Matt, but that didn't mean I fancied them. The two women on *Lovers and Sinners* didn't count either; I just admired them for the way they were acting out this perfect love story on my TV. That *certainly* didn't mean I was gay.

But with Fickle it was different, and by the third night of my self-imposed cold turkey from the message board, I was missing her like I'd never missed anyone in my life. It was much more than missing just Fickle, though; I missed the message board itself and everyone else on there—Twiggy, Joey, even Betty Blue Rinse—so much it was beginning to hurt. I particularly missed talking to Joey and Twiggy on MSN, I missed the banter on the message board, I missed catching up with everyone's news.

Whatever it was that was going on with me, I did know that I needed to do something about this growing fascination with Fickle and decided there and then that I must find enough willpower not to speak to her anymore. If I didn't talk to her, then I couldn't be confused by my feelings for her, and I'd have more time to focus on being a better, more attentive girlfriend to Matt. The more I saw of Matt, the less I'd think of Fickle, and that was the way I wanted it. Simple.

I snatched up my phone and on an impulse rang Matt.

"Hey, babe." Matt's familiar voice sounded at the other end.

"Hey."

"What you up to?"

"Nothing much."

There was a short, awkward silence.

"You fancy doing something?" I found myself saying, trying to make my voice sound light, as if I really meant it.

Matt sounded pleased.

"Sure! I can meet you in town if you want?"

I did want. I had to want to see him. It made sense.

"Cool. See you at the usual spot?" I looked at my watch. It was 6.30 p.m. "Seven-ish?"

"I'll be there, babe. Looking forward to it," Matt said before ringing off.

I looked at my phone and bit my lip. This was the right thing to do. Matt was my boyfriend; Fickle was nothing to me. I knew nothing about her. She was a stranger on the other end of a computer, so she shouldn't even be in my head. She could be married for all I knew! I didn't even know what her name was, for goodness sake! Matt was real. Fickle wasn't. Matt wanted me; he was flesh and bones, he was there. What was Fickle? A photo on my computer screen, that was all.

I hauled myself up off my bed and grabbed my coat, taking the stairs down to the hallway two at a time, jumping the last three steps just for the hell of it. I poked my head round the kitchen door, watching briefly as Mum loaded our dinnertime crockery and pans into the dishwasher.

"I'm heading out," I called from the doorway.

She swung round.

"Matt?" she asked, raising her eyebrows.

"Yeah," I said, hauling my coat on and stuffing my beanie on to my head. "We're just gonna grab a quick drink in town. I won't be back late."

She nodded, smiling.

"And he'll walk you home? Your dad'll want to know in case he has to come and pick you up." Mum jerked her head in the direction of the lounge, where I assumed Dad was sitting watching TV.

"Yeah, he'll see me home okay." I grabbed my purse from the kitchen sideboard.

And he would. Matt was nice like that. "A good lad", as Dad would say.

I left the house, ambling down over the canal bridge, the same one Matt would walk me to later and stand on to watch me as I made the short trek back up to my house. The same bridge that we would kiss on, like always…

I squeezed my eyes tight shut and opened them again quickly, trying to shake the thought from my head. I walked under the railway bridge and rounded the corner, seeing Matt already waiting for me by the fountain where we always met. He was sitting on the steps of the fountain, fiddling with his phone, presumably texting someone; he seemed lost in thought and jumped slightly as he heard my footsteps next to him.

I looked down at him and nodded at his phone.

"Secret admirer?" I have no idea what made me say that.

He lazy-grinned up at me.

"There's only you, Immy. You should know that by now."

He hauled himself to his feet and kissed me on the cheek, linking his fingers in mine as we walked together towards a pub on the corner that we both liked. After fetching us both a drink, he straddled his long, lean legs across either side of a stool and sat heavily. He pulled his hand through his hair and looked at me. "So how's your day been?" he asked, taking a long sip from his beer.

"Yeah, okay," I replied. "You?"

"Not bad. Better since hearing from you. That was a nice surprise." He eyed me over his glass.

I didn't want to tell him that the only reason I'd rung him was because every part of me had been aching to log on, to talk to Fickle. If I hadn't arranged to meet up with him, I would have ended up going online to find her. I didn't want to tell him, either, that it had taken every last ounce of my willpower to come away from the house, away from the computer. Away from her.

Matt and I talked that night about nothing in particular. He told me Anathema had a string of gigs coming up in the following weeks, and as he was telling me about the band and the gigs I could see the excitement in his eyes—eyes that were alive with the joy of doing something that he loved. That pleased me.

"It might mean I'm a bit quieter than normal, you know?" Matt reached across the table and took my hand in his. I looked down at my hand, sitting limply in his, and wondered why I didn't feel dismay or upset at what he'd just said.

"Don't worry about it." I stared kinda blankly at him.

"It'll just be a bit mad for a bit, practising, moving gear around, shit like that." Matt squeezed my hand. "But it doesn't mean I won't be thinking about you all the time."

I nodded.

"Like I said, don't worry. I got heaps of work for college anyway, so…" My voice trailed off.

"Well, our first gig isn't until Saturday, so if you fancy doing something Friday?" Matt cocked his head to one side.

"Sounds good." I smiled tightly, aware I was being pretty monosyllabic, but struggling to find additional words.

It was amazing, I suddenly thought, how I never struggled for words with Fickle, yet here I was with my boyfriend, racking my brain to find something, anything, to talk to him about. I looked over at him and wondered why I'd bothered dragging him out, encouraging him, making him think I wanted him when all along I wanted…

What did I want?

I wanted Fickle.

❖

On the fourth night away from the computer, I finally conceded defeat and logged on, bored with night after night in front of dull programmes on the TV, and even more bored of all the work I'd been doing during my abstinence. Anyway, I figured even if Fickle was there, I didn't have to talk to her, did I? I could just tell her I was busy. My life didn't have to revolve around Fickle.

But even as the computer booted up, I couldn't help but think about her sitting wherever it was she sat to talk on the Internet. I closed my eyes and pictured her as I'd seen her in her photo, looking out at me with those incredibly expressive and beautiful eyes. Before I'd even had the chance to see who was around, and before I could even disable my MSN, Fickle had messaged me.

Fickle: Hey, stranger!

Just the sight of her name made my heart beat faster. My hands shaking, I wrote:

Barnaby Rudge: Hey!

Fickle: Where you been?

Then, before I could answer her, this:

Fickle: I've missed ya!

I looked at her message. She'd missed me. Maybe she was just saying that? I didn't know what to say to that, so I just ignored it.

Barnaby Rudge: Just been busy, is all.

Fickle: Too busy for me?

Was she flirting with me? Why would she flirt with me?

Barnaby Rudge: LOL.

There was a long pause. I stared at my computer screen, not really knowing what else to say. Actually, scrub that. I knew exactly what I wanted to say, and it was something along the lines of: What the fuck was going on with me? Or, what the fuck did your picture do to me the other night? Or even, what the fuck are *you* doing to me?

I carried on staring at the screen.

Fickle: You okay?

Barnaby Rudge: Yeah, just tired. Soz.

Fickle: Ah! Long day?

Barnaby Rudge: Something like that.

Fickle: Do you want me to go?

Barnaby Rudge: No!!

I'd written it without even thinking.

Fickle: K.

Do you know that feeling of being guilty about doing something that you feel you shouldn't be doing, but loving it at the same time? I had that feeling right then. Everything inside me was telling me to stop talking to her, that it would just make matters worse, confuse me even more. And yet, I loved talking to her. Even though we'd barely spoken, she was making me so happy that I just couldn't bring myself to log off again.

Barnaby Rudge: So you missed me then, huh?

Why did I write that? Because I wanted to. I wanted to draw her in.

Fickle: Yeah, 'course I missed you!!

Barnaby Rudge: What have you been up to lately?

Fickle: Ah, this and that. You?

Barnaby Rudge: College work, shit like that.

Fickle: That's 'cos you're a good girl, Barnaby Rudge!

Barnaby Rudge: What about you? Are you a good girl?

Fickle: Always!!

Then:

Fickle: Well, sometimes.

She posted me a winking sign. I felt my tummy flip again and suddenly felt like the four nights away from her had been for nothing.

Fickle: And my mum's not been so well so I've kinda been looking after her.

Barnaby Rudge: I'm sorry. Is she okay?

Fickle: Better now. Thanks for asking. She has MS, y'see?
Some days she's okay, some days not so okay. The
days she's not so okay, I look after her.

I felt like my heart might melt right there and then.

Barnaby Rudge: And I'm sure she's glad to have you
around to help her.

Fickle: Ah, I'm not so sure about that! I still cause her grief
sometimes!

There was a pause while I guessed Fickle went off to do
something else. I looked at her last messages and read them again;
Fickle had a good heart, I was sure of it. So she was lovely and had
a good heart. The perfect girl.

Fickle: Hey, BR, you fancy swapping mobile numbers? Be
good to text, don't you think?

I did think so.

Barnaby Rudge: Sure!

Fickle: Then I can keep in touch with you throughout the
day, stuff like that. We can text each other during
lessons. I think that'd be kinda cool, don't you?

The thought of being in touch with Fickle outside of MSN
seemed appealing, and even though I knew it was going to make me
closer to Fickle than ever, and a loud voice was screaming in my ear
not to give her my number, I did.

And so we did.

Text, I mean.

She gave me her number that night and I put it into my phone
straight away, looking at the number until I knew it off by heart. She
sent me a text the next morning, just the briefest of messages to say
"Hi", but I didn't text her back until later the next night because, I
guess, I wasn't sure what to say to her. I sat up in the darkness of my

room and turned my mobile over and over in my hands, wondering whether what I was about to do was a good idea. Oh, I knew I was going to text her eventually, and I knew that once I'd done that there was no going back.

You see, I knew I could monitor how much or how little I spoke to Fickle on the computer. But texting? That was a whole different thing as far as I was concerned. Her messages would always be there, stored in my phone until I chose to delete them, so I could read them over and over again, never giving her a chance to leave my thoughts. I took a deep breath and texted her back, a nondescript message that just kinda asked her how she was. It seemed she'd been waiting for me to text her though, 'cos she answered with: *Much better from hearing from you. I've been waiting all day for you to text me!*

I looked at her text and my heart fluttered. She always managed to cause that. It all began to make sense in the dead silence of the night; I knew I'd become hooked on the message board where I still chatted to Twiggy and Joey and some others on there, and I'd become almost reliant on MSN, far more so than Facebook or Twitter, mainly because I enjoyed the privacy and anonymity of MSN more than either of those. But what I hadn't realised, not until recently anyway, was that I was logging on more frequently now, supposedly to put messages on the board, or to read others' comments, or to see how Twiggy was. But my heart leapt if I saw that Fickle was online too, and more worrying was the feeling of, well, wretchedness—I can't think of a more appropriate word—if she wasn't there. Seeing her picture, it seemed, had only set alight something that was already inside me—I just hadn't known it.

I was mesmerised by her, thought about her all the time. If Fickle didn't log on during the times I was online, I'd wait and wait, finding random things to look at on the web, hoping that if I waited around long enough, she'd log on, just hanging around on there doing jack shit until I'd eventually concede defeat and finally log off. I always left with this feeling of emptiness, a feeling that would stay with me until I caved in and logged on again, knowing that I shouldn't, knowing that I had other things to do, knowing this…crush?…had grown out of control. And then saw she was there. It was during those times that my heart would beat faster and my palms—yes, my palms!! Crazy, huh?—would sweat. You read about this stuff in slushy romantic novels, right? It didn't happen to normally sensible eighteen-year-old college students like me.

Our MSN conversations grew increasingly flirty night after night, long into the night. Her spirit and sense of fun and extroverted nature—and her flirting—all combined and conspired to pull me towards her, closer each time we spoke. I'd never felt like this about anyone before—certainly never with Matt—and I was scared and excited at the same time.

I knew by now that I wanted her—I just didn't know how I was going to get her.

❖

"So you'll have to fend for yourself tonight, okay?" Mum was fussing round me like, well, like mums do.

"I told you just now, yeah, it's no problem." I was in the kitchen, rooting round for something to eat. "I *can* cook, you know!"

"Now, your dad and me will be out until midnight, I reckon," Mum said, pulling down a packet of pasta from the cupboard. "You know how these things drag on. Have a pasta bake." She waggled the packet of pasta in my face.

"What about Sophie? Do I have to feed her as well?" I sighed.

"Sophie's gone to Megan's for a sleepover, so she won't be back till morning, okay?"

The house to myself! A shiver shot through me at the thought of an uninterrupted evening in front of the computer, talking to Fickle.

My parents left shortly after seven p.m., leaving me alone in the house for the first time in what seemed like ages. It had been just over a week since Fickle and I had exchanged phone numbers, during which we'd texted and MSNed pretty much daily, but the excitement I felt, knowing I'd have her all to myself for an entire evening, was something else. After I'd eaten, I took myself up to my room, wriggling with an overwhelming sense of anticipation as I watched the PC boot up. I logged myself onto MSN, hoping desperately to see Fickle's name.

She was there.

A wash of excitement cascaded down my back.

Barnaby Rudge: Hey!

Fickle: Hey yourself! How's tricks?

Barnaby Rudge: Yeah, good! 'Rents just gone out for the night so I'm home alone!

Fickle: Ooooh, are you to be trusted??

Barnaby Rudge: Of course!

Fickle: I'm not so sure! I've heard about girls like you!

She did one of those poking-tongue smilies. It made me feel almost as weird as her winking ones.

Barnaby Rudge: I hope you're not flirting with me!

Fickle: Now, would I do that?!

Barnaby Rudge: Hmm.

Fickle: Don't hmm at me, madam! LOL.

Barnaby Rudge: Sorry.

Fickle: Chillax! I'm kidding ya! Hey, you got another photo for me, then?

Barnaby Rudge: You want one??!

Fickle: Sure! I can't keep looking at this one all the time, can I?

Okaaaaay, that was flirtatious, wasn't it?

Barnaby Rudge: OK, if you think you can stand it! Here's
    one taken last year in Crete. My parents are in the
    photo too, but you can ignore them!

I remembered I had a photo, taken in Crete the year before, of
me on the beach in my shorts and T-shirt. The picture showed off my
legs to their best, and I kinda wanted Fickle to see them too.

Barnaby Rudge: You got it yet?

Fickle: It's just coming now. You send it by pigeon post or
    what?

She sent me a winky; this time I grinned at it.

Fickle: Here it is.

I waited, dying for her to make some comment about my legs.

Fickle: Hey, nice! Where was it taken again?

Barnaby Rudge: Crete.

Fickle: Never been there myself. Is it nice?

I wanted her to mention my legs, not bloody Crete!

Barnaby Rudge: Yeah, it's all right, not bad, y'know?

Fickle: You're lucky. All we get to go to is the coast
    each year. Dad has this mobile home thing down
    there, so he reckons we have to go to get our
    money's worth!

Why hadn't she mentioned my legs? I'm not blowing my own
trumpet or anything, but my legs are good! Anyone can see that!
The photo shows that!

I suddenly looked at her name, flashing away on the screen in
front of me. Fickle. That was all I knew her as. It was crazy! I was
beginning to have feelings for Fickle and I didn't even know her
real name.

Barnaby Rudge: What's your real name, Fickle?

There was a pause and I wondered if I'd pissed her off, or
whether she just didn't want to tell me. The great thing about the

Internet is the anonymity. Maybe she was happy for me to just know her as Fickle. After all, who was I to her?

I winced inwardly, sure that she was going to tell me to mind my own business.

Fickle: Soz, went to the toilet! LOL. My name? It's
Gemma.

Toilet? She should have been looking at my legs, not going to the toilet!

Barnaby Rudge: That's a nice name.

I meant it too.

Fickle: LOL. What's yours?

Barnaby Rudge: Imogen. Everyone calls me Immy
though.

Fickle: That's well sexy.

She added a winky sign. Why did that winky sign make me feel so weird?

Barnaby Rudge: Sexy? LMAO! You think so?

Fickle: Yeah. I love it when people shorten their names.
Very hot!

I didn't think it was sexy at all, but each to their own, I supposed.

Fickle: Why did you wanna know my name, Immy?

Barnaby Rudge: I dunno. We've been talking for a while
now, I s'pose I just wanted to know who you really are.

Fickle: Well, I'm glad you asked. I wanted to know what
your name is for ages. Even more so since I've seen
your photos. Now I know, I like it. It's nice.

Barnaby Rudge: Thank you! So's yours!

My legs! Was she going to mention my legs?

There was a pause, then:

Fickle: Ah crap, BR, I gotta go.

Damn!

Barnaby Rudge: So soon?

Fickle: I'm sorry, yeah. I'm going out tonight.

Barnaby Rudge: Oh, okay. Going anywhere nice?

Fickle: Meeting my ex.

Barnaby Rudge: Ah, right.

Fickle: And I wanna grab a bite to eat before I go…and of course, make myself look shit hot. Might smooth things along better with her, you know what I'm saying? LMAO. Kidding ya.

Her…?

Barnaby Rudge: You're, uh, you're gay then?

Fickle: LMAO! Uhh, yeah, durr! Hadn't you already guessed that?

Barnaby Rudge: Oh, um, I hadn't really thought about it.

Yeah, right! Who was I kidding?

Fickle: Really? Surprised about that!

Barnaby Rudge: Sorry?

Fickle: Nothing. LOL. Did I tell you about my ex? All very nasty, it was, towards the end.

Barnaby Rudge: You didn't, no.

Fickle: It'll have to be another time, BR. I really gotta go. Wish me luck!

Barnaby Rudge: Good luck, Fickle.

Fickle: See ya.

Barnaby Rudge: See ya.

I watched as Fickle's status changed from online to offline and leant back in my chair, rubbing irritably at my eyes with the balls of my palms, my head filling up with a thousand thoughts.

So Fickle was gay. I supposed I'd kinda already guessed that, just by all the flirting, but seeing her write it in black and white confirmed it for me. And she had an ex too. Why couldn't I have seen that? Of course she was going to have an ex! Everyone has a bloody ex! And if Fickle had her way, whoever she was, she wouldn't be an ex for long.

Anger pulsed through me, for no apparent reason, like there was some kinda rising tide of frustration and rage that I couldn't control or stop. On an impulse, I snatched up my phone and called Matt, listening half in disappointment and half in relief as I heard it ring out and go to voicemail. I closed my eyes and spoke into the phone, telling Matt I wanted to see him. I don't know why I wanted to see him—I just did. Or did I? Who the fuck knew? "Be good to hook up, Matt," I said, squeezing my eyes tight shut. "Ring me when you get this message, yeah?"

I flipped my phone shut and wandered to my bed, lying out on it with my hands folded behind my head, enjoying the silence of the house. I stared up at the ceiling and tried not to think about Fickle and her ex, but no matter how hard I tried, images of her—of them—floated in and out of my mind, until I thought that I would go raving mad. The ringing of my mobile a short while later punctured the silence, and I jumped. I blinked my eyes open, surprised to see my bedroom now in complete darkness, except for the flickering light of my computer, which had evidently given up any hope of my return and had gone into standby. I must have fallen asleep. I looked at my phone; Matt's name flashed at me.

I sat up, flipped the phone open, and spoke.

"Matt," I said groggily.

"You okay? You don't sound so good." Matt's voice rumbled with concern.

"I was asleep, I dunno, I just, uh, I just fell asleep on my bed." I laughed, rubbing at my eyes and yawning loudly.

"Hard day, huh?"

"I guess."

"You said you wanted to hang out, yeah?" Matt sounded breathless, as if he was walking and talking at the same time.

I looked at my watch. Fickle would be out by now. With her ex.

"Yeah, fancy it?" I tried to forget about Fickle and focus on talking to Matt.

"Sure. You wanna meet in town?" Matt asked.

I mean, who the hell was Fickle's ex anyway? And why hadn't she told me she had an ex? I frowned. More importantly, why was she always flirting with *me* when she had an ex whom she was still interested in?

"Immy? You there?" Matt again.

Where was she now, huh? Why did she have to go out when all I wanted to do was talk to her, get to know her more? Did she have any idea how much I thought about her? How much I wanted her? How could I ever get to know her better if she wasn't around? You know what? Fuck her.

"No, come over here," I suddenly said to Matt. "Mum and Dad are out. Sophie's at a mate's."

"You sure?" Matt sounded cautious.

"Very sure," I replied.

❖

Matt arrived at the house just after seven, slightly out of breath.

"I was walking through town when you rang, so I just ran up straight from there." He grinned at me, shrugging apologetically.

I stepped aside to let him in.

"You had a good day?" I asked, shutting the front door behind him as he brushed past me, bringing a rush of cool evening air from outside in with him, and stood in the hallway.

"Not bad. Just been given a pile of work at college, but nothing that can't wait." Matt pulled his coat off and placed it over the banister. He looped his arms over my shoulders and pulled me to him, kissing me briefly.

"Drink?" I removed myself from his hug and walked towards the kitchen.

"You got a beer there?" Matt followed me into the kitchen and leant against the sink, watching me.

I retrieved a beer from the fridge and flipped the lid from it before handing it to him, nodding as he thanked me and took a large drink from it. I watched as the bubbles settled back in the bottle and wondered briefly if Fickle was drinking beer, wherever she was right now. I shook my head, almost as if to shake the thought of it from my head, and grabbed myself a beer, flipping the lid from it and drinking it back.

"You okay?" Matt was still leaning against the sink.

I looked at him.

"Bit of a headache, thassall." I thought I saw a brief flash of disappointment on his face.

"C'mere." Matt placed the beer bottle down on the side and held his arms out to me. He wrapped his arms tight around me as I leant against him, burying my head in his shoulder, my beer bottle still grasped tightly in my hand.

"I've missed you," he whispered into my hair. "You do know how I feel about you, don't you?"

I nodded into his shoulder, then watched as he took the beer bottle from me and placed it on the side. I followed resignedly as he took my hand and led me from the kitchen. We paused at the bottom of the stairs as Matt took my face in his hands and kissed me again, softly at first, then harder, his lips cold and wet against mine. My head started spinning and I found myself kissing him back, hard, as visions of Fickle swam into my head over and over again.

Without another word, I took his hand and climbed the stairs, leading him to my bedroom and pushing him down onto my bed.

I clambered on top of him and kissed him again, before we both flipped over so that he was now on top of me, regaining the upper hand once more.

"Are you sure?" he asked, voice husky, eyes intent.

I nodded.

Matt leant back and pulled his jumper off over his head, throwing it onto the floor, then nuzzled at my neck, telling me to take my top off too. I did what he wanted and lay back down, letting him kiss his way down my body, before he started undoing my jeans.

I lifted my hips up and let him pull my jeans down, wriggling my legs a little to help them down and watched, almost in slow motion as Matt raised himself up and unbuckled his belt, pulling his jeans down too. He leant back over me, hands either side of my head, and dipped his mouth to mine, kissing me more urgently.

"I've waited soooo long for this," he whispered, tugging at my knickers. "You have no idea how long I've wanted this, Immy."

His words washed over me as I lay back and closed my eyes, hating the feeling of Matt's rough body pressed against mine. Images of Fickle burned into my eyes as I squeezed them tight shut, almost as if to keep them safe inside me, and away from Matt. Images of Fickle being with her ex, images of Fickle being with me and doing this with me swam through my head as I felt Matt's body start to move against mine.

Afterwards, as we lay spooning, tears rolled down my face, soaking my pillow. But I knew I'd done the right thing. Sleeping with Matt had been the barrier I'd needed to break for months. Now I'd done it, I could start to forget about Fickle and finally be a proper girlfriend to Matt.

I wasn't gay. I was straight. And you know what? I'd just damn well proved it.

CHAPTER SIX

After Matt had gone, kissing me tenderly good-bye at the front door and telling me how happy he was, I returned to my room and lay on my bed in the darkness, just staring up at the ceiling. I remembered everything we'd just done and tried to stem the feeling of panic about to overwhelm me.

Why had I done it? Why?

I knew darned well why. Fickle.

I wanted to prove something to myself, but what was it? That Matt was important to me and that Fickle didn't matter? Was I trying to punish her? Punish myself? Ridiculous! Fickle was nothing to me, yet here I was imagining that I'd just slept with Matt so that it would punish her for going out when all I'd wanted was for her to be with me, even if only in cyberspace.

I rubbed at my eyes, trying to stop the tears I knew were only one more thought away. I was going mad; there was nothing else to explain it. I was infatuated with someone I'd never even met, infatuated to the point that I'd slept with my boyfriend and hated every second of it. Just to prove a point.

I looked across to the computer and, hauling myself from my bed, set myself down in front of it and brought up MSN again. I knew Fickle wouldn't be around, but a small part of me kept hoping that she might show, even though the last thing I needed was her telling

me about her fabulous night out with her ex. As MSN flickered
into life, I secretly prayed that her name would be there. It wasn't.
Instead, I went to the message board, seeking comfort that I knew
I'd get from an hour or so of inane chatting.

I posted a few hellos and answered a few threads, but my heart
wasn't in it. Despite every part of me telling me I was being stupid,
I knew that what I really wanted was Fickle. Joey's name flashed
up on MSN and I smiled. Relieved to have the chance to talk to
someone, I sent her a message:

Barnaby Rudge: Hey!

Joey: Hey! You okay? You sound a bit down in the dumps
on the board tonight.

Barnaby Rudge: Bit fed up, is all.

Joey: That doesn't sound like you! Wassup?

Barnaby Rudge: Oh I dunno, Joe. My life's just a bit
confusing right now.

Joey: You wanna talk about it? I'm having an argument
with someone called HoBo on the board, so I think I'm
kinda gonna be here for the night!

Barnaby Rudge: It's just, I dunno. I'm going out with this
guy, right?

Joey: Uh-oh, man trouble alert!

Barnaby Rudge: And he's nice and he's good looking and
he's attentive and he treats me well and all.

Joey: Uh-huh.

Barnaby Rudge: But I'm not getting it, you know?

Joey: Not getting what? Sex?

Barnaby Rudge: LMAO! Noooooo! I'm not getting HIM.

Joey: Ah! Phew! 'Cos it's best not to ask me about yukky
things like boy sex, y'see. I bat for the other team,
kiddo, so I wouldn't be much cop advising you about
that.

Barnaby Rudge: Ah, right!

Joey: But lemme tell you, I've been out with enough women to help you with the whole 'not getting it' vibe. Ooooh believe me, mate, I've been there and bought the T-shirt. Mind you, there've been times I wished I'd kept the receipt…

Barnaby Rudge: And what did you do?

Joey: Well the thing is, you know when a person's right for you, don't you?

Barnaby Rudge: Yuh huh.

Joey: 'Cos you get, like, the butterflies, the whole 'can't eat' thing, the 'can't stop thinking about them' thing, don't you?

Barnaby Rudge: Yeah.

Joey: So are you getting all that with your bloke?

Barnaby Rudge: No, that's just it. I mean, I like him. I like him a lot. He's a good guy, you know?

Joey: But he ain't setting your candle alight?

Barnaby Rudge: Doesn't even have the matches.

Joey: LMAO! I like that.

Barnaby Rudge: And I try, y'know? I try sooo hard to feel something resembling attraction to him, but I can't. I mean, it's like, I look at him and I can see he's good looking but there's nothing there. And we've been out on loads of dates, so you'd kinda think there'd be some sort of spark by now, wouldn't you?

Joey: You would. It's getting you down, is it?

Barnaby Rudge: Yeah, because I don't know what to do. We, uh, we slept together for the first time tonight.

Joey: K, toooooo much information!

Barnaby Rudge: Soz!

Joey: LMAO, s'ok! So you slept with him, and?

Barnaby Rudge: Nothing.

Joey: Erk.

Barnaby Rudge: Indeed. I mean, I must have wanted to do it with him, why else would I have done it? I dunno, I s'pose I was curious to see if I'd feel anything more for him, you know?

Joey: I do know. And so you did it and…zippo?

Barnaby Rudge: Complete zippo. I just lay there like a dead fish on a harbour wall or summat. I dunno what to do, Joe!

Joey: Well, if you ask me, I'd say move on. Find someone who does float your boat. It's not fair on him, and it's certainly not fair on you. Sounds like you're wasting your time, kiddo.

Barnaby Rudge: But why it is he doesn't do anything for me?

Joey: Blimey, loads of reasons! I've been out with girls before who I've liked on our first date, but by the third date or whatever it's been obvious they're not the one for me. It's kismet innit? Stars colliding and all that. And when you do meet someone that lights up your life, makes you feel all mushy inside, and kinda makes you grin stupidly just thinking about him, well, then you'll know he's the one for you.

I looked at Joey's words. I'd already found that person, hadn't I?

Barnaby Rudge: Joey, can I ask you something personal?

Joey: Sure! As long as it's not about my weight, ha ha!

Barnaby Rudge: What's it like being with a girl?

Joey: Oooh, now that IS personal!

Barnaby Rudge: Sorry. Don't answer if you don't want.

Joey: Nah, you're cool. It's, well, it's amazing actually. Women are nice, y'know?

Barnaby Rudge: I know!

Joey: And they're softer and they sure as hell smell nicer than men!

Barnaby Rudge: Ha, ha! I'll bet!

Joey: And women kinda get other women, know what they want. They're probably just a bit more in tune with another woman's feelings 'cos it's only what they're thinking too. But, hey, that's not to say they can't hurt you too. It ain't just men who can break your heart, you know!

Barnaby Rudge: When did you know you were gay?

Joey: Flip, Barnaby! This is deep stuff for a Saturday night, you know!

Barnaby Rudge: Soz. I'm just interested.

Joey: I think I'd known since I was little, and I kinda had crushes on girls all the time, but then I fell madly in love with my best friend at school and then I knew for sure.

Barnaby Rudge: Did your best friend know?

Joey: Nope, I kept it to myself for ages and it was agony. I couldn't sleep, I couldn't eat, I couldn't function when I was around her. I eventually withdrew into myself 'cos I couldn't cope with it all and then one day she asked me if I was okay and I told her I loved her.

Barnaby Rudge: And?

Joey: And she was disgusted. She never spoke to me again.

Barnaby Rudge: Jeez, Joe! That's awful!

Joey: It was. Some friend, huh? But, hey ho! That was

three years ago and we haven't spoken to each other since. It was hell seeing her every day at school afterwards, but I got through it, and then eventually I met someone else and we fell in love and suddenly everything fell into place.

Barnaby Rudge: You still with her?

Joey: Nah. We drifted apart, but being with her was just what I needed at the time 'cos at least it let me know who I was. Loving someone and being loved back was the most awesome thing in the world, and it was brilliant while it lasted, but sometimes people drift apart. That's what happened to us.

Barnaby Rudge: That's kinda neat. Apart from the drifting apart bit!

Joey: And now I'm with a girl called Claire and, yeah, I like her a lot and, well, we'll see!

Barnaby Rudge: And you're happy?

Joey: Very.

Barnaby Rudge: Y'see, that's what I want. To be happy with someone.

Joey: But you're not happy with your boyfriend?

Barnaby Rudge: No.

Joey: Then it's like I said. As harsh as it sounds, maybe you gotta move on! Life's too short, kiddo.

Barnaby Rudge: I think you're right.

Joey: Ah, I'm ALWAYS right! You'll find someone, you'll see.

I took a deep breath, feeling my heart beat a bit faster all of a sudden.

Barnaby Rudge: I think I may already have found someone else.

Joey: Woop woop! Good on ya, kiddo! What's his name?

I stared at the screen and screwed up my hands into tight balls, gently knocking my knuckles against each other, wanting to tell Joey, but hardly daring to. This would be the first time I'd admitted to anyone that I had feelings for Fickle, but more importantly, this would be the first time I'd admitted I fancied a girl. It felt strange.

Barnaby Rudge: Thing is, Joey, it's a girl.

Joey: Woohoo! Welcome to my world!

Barnaby Rudge: Aaaand I dunno what to do.

Joey: Does she know?

Barnaby Rudge: No.

Joey: Is she gay?

Barnaby Rudge: Yes.

Joey: Well, that's a start! LOL.

Barnaby Rudge: I know. But the thing is, I don't want to scare her off by telling her I fancy her, because I like talking to her. I'd miss her if she wasn't around.

Joey: Amen to that. Where did you meet her?

Barnaby Rudge: On the Internet. Don't laugh.

Joey: Hey, who's laughing? It's where I met Claire!

Barnaby Rudge: Really? That's wicked! I actually met this girl on the L&S message board.

Joey: Cool! Do I know her?

Barnaby Rudge: She's called Fickle on the board. Her real name's Gemma.

There was a brief pause.

Joey: The name Fickle rings a bell, I think, but I've never spoken to her, I don't think. So do you think the whole business of you not feeling anything for your boyfriend has anything to do with Fickle?

Barnaby Rudge: I dunno, Joe. I don't think it helps.

Joey: Are you gay, then? I mean, have you fancied other girls before her?

Barnaby Rudge: That's just it, I don't know what I am at the moment. I mean, yeah, I think I've fancied girls before but it's been nothing like this! This is real intense, you know? And I'm so confused right now, it's making me miserable. I feel like I'm someone I'm not…I feel like it's all an act at the moment, like I'm hanging on by my fingertips.

Joey: I figured you were down. I'm very astute like that!

She'd added a winky sign, like Fickle does, making me suddenly wish for the umpteenth time that Fickle was online.

Barnaby Rudge: She sent me her picture, right? And the minute it came through it made me feel all weird.

Joey: But weird-good, yeah? Not weird-bad?

Barnaby Rudge: A bit freaked out but yeah, weird-good.

I paused. Then:

Barnaby Rudge: How do you know if you're gay, Joe? I figure if I knew then I could at least do something.

Joey: It's tricky, kiddo. It's not like we wear a rainbow-coloured silk sash round our shoulders proudly declaring it each and every day.

Barnaby Rudge: She told me she has an ex-girlfriend as well.

Joey: But not a current one?

Barnaby Rudge: Don't think so. She knows I have a boyfriend, though.

Joey: OK, well, if you do decide to dump your boyfriend—and I have a sneaky feeling you're gonna—how about telling her you've dumped him only because you're confused about her? She might be hanging back 'cos she knows you have a boyfriend. And then if you do dump him, then two birds, one stone and all that.

Barnaby Rudge: Sounds like a plan.

Joey: I know. I'm so perfect sometimes it frightens me.

Barnaby Rudge: How'd you get such a wise head on such young shoulders, Joe? We're the same age but you sure as hell talk a lot more sense than I do!

Joey: LMAO! Life experiences, kiddo. Life experiences.

There was a pause. Then:

Joey: Hey, you wanna see MY picture? I can guarantee it'll make you feel weirder than weird LOL.

Barnaby Rudge: Sure! I'll send you mine too!

I switched across to my Hotmail and attached a picture, the same one of me in Scotland that I'd sent Fickle that first time. After I'd sent it, I noticed Joey's e-mail to me, waiting patiently in my in-box, her photo attached.

It was a photo taken of her with a Christmas party hat on and what looked like a fake cigar in her mouth. She was pulling a silly face to the camera and, I dunno, she looked exactly as I'd expected her to; zany as hell.

Barnaby Rudge: I presume this was taken at Christmas, yeah?

Joey: No, I always wear Christmas hats, don't you??!

She posted a poking out tongue at me, making me laugh.

Joey: That looks like Edinburgh in your pic. Is it?

Barnaby Rudge: Yeah. Near the castle.

I suddenly heard my parents come in the front door downstairs and looked at the yellow clock on my wall. It was nearly midnight.

Barnaby Rudge: I better go, Joe. Parents just came home, so I ought to go speak to them.

Joey: K, chick.

Barnaby Rudge: You've been brilliant. Thank you so much for listening to me!

Joey: Any time. You know that. And thanks for the picture!!

I grinned to myself as I watched Joey change her status to

"Busy", evidently heading back to the message board to argue some more with HoBo, whoever he or she was. I logged off the computer and sat a while at my desk, eyes closed tightly, thinking about everything Joey had just said to me. When I opened my eyes again, everything seemed just that little bit clearer. I suddenly knew exactly what I had to do, and I knew Matt wasn't going to take it well.

CHAPTER SEVEN

I spent the whole of the next day, Sunday, lost in my thoughts, knowing what I had to do, but dreading having to do it. My worry about what I was going to do was not helped one little bit by at least a dozen texts from Matt telling me how much he'd "enjoyed" last night. I think I answered about three of them.

Lunchtime, as it turned out, was an absolute nightmare. Dad's sister, my fragrant and forthright Aunty Julia, came to eat with us, and although she was a welcome distraction from my thoughts, as usual Sophie and I had to run the gauntlet of questions about our love lives.

"Are you still with Mark?" Aunty Julia was now saying through a mouthful of roast potatoes.

"Matt," I replied, probably more sharply than I should have done.

"Matt, that's right. Are you still together?"

"Yup," I nodded, trying not to add, *"For now."*

"They seem very smitten, don't you, Immy?" Mum offered a bowl of potatoes to Aunty Julia and I watched, amused, as she stabbed up three in quick succession with her fork and plopped them down onto her plate.

"Mmm," I grunted, concentrating on my food.

"And really, Immy couldn't ask for a nicer boy," Mum was now saying.

"She's in love with him, Aunty Julia." Sophie leaned conspiratorially towards Aunty Julia. "She wouldn't ever say it, but she is. Who'd have thought it? My sweet sister in love."

Sophie looked at me and grinned sarcastically, shoving a piece of carrot into her mouth and chewing it noisily.

"Well, I think it's lovely." Aunty Julia smiled across the table. "I remember how it felt, only too well." She sighed and looked down at her potatoes again.

"But she gets dreadfully embarrassed talking about him, don't you?" Mum was pouring gravy over her dinner and I watched, suddenly feeling sick, as the thick, brown goo spread across her plate.

"Immy and Matt sitting up a tree, k-i-s-s-i-n-g," Sophie sang, poking her tongue out at me.

I glared, mouthing *"piss off"* to her as I heard my phone beep out at me from somewhere in my pockets.

"That'll be Matt," Sophie said matter-of-factly to Aunty Julia, who smiled a twee smile at me, making her eyes crinkle alarmingly at the corners.

I fished out my phone from my pocket and flipped the lid. It was from Fickle.

Where are ya? it said. *I'm lonely. Come and play with me.*

I snapped the phone shut again and put it back in my pocket.

"And what about little Sophie?" Aunty Julia was now saying. "Are you courting?"

"Courting?" Sophie snorted, making a small piece of carrot she was chewing shoot across the table from her mouth and earning her a look from Dad.

I put my knife and fork together and wiped my mouth with my napkin, turning to look at Mum.

"Can I be excused? I've had enough to eat, thanks," I said, hoping she wouldn't make me stay at the table and endure further agony of small talk with Aunty Julia.

"Do you have college work to do?" Mum frowned.

"Yeah," I lied. "I just wanna tweak an assignment I gotta hand in next week."

"Okay, off you go." Mum jerked her head in the direction of the door.

I smiled at Aunty Julia and bumped my chair into Sophie's as I rose from the table, catching the side of her head with my elbow for good measure as I brushed past her on my way out of the room.

Out in the hall I flipped open my phone and read Fickle's message again.

I'm lonely. Come and play with me.

I took the stairs two at a time, levering myself into my computer chair with a contented sigh, grateful to have a bit of peace and quiet away from everyone else downstairs.

I switched my computer on and watched as it booted itself up, feeling a shiver of excitement as I logged onto MSN and saw that Fickle was there waiting for me.

Fickle: 'Bout bloody time! Where ya been?

Barnaby Rudge: Lunch with the family.

Fickle: Nice!

Barnaby Rudge: It wasn't, trust me!

Fickle: Me mum's having a bad day today so I've decided to keep out of her way.

Barnaby Rudge: Oh! Is she okay?

Fickle: Yeah, just not so good, is all. She's downstairs watching the TV so I thought I'd just leave her to it.

Barnaby Rudge: So how was your night last night?

Fickle: Nothing special. We just went for a drink but like I say, it was nothing special. The ex is still very much an ex and I'm still single!!

My mind was racing and I suddenly grinned, but I didn't know why I was grinning like that. Her ex was still an ex. I liked that. It put a new edge on things again, I supposed. Made her more available.

What? I leant back in my chair, aware of what it was that I was thinking.

Fickle available? Who was I kidding? I knew nothing about her. All I knew was what she looked like, that she was eighteen and went to school somewhere. I didn't know who she lived with other than her mum, if she had brothers or sisters. Nothing. Yet here I was grinning like the cat that got the cream because Fickle had told me she was single.

I wanted to change the subject—and fast.

Barnaby Rudge: You see the football yesterday?

Fickle: Yeah, it was all right. Nothing special, was it?

Anyway, how was your Saturday night?

Barnaby Rudge: Not bad. My boyfriend came over.

I have no idea what made me mention Matt to her at that precise moment. Maybe it was because we'd just been talking about Fickle's ex, maybe it was a surreptitious way of seeing what her reaction would be. Maybe it was something deeper. Who knows?

Fickle: You have a boyfriend?

I'd told her I had a boyfriend practically the first time we ever spoke to each other. Why hadn't she remembered that?

Fickle: You never said.

I had said! I had!

Why was I so pissed off that she hadn't remembered that I had a boyfriend? Wasn't it important enough for her to remember?

Barnaby Rudge: Yes I did. I told you before, Gemma! His name's Matt. He sings in a band.

Fickle: Did you? Kewl. What sort of music?

Barnaby Rudge: Grunge, Emo, that sorta stuff.

Fickle: Niiiiiiiiiice.

I wanted to tell her that he wasn't that special, that other people were keener on him than I was, and that I'd been trying to figure out the best way to finish with him all day. I wanted to tell her all these things but something kept stopping me. Instead, I wrote:

Barnaby Rudge: Sorry, I did tell you about him before, you know.

Fickle: You know what I love about you, Immy?

Barnaby Rudge: Hit me.

Fickle: You're always apologising. It's cute, but you kinda gotta stop it!

She put a winking sign, which sent shivers down my spine. She said I was cute. Well, fine, she said *it* was cute, but that's the same thing, isn't it?

Barnaby Rudge: I know. It's a bad habit of mine.

Fickle: I can think of worse!

Barnaby Rudge: Such as?

Fickle: Having a boyfriend!

Barnaby Rudge: You got a point there! BRB, Fickle!

I heard footsteps on the stairs outside my room and immediately minimised the page I was talking to Fickle on and brought up a website on Vietnam, in the hope that it would look like I had actually been doing some work in the time I'd been up in my room.

A soft knock on my door was followed by Mum's face peering round into my room at me.

"You doing fine?" she asked, looking over my shoulder at the website.

I hastily picked up a pen and made to write out some notes on a piece of paper that was on my desk.

"Yeah." I nodded. "Trying to make head and tail of Vietnam—as you do!" I tapped my biro on the computer screen.

"We're eating chocolate pudding downstairs if you want some?" Mum was now asking.

"Nah, I'm not hungry," I replied, itching to get back to Fickle.

"I'll keep some back in case you want it later." Mum's head disappeared from sight again. "Don't work too hard," I heard her call as she went back downstairs again.

I opened up MSN and felt a ripple of pleasure as I saw Fickle's messages to me.

> **Fickle:** Where are yoooooo? Bored, bored BORED without yooooo.
> **Barnaby Rudge:** Okay, okay, keep your hair on! I'm here.
> **Fickle:** Missed ya!
> **Barnaby Rudge:** You really are bored, aren't you?!
> **Fickle:** No, I really did miss you.
> **Barnaby Rudge:** Yeah, right!
> **Fickle:** So tell me about this boyfriend of yours, Immy. How long have you been with him?

Why did I have to talk about Matt? I wanted to talk about Fickle's ex, not my boyfriend.

> **Barnaby Rudge:** Uh, dunno, 'bout six weeks or so.
> **Fickle:** Sweet! You in love?
> **Barnaby Rudge:** Next question. LOL.
> **Fickle:** Oh right. Soz.
> **Barnaby Rudge:** No worries. How long were you with your ex, then?
> **Fickle:** Not long.
> **Barnaby Rudge:** Right.
> **Fickle:** It all ended pretty nastily, to be honest.
> **Barnaby Rudge:** So you on the lookout for someone else?

Fickle: Sure am. And I've got my eye on someone already.

She put that damn winking sign up after that and yet again my heart fluttered at the sight of it. We chatted on for ages after that, flirting and generally teasing each other and, without even me realising it, I suddenly discovered I'd been chatting to Fickle for nearly two hours. Time flies when you're having fun, huh? I thought about everyone downstairs and, reluctantly, thought I'd better show my face to them again.

Barnaby Rudge: Gemma, I'd better go. I've been up in my room for ages.

Fickle: Do you really have to?

Barnaby Rudge: I should. The 'rents'll wonder what's happened to me.

Fickle: Get your 'rents up here on the computer! I'll tell 'em I've abducted you!

Barnaby Rudge: If it meant I didn't have to go downstairs and make small talk with my Aunty Julia, I'd say go for it!

Fickle: I'd happily abduct you, Immy. Whisk you away from it all!!! Anything has to be better than having to make polite conversation with a visiting relative!!

I looked at my watch again. Everything was urging me to stay talking to Fickle, but the polite and guilty girl inside me was telling me to go down and say hi to them.

Barnaby Rudge: Are you going to be here all afternoon?

Fickle: Probs. Shit all else to do.

Barnaby Rudge: I'll be half an hour. Will you wait?

Fickle: For you, Immy, forever!!

Was that sarcasm or flirting? I was darned if I knew, but what I did know was that the sooner I got myself downstairs and made a show of speaking to everyone, the sooner I could come back upstairs. Back to Fickle.

I logged off and wandered down to the lounge where Mum, Dad, and Aunty Julia were deep in conversation about the state of the health service or something, whilst Sophie was slumped on the sofa, furiously texting away on her mobile, totally oblivious to the chatter going on around her.

"All done?" Mum looked up at me and smiled as I perched on the edge of the sofa.

"Not quite," I replied, leaning over to grab a biscuit from a plate on the coffee table.

"Immy's got assignments up to her ears at the moment, haven't you?" Mum looked across to Aunty Julia then back at me.

"Mmm," I half grunted, reaching for another biscuit.

"What are you doing up there at the moment?" Aunty Julia smiled over at me, her eyebrows raised questioningly.

Of course, what I wanted to tell her was that I was up there talking to someone who I barely knew, but who I kinda wanted to get to know a whole lot better, and that because she, Aunty Julia, was visiting, I didn't feel like I could, and could she, Aunty Julia, *please* go home so that I didn't have to feel guilty about secreting myself away in my room talking to someone who I just happened to fancy the very arse off, thank you very much.

Instead I smiled back at Aunty Julia and said, "Oh just an essay on Vietnam and Sino-U.S. *Rapprochement* 1968–72." That seemed to stop her in her tracks. I was secretly pleased that I'd come back at her with such a stunning reply, and even more pleased that I'd actually remembered what work it was I was supposed to be doing, and it really did seem to work because Aunty Julia reached for another biscuit and simply said, "Well, if you have to get on, my love, don't let me stop you."

I immediately thought of Fickle waiting for me online and looked to Mum for confirmation, receiving it in the form of a nod and warm smile, which was enough for me to leave the room and take the stairs back up to my room, two at a time, heart thumping wildly in my chest, hoping that Fickle had kept her word and would still be there.

She was.

Barnaby Rudge: I'm back!

I leant back in my chair and grinned at the screen, waiting for Fickle to reply, watching and waiting for the flashing message to appear on screen, telling me she had written back. I waited for around five minutes, wondering where she'd gone, when suddenly I saw her name appear.

Fickle: There you are! I was just texting you!

Barnaby Rudge: You were? To say what?

Fickle: Just that I was waiting for you and I missed you!

Barnaby Rudge: I was only gone two minutes!

Fickle: Two minutes too long.

Barnaby Rudge: Blimey, you must be bored!

Fickle: Something like that. So how's your Aunty Julia? LOL.

Barnaby Rudge: Okay.

Fickle: Just okay?

Barnaby Rudge: Yeah. At least she didn't start quizzing me about my bloody love life again like she did over lunch!

Fickle: About boyfriends and shit? I hate that! Why do they all do that? My relatives are just the same. Drives me crazy.

Barnaby Rudge: They don't know you're gay?

Fickle: Nooooo! And that's the way I like it. It's no one else's business anyway.

Barnaby Rudge: And all the questions wouldn't be so bad if I was enthusiastic about my boyfriend, but, y'know!

Why did I write that? Why did I have to let Fickle know that?

This wasn't Joey I was talking to now. Fickle would seize on it, I knew. And she did.

> **Fickle:** You're not so hot on him, then? I do remember you saying something to me about him now, but it was a while ago, I think.
>
> **Barnaby Rudge:** See? I told you I had! Yeah, I'm kinda lukewarm on him, I guess!
>
> **Fickle:** Aaaaaand yet you're still going out with him?
>
> **Barnaby Rudge:** Yeah, yeah I know.
>
> **Fickle:** You shouldn't be with him if you're not hot on him, Immy! Life's too short. Get out there and have fun!
>
> **Barnaby Rudge:** That's what someone else told me today as well!

I knew they were both right, of course, both Fickle and Joey. But it's not easy dumping someone, is it? I knew darn well I had to finish with Matt, but every time I thought about ringing him, my blood ran cold. I'd even thought about texting him, but that would just be too cruel.

I might be totally pickled with confusion, and as miserable as sin, but I'm not that much of a bitch.

Chapter Eight

I eventually finished talking to Fickle around nine that night, missing dinner with my parents with the excuse that I wanted to get my assignment finished and printed before the next day. Aunty Julia had long gone by then, allowing me to indulge in stupid but wonderful Fickle chatter, totally uninterrupted. Brilliant.

Twiggy had logged on shortly after six, so I'd had the pleasure of her company for a few hours too, something I was grateful for, having not spoken to her in what seemed like ages. Despite my obsession with Fickle, I was still extremely fond of Twiggy, with her silly jokes and funny ways. After all, I reasoned, if it hadn't have been for Twiggy first contacting me on the board and introducing me to the wonderful world of MSN, I might never have hung around long enough to ever meet Fickle. For that alone, I was incredibly grateful.

I'd wanted to talk to Twiggy about Fickle too that night, but something had held me back; mainly worry that her reaction might not be what I'd wanted. After I'd finally logged off, reluctantly leaving Fickle, who kept telling me she'd miss me, I returned downstairs to sit with Mum and Dad in front of the TV for a bit. But every time I tried to concentrate on the TV programme they were watching, my brain just kept turning things over and over, replaying my conversations with Fickle, and distracting me so much that eventually even Mum noticed that I seemed preoccupied.

"You worried about that assignment you've been working on?" Mum picked up a magazine and started flicking through it. "You're away with your thoughts tonight, Immy."

I stretched my legs out in front of me. "Mmm?" I said, "Nah, it's just, I'm just, uh, just thinking about what I've got coming up next week, that's all."

"You're not worried about any of it, are you?" Mum patted my outstretched leg.

I smiled.

"No, not worried."

Mum lowered her voice as Dad continued staring at the programme on the TV. "You've been awful quiet lately."

"Have I?" I shrugged. "I don't mean to be."

"Everything all right with Matt?"

"Fine, yeah." I nodded, probably more enthusiastically than was required.

"And you'd tell me if there was anything, wouldn't you?"

"No." I laughed, then, "Yes, of course. There's nothing, honest."

What could I say to Mum? That I was thinking about dumping my doting boyfriend because I was having feelings for a girl I'd only just met on the Internet? Yeah, that'd go down well!

I sure as hell couldn't tell her that I thought I might be gay. Now that *definitely* wouldn't go down well! I'll be honest here and say that gayness is not the kind of subject that my family regularly talk about around the dining table of an evening. Of course, I've thought about hardly anything but gayness over the last few weeks, and I've often thought that Mum would be okay with it. Not Dad.

I'd hate to use the word *homophobic* to describe Dad, but it doesn't sit comfortably with him, Dad being the sort who would get up and leave the room if there's something remotely gay on the TV, rather than actually having to watch it.

But that's his problem, not mine or anyone else's. Right?

It didn't make the thought of broaching the subject with them any easier, though. I sat and stared into space, ignoring the TV programme, and tried to figure out the best thing to do. The one thing I did know for sure was that if I was to sort out the confusion in my head, then I needed to finish with Matt, however horrible it was going to be. I needed to be prepared for the questions that would follow too, questions from Mum and Dad, as well as Emily and Beth, both of whom would think I was totally mad.

I sighed, earning another sideways glance from Mum. Finishing with Matt was going to be the hardest thing I'd probably ever have to do, but I knew it needed to be done, both for his sake and mine. How could I be sure what it was I wanted, or what it was I thought I might be? I needed to be 100 percent sure I was gay, and the only way to find that out was to try and get to know Fickle better. I couldn't do that while I was still seeing Matt. I needed to be true to myself, right? Maybe I was seeing Fickle as a way out of my dead-end relationship with Matt, or maybe I was just fascinated by her and was reading her friendliness as flirting. One thing was for sure, though. Unless I cranked it up a gear and found out for myself, I'd never know.

I looked at my watch; it was a little after ten p.m. Suddenly needing to talk to someone, I made my excuses and wandered back up to my room, firing up the computer, hoping that either Twiggy or Joey might be around, hoping even more that they wouldn't mind lending me an ear for an hour or so. To my relief I saw that Joey was online, chatting to someone on the message board about the previous week's episode of *Lovers and Sinners*. I grinned. A dose of Joey was just what I needed.

Barnaby Rudge: Hey Joe!

Joey: Hey, chick! How's tricks?

Barnaby Rudge: Not bad, not bad. You?

Joey: Yeah, cool. I was just telling SpyderWoman that next week's L&S is on Thursday, not Wednesday.

Barnaby Rudge: Ah right. Thanks, I didn't know.

Joey: No probs. Do you know, SpyderWoman's real name is Cynthia. I mean, who's called Cynthia anymore??

Barnaby Rudge: She sure doesn't talk like a Cynthia. LMAO!!

Joey: I'm really Joanna, btw. Now can you see why I prefer Joey? LOL

Barnaby Rudge: Uh, yeah I can, Joe! Sorry!

Joey: What's your name?

Barnaby Rudge: Imogen—Immy.

Joey: My neighbour's got a guinea pig called Immy.

Barnaby Rudge: Is that your useless fact for the day?

Joey: Cheeky bugger! Anyway, how're you? You having a good day?

Barnaby Rudge: Yeah, apart from having to entertain my Aunty Julia. She came over for lunch today.

Joey: Eek! Whatchoo do to entertain her? Balance a ball on your nose? Give her your paw?

Barnaby Rudge: Funny! Nah, just had to bat away questions about my love life.

Joey: Shudder! Been there, done that. I sympathise!

A pause ensued.

Joey: So how are things going with Fickle? You come onto her yet?!

Barnaby Rudge: No!! I've never come onto anyone in my life! Wouldn't know what to do, Joe.

Joey: You can drop her some subtle hints, though, see if she bites, so to speak.

Barnaby Rudge: Like flirt with her, you mean?

Joey: That's exactly what I mean!

Barnaby Rudge: I could try, I suppose. What if I've been reading her all wrong, though, and she doesn't like me like that?

Joey: Well, she must have given you some encouragement, otherwise you wouldn't say you think she's flirty with you. What sort of things does she do?

Barnaby Rudge: Hmm, dunno. Lots of winking, she tells me she misses me when I'm not here, she texted me today and asked me to get online 'cos she said she was lonely without me.

Joey: Fllliiiiiiiiiiiiirt Alerrrrrrrrrt! Yeah, that's kinda flirty, isn't it?!

Barnaby Rudge: So it's not my imagination?

Joey: Well, unless she's like that with everyone, male and female, I'd say she was flirting. I mean, you don't tell people you miss them and you don't wink at them unless you want to let them know you're being flirtatious. Just my opinion, kiddo.

Barnaby Rudge: I really like her, Joe. It's proper messing with my head, all this.

Joey: I bet.

Barnaby Rudge: Yeah, #groan#. I'm still confused about why I slept with my boyfriend too.

Joey: You still don't know what to do, then?

Barnaby Rudge: No…I still wanna finish with him, which is why sleeping with him was all the more mashed up.

Joey: So why DID you sleep with him?

Barnaby Rudge: You tell me, Joe! Maybe I wanted to see

if it sparked anything off, some sort of feelings towards
him, I dunno.

Joey: But you said that it didn't?

Barnaby Rudge: Nope. It just made me feel ashamed of
myself.

Joey: Ashamed?

Barnaby Rudge: For using him. I think I did it as a knee-
jerk reaction 'cos Fickle had just told me she was
meeting her ex for a drink.

Joey: Blimey! I can see why you're confused! Although I
wouldn't feel too guilty about using him, Immy. He's a
man; he wouldn't have felt used! For him it was just
sex.

Barnaby Rudge: But it's, like, totally stoopid, isn't it?
Sleeping with someone I'm planning to dump just 'cos
someone I've never met but fancy the arse off just
happens to go out with her ex-girlfriend for a drink.

Joey: And I'm sure there'll be plenty of guys and girls all
up and down the country who've done something
similar, trust me! It's just called being confused.

Barnaby Rudge: And I am gonna finish with Matt. It's
just…it's hard, isn't it?

Joey: And not a very nice thing to do. I know, it's tough,
isn't it?

Barnaby Rudge: And it's like, having to explain to
everyone why I did it. That's what I'm dreading.

Joey: Well, at the end of the day it's nothing to do with
anyone else. It's your life, your decision. But if you
ask me, you can't even begin to get your head around
the whole Fickle thing as long as you're still with your
boyfriend, being eaten up with guilt about it all. So I
guess either you stay with your boyfriend, not getting

much out of being with him, and forget all about
Fickle, or you finish with him and turn your whole
attention to her.

Barnaby Rudge: That's what I've been thinking. I can't
forget her, Joe. I can't stop thinking about her! It's all
I do from the moment I wake up until the second I fall
asleep at night, and then I even sometimes bloody
well dream about her! She's in my head 24/7 and it's
killing me!

Joey: Sounds like you got it bad.

Barnaby Rudge: I think I have. I feel miserable when
she's not 'around' on MSN and then I feel like my
heart's gonna burst with joy whenever she's online.
She makes me happy and she's all I ever think about,
all day at college all I can think about is her, what
she's doing, where she is, and then I can't wait to get
home and talk to her on MSN. Or, like, if my phone
beeps and I see it's her sending me a text, it makes
me feel soooo happy! Is that crazy?

Joey: No, it's not crazy, kiddo. I think it's what they
commonly call Fancying Someone.

Barnaby Rudge: But it feels great and shitty at the same
time. What's that all about?!

Joey: Welcome to the world of loopy-love bunnies! LOL.
It's just crap when you're so into someone but you
don't know how they feel, and you don't know what to
do about it, isn't it?

Barnaby Rudge: Like with you and your best friend?

Joey: Exactamundo. Listen, kiddles, I gotta go, I'm sorry.
I've gotta get some sleep.

Barnaby Rudge: No worries, Joe.

Joey: I'm off on a field trip with college tomorrow to
Scotland until Friday. The minibus leaves at six in the
morning, then a ten-hour coach drive. Yuk!

Barnaby Rudge: So you don't live near Scotland, then?
LOL!

Joey: Very astute, Imms! Nah, I live in a town called
Abingdon. It's in Oxfordshire, so hence the ten-hour
drive!

Barnaby Rudge: No shit? I live in Oxford! I'm only about
10 miles from you, thassall!

Joey: LMAO, really? It's a small world innit, kiddo?!

Barnaby Rudge: Too right it is! So you're gonna be away
all week, then?

Joey: 'Fraid so.

This wasn't what I wanted to hear. I was kinda hoping Joey
might be around to guide me through what I had a feeling was going
to be the week from hell for me.

Barnaby Rudge: Well, have a good one won't you, Joe?

Joey: I'll try. Hey, look, here's my mobile number. Text me
if things get too heavy, yeah?

Joey typed up her phone number and I jotted it down quickly.
I'd use it too. I was sure of that.

Barnaby Rudge: I'll try not to bother you too much!

Joey: It'll probably be a welcome distraction from studying
amoeba in some murky Scottish loch!!

After we'd said our good-byes and Joey had logged off, I hung
around online for a while, secretly hoping that Fickle might log on
briefly before bed. I glanced down at my mobile and remembered
what Joey had just said about perhaps giving Fickle the come-on,
let her know I was interested. I wondered if I should text Fickle,
say to her some of the things she says to me; tell her I missed her,

that I wanted her to come online and talk to me. Then I remembered Matt and I felt the familiar sinking feeling in my heart, as I always seemed to when I thought about him.

Joey was right. There was no way I could even begin to think about letting Fickle know I liked her until I did something about Matt. I looked down at my phone again and without really knowing what I was going to say to him, dialled his number, my heart thumping wildly in my neck.

CHAPTER NINE

"It sounded urgent on the phone." Matt frowned across the table at me the next night. "What's up? Is something wrong?"

I'd met Matt at our favourite local café, where you could get a burger, chips, and drink for under a fiver, so it did us quite nicely. It was nothing special, more the sort of place where if you wanted to know what else was on the menu, you just had to look at the stains on the cook's apron. You know the sort of place.

I looked over at Matt, taking in every detail of his face. I tried, for the last time, to find some spark inside me, something that might stop me from doing what I was about to do. But there was nothing. No lust, no fancying, no love. Genuine affection, sure, but no fireworks, no fire at all. Nothing that came even close to what Fickle ignited inside me.

I watched as Matt picked off a chunk of burger roll and shoved it into his mouth.

"It's not urgent, nothing's wrong." An image of Matt's face looming over mine, just as it had done the night we slept together, entered my head, making the skin on the back of my neck prickle. "Well, kinda wrong, but everything's okay. At least I think it is. Well, it will be. I hope so, anyway." I was stuttering now. "I just need to talk to you, Matt." I heard myself sighing at him.

"Okaaaay." Matt squinted, peering at me quizzically. He put down his burger and wiped his mouth with his napkin. "I think I know what this is about." He nodded.

"You do?" I frowned at him.

"It's about the other night, isn't it?" Matt reached for his drink and took a sip, watching me carefully over the rim of the glass.

"What about the other night?"

"You regret it, don't you? I was getting vibes off you even before I'd left the house."

I hesitated, thinking about what I was going to say next.

"You wish you'd never done it, I think." Matt pursed his lips.

"I do," I said slowly, feeling grateful to Matt for leading me into this conversation, so that I didn't have to kinda start from scratch.

Matt nodded and picked up his burger again, biting a chunk from it. I looked down at my own, half-eaten burger. A wave of nausea threatened to overwhelm me.

"I hope you don't think I forced you into anything, but you kinda seemed up for it when I came round." He shrugged. "I love you, Immy, and you love me, and it's what people in love do. Simple."

He loved me? Worse than that, he thought that I loved him too? I stared at him, kinda dumbstruck.

"You do realise that I love you, don't you, Immy?" Matt reached over and took my hand, stroking the palm of my hand with his thumb. "I guess I should tell you more often than I do, but it's kinda obvious, isn't it? That we're made for each other."

I guessed it was now or never.

Taking a deep breath, I slowly said, "I do wish I hadn't slept with you, yes, and I'm sorry for that," and watched as Matt blithely stabbed up some chips with his fork. "And I kinda…I kinda don't want to do this anymore either."

Matt's head sprang up and he stared straight at me. "Don't want to do what anymore?"

"This," I said feebly. "Us."

"Eh?" Matt frowned. "What do you mean?"

I tried not to sigh, wondering just how blunt I needed to be before he got the message, but before I'd even answered, the look on his face told me that the penny might finally be dropping.

"Wait a minute. I don't understand where all this is coming from. I thought you meant you just weren't ready to sleep with me. I was fine with that," he said. "I didn't think you wanted us to split up!"

"I'm sorry," I said, suddenly thinking what an insipid, crap word "sorry" can be in situations such as these.

"Sorry? So you're actually going to dump me?" I heard the words choke in his throat as he said them.

Silence. What could I say?

"Jesus, Immy! You're kidding me, right? Tell me you're joking, for shit's sake!"

"It's not a joke. I'm sorry." I reached over and took his hand again, not sure what else to do.

He snatched his hand from mine and shoved back in his chair, turning his head to stare out the window, like a petulant child.

"It happens," I added, probably not very helpfully.

He turned and looked back at me. "Not to me, it doesn't," he said.

That kinda pissed me off, I dunno why.

"But I love you," he said. "I've proper fallen for you, you know?"

Another silence.

"So…you *don't* love me?" Pain threaded through Matt's tone.

I shook my head, just wanting this to be over. "I do like you, Matt, I do. It's just, I dunno."

"Just liking me's not enough?" Matt's voice began to rise, while his face looked like it might crumple at any moment, and I suddenly thought how awful it might be if he started crying.

I shook my head again.

Matt picked up his napkin and stared at it, turning it over and over in his hands. "I don't understand where this has come from."

"It's not you, Matt. It's me," I said quietly, cringing at the cliché, even though it was a cliché that was actually true for once.

Matt robotically shredded the napkin, as if unaware of his actions. "How long have you felt like this, Immy?"

"A while."

"You should have said you weren't happy!" Matt's voice rose again, and people looked over at us, curiously.

I desperately wished this were over so I could get the hell out of that damn café. "I just did," I replied, probably more sharply than he deserved.

"So who is he, then?" Matt's voice was still louder than I wanted it to be.

I blinked, confused. "What?" My face flamed with embarrassment.

"There must be someone else." Matt leant closer. "That dickhead from your economics class, I knew he fancied you."

I leant back in my chair and ran my hand through my hair, staring across the table and resisting the urge to roll my eyes. "There's no one else," I lied. "You and me just doesn't feel right, thassall."

"Bollocks!" Matt angrily shoved his plate away, his fork spiralling off the edge and clattering onto the table.

"You're a really nice guy, Matt." I paused. Swallowed. "And you deserve someone better than me, someone who…values that."

"Fine." He suddenly rose from his chair, scraping it back so loudly that the couple sitting across from us turned in unison to gape. He dug into his jeans pocket and pulled out a tattered-looking £10 note, flinging it, still crumpled up, onto the table. "Dinner's on me." He yanked his coat from the chair and stalked from the café without so much as a backward glance.

Part of me shuddered with relief. The other cringed with embarrassment. I stayed at the table, staring at the crumpled £10 note without really seeing it. I sensed the couple on the next table still sneaking surreptitious glances, evidently clear about what had just happened, and decided to stay where I was a while longer, trying to look as casual as possible.

Was that it, then? Had I finally done it? A small surge of relief inside me mixed in with gut-wrenching guilt, and I prayed that Matt wouldn't come back to the table to talk more. I suppose part of me felt surprised at how readily he'd accepted it and, if I'm honest, a bit peeved that he didn't put up more of a fight, but I supposed that had to be an ego thing.

But I *had* done it, yeah. I'd finished with Matt and, yes, the sense of release felt amazing. However, it had been the most toe-curlingly awful thing I'd ever done in my life. I wondered where Matt had gone, wondered briefly if I should go and find him, but my head told me to leave him alone. I finally summoned the courage to look around, feeling just a bit lost, not wanting to leave the café for whatever dumb reason, then slowly ate the rest of my burger, feeling the waves of nausea that had seemed to have lived with me for weeks gradually start to disappear.

❖

I walked home alone, of course, over the canal bridge that Matt normally walked me to, and felt…well…nothing really. I wondered if Matt might ring or text me, ask to see me again, to talk things over, but he didn't. Thank God. The last thing I wanted was to see him and go over everything again. As far as I was concerned, I'd done what I'd wanted to do for ages; now all I wanted was go home and not have to think about anything for the next few hours.

As I stepped into the house, I peered briefly at my phone to see if there were any messages. Nothing. I poked my head around the corner of the lounge door but all I could see was Sophie sitting on the chair in the corner of the room, legs tucked up under her, deep in conversation with someone on her mobile phone. She looked up when she saw me but didn't acknowledge my presence, choosing instead to carry on her conversation about "how fit Brett McManus is and, like, did you know he, like, *totally* looked at me today".

I rolled my eyes and retreated to the kitchen, finding Mum sitting at the breakfast bar reading the daily paper. She looked up and smiled at me when she saw me and pushed the newspaper away from her a little way.

"I've sought refuge in here." She grinned. "Your sister's on the phone to Rhian and I couldn't bear to have to listen to her talking about Brett McManus a minute longer." She patted the stool next to her. "How was your evening?" she asked as I lifted myself up onto the stool and leant my elbows on the breakfast bar.

"Yeah, all right." I pulled my hands through my hair and sighed.

"As good as that?"

I looked at her from the corner of my eye.

"Me and Matt aren't seeing each other anymore," I said, waiting for her reaction.

"Oh?" she sounded surprised. "That's a shame. He's a nice boy. I liked him."

"Mmm." I nodded slowly.

"Did you have an argument? It'll blow over, it always does." Mum put her hand on my arm. "You'll see, he'll be all apologies tomorrow, they always are."

"We didn't have an argument." I turned my head briefly as I heard my phone beep somewhere out in the hall.

"And that'll be him, mark my words." Mum jerked her head towards the door. "Texting to tell you he loves you." She smiled softly.

"It was me that finished with him," I said simply, staring down at my hands in front of me.

"You finished with him?" Mum repeated, her brow knitting. "Why?"

"Just…'cos."

"You finished what?" Sophie's voice sounded from the doorway.

"Nothing, Sophie. Immy's just not seeing Matt anymore, that's all," Mum said, looking sympathetically at me and patting my arm, as if my hamster had just died or something. I don't even have a bloody hamster.

"You did *what*?" Sophie gaped incredulously at me.

"You heard," I snapped back at her.

"Er, like, *why*?" Sophie raised her eyebrows and put her hands on her hips.

"Er, like, 'cos I *wanted* to," I replied sarcastically.

"Er, 'cos you wanted to? Do you know how many girls *want* to date Matt? You're crazy, you are."

Wasn't that enough reason? I suddenly felt like an animal trapped in a cage, having to justify myself to my idiot younger sister.

"I have my reasons." I stared down at my hands.

"But he's buff, man." Sophie still had her fists on her hips.

"Buff? Man? What freaking language are you speaking, you jerk?" I glowered at Sophie.

"Immy," Mum warned, still managing to glare at both me and Sophie.

"And what freaking planet are you on, *you jerk*, if you think dumping a guy like Matt is a wise move?" Sophie waved a dismissive hand at me.

"Fuck you, idiot," I muttered under my breath, staring petulantly into the distance.

The abrupt scrape of Mum's stool across the kitchen floor made me jump as she stepped down from it and stood in the middle of the kitchen. "Enough." She ushered Sophie back out of the room, muttering something to her before turning back to me. "Immy, I'm sure you had your reasons for ending things with Matt, but whatever they were, don't go taking it out on Sophie, okay?"

"Sure," I replied, getting down from my stool and brushing past her into the hall. I grabbed my phone and flipped it open as I walked up the stairs to my room, grinning with relief as I saw it was from Joey and not Matt. I'd texted Joey earlier in the day, wishing her a safe journey up to Scotland. I guessed she'd arrived safely when I saw that her text just said:

Och aye and a hoo, hoo, hoo from bonny Scotland.

I sent her a quick message back, asking her how she was and that, oh yeah, I'd just broken up with Matt. Then I sent Fickle a text too, writing some silly message to her, hoping that we might have a silly, flirty text conversation for the rest of the evening. I flopped myself down on my bed and stretched out, waiting for her to reply, but only Joey sent me a text, just asking me if I was okay. I thought I was probably a lot better than Matt, then kinda lay there for a bit thinking about him, wondering how he was, and thinking I ought to text him, see how he was.

I didn't.

Instead I waited for ages for Fickle to text me back, looking at my phone over and over again, in case I hadn't heard it. When I still hadn't heard from her after an hour, I sent a text back to Joey telling her not to drink too much Scotch whisky and went to bed, my mind swirling with images of Matt, flinging his tattered money at me across the table and stalking out of my life for the last time.

Chapter Ten

I suffered an awful night's sleep, turning stuff over and over in my head, wondering if I'd done the right thing, worrying that I was turning into the bitch from hell because I'd dumped Matt so coldheartedly, then hadn't bothered to try and find out how he was handling it.

I couldn't face yet more snide remarks from Sophie at the table, so I skipped breakfast altogether, choosing to sneak out of the house before anyone could realise I was up and about. I switched on my phone as I was walking into college, kinda still wondering if Matt might have texted me, but more desperately hoping Fickle had sent me a message instead.

She had.

I felt my heart jump as I saw her name appear and stopped walking for a second, just enjoying the sight of her name sitting there in my in-box, waiting for me.

Fickle.

I clicked on her message and giggled as I read it, her message just saying, *Hey you! Soz 4 late reply. H8 2 keep a girl w8ing, specially u! U OK? Hv a gd day, F xxxxxxx*

I sent her one back telling her to have a good day as well, and kinda didn't expect to hear back from her all day, so when another one came back from her just as I was getting to college, I suddenly felt like my day was going to be a really good one. It just said,

Day just got better hearing from u! Be on MSN l8r? Missing u xxxxx

And suddenly, you know, I reckoned I'd done the right thing ending it with Matt. I read her messages again. This couldn't be anything other than flirting, could it? Why else would she say to me she hated to keep me waiting, and that she missed me? She wouldn't do that unless she was giving me the come-on, surely? I hugged myself, suddenly feeling real happy, knowing that later I'd get to do the only thing that seemed to matter in my life right now: spend the evening talking to Fickle.

Still pumped, I turned into the college canteen and, seeing Emily nursing a hot cup of coffee in the corner, grabbed myself a cappuccino and headed over to join her. She held up her hand in front of her when she saw me coming and looked at me through bleary eyes.

"Hangover from hell. Sit down but puh-lease don't speak too loud at me 'cos I'm likely to spontaneously combust." She put her head in her hands and groaned softly.

"That'll teach you." I scraped my chair back and chuckled as I saw her wince behind her hands.

"Never again, I'm telling you! If I *ever* tell you I'm hitting the town with Naomi Watson again, just shoot me, right?"

"I could shoot you now." I peered at her. "You look like you need putting out of your misery."

Emily drank a little of her coffee and grimaced. "You're a pal." She grinned sarcastically at me. "You doing well, anyway? Not seen you around for a while."

"Yeah, I'm good," I replied, taking a sip from my steaming cappuccino. "Just been busy, you know how it is." I mock rolled my eyes at her.

"Tell me about it." Emily scratched irritably at her eyes. "I've got, like, three assignments due by the end of the week. It's worse than being at school here, sometimes."

"And yet you still thought to go out and get splattered last night?" I sat back and folded my arms, trying to look as sanctimonious as I could.

"Pff, you're only young once, that's what I say." Emily laughed then winced, cradling her head in her hands like it was a piece of fragile porcelain.

I turned my head as I heard some people clatter noisily through the door of the canteen, bringing a blast of cold air from outside in with them and saw, in amongst the group, Matt, skulking somewhere near the back of the group, head bent, texting away on his phone.

Terrific. The very day I really didn't want to see Matt and he was there. I tried making myself smaller in my seat, kinda slumping down slightly, hoping he wouldn't see me. I took a sideways glance at him and saw he was still texting, one hand in his jeans pocket, the other wrapped round his mobile, thumb bouncing up and down off the buttons. His hair was down over his eyes, the way he always liked to have it, so I couldn't see his face. I kinda wanted to see what sort of expression he had on his face, I don't know why.

Just as I was looking at him, he looked up from his phone and stared right back at me, making me quickly drop my eyes and stare back at Emily, probably making me look a bit like a startled deer.

"Isn't that Matt?" Emily was still cradling her head in her hands and now looked across the canteen through her fingers. "Get him over if you like. I won't mind."

"No," I said, probably more sharply than I should have done. "It's cool." I fussed about with my bag, pretending to look for something.

"Hmm, he's gone anyway." Emily was straining to see. "Maybe he didn't see us."

"He did, that's why he went the other way." I sipped at my coffee.

"Trouble?" Emily raised her eyebrows.

"Yup." I took another sip. "I, er, I kinda ended it with him last night."

Emily took her hands away from her head and stared at me.

"No shitting me?"

I shook my head.

"Blimey, Immy." Emily gingerly picked up her coffee cup and nursed it in both hands. "Wanna talk about it?"

"Not really." I laughed. "It was the right thing to do—for me, anyway—but it still doesn't make it easier, does it?"

"Breaking up is hard to do, as Neil Diamond once sang." Emily nodded and grimaced.

"It was Neil Sedaka, wasn't it?" I frowned.

"Whatever. Neil Diamond, Neil Sedaka, Neil Armstrong: who gives a shit? Still bloody tough, isn't it?" Emily pulled a face.

"It is. It was." I sighed, casting an eye round the canteen on the lookout for Matt.

"How did he take it?" Emily put her coffee cup back down and leant back in her chair.

"As well as could be expected, I suppose," I said. "He said he couldn't understand why, then told me he thought we were in it for the long run, then paid for dinner and left." I laughed slightly self-consciously.

"But you didn't see you as being in it for the long run?" Emily asked.

I shook my head. "I didn't, no. I hadn't been getting anything from 'us' for a while, so kinda thought, what's the point?"

"Seems a shame. I always thought you made a cute couple." Emily raised an eyebrow.

"Nah." I shook my head again. "I mean, he's lovely, don't get me wrong. But I think he'll be happier with someone else. Someone that appreciates him more than I can."

"Like Beth?" Emily suggested. "She'll be after him now, you just watch."

I shrugged.

"Sorry." Emily leant across the table and grabbed my hand. "That was insensitive."

"But she can go after him!" I implored Emily. "That's just it, I really don't mind."

And I didn't. In fact, a small part of me really hoped that Beth *would* go after Matt. At least it might stop me feeling so guilty about everything.

I heard my phone beep from somewhere in my bag and leant down to fish it out, catching sight of Matt leaving the canteen again as I did so. He looked over to where Emily and I were sitting, but nothing registered on his face; instead he carried on walking out through the door as if he'd never seen us at all.

"Matt?" Emily jerked her chin towards my phone.

I read the message.

"No, not Matt," I said, as casually as I could.

It was another message from Fickle, and when I read it, her telling me she was thinking about me, it was all I could do to stop the biggest, stupidest grin from spreading across my face.

❖

The next few days went in a bit of a blur. Thankfully I managed to avoid seeing Matt again, but the gossip-mongers at my college had evidently been hard at work, as, by the Thursday, at least two different girls from my Maths group, neither of whom I knew particularly well, nor wanted to, asked me if it was true what they'd heard about me and Matt.

When a third girl asked me the same question, shortly before my last lesson of the day, I sent a curt text to Emily asking her, *Just how many peeps have u told 'bout me & Matt?* to which she replied, *None. If peeps know it's 'cos Matt's a popular guy. Nothing 2do with me.* I thought about replying, but figured she was probably right. News travels fast, especially when the subject of that news happened to be one of the hottest guys in the college. That would be the hottest guy I'd just dumped, then.

I went straight to my room when I got home, resisting the temptation to go onto the message board, even though I knew what I needed was a pick-me-up from the people on there. I put the finishing touches to a couple of assignments, all the while my mind on MSN and Fickle, hoping she'd be around when I finally finished my college work and felt I'd done enough studying to allow myself time on MSN.

She was already there when I eventually signed in, and I felt the familiar flutter of excitement in my tummy the minute I saw her name.

Fickle: At last! Pleeeease save me from the boredom that is Daisy2011!

Barnaby Rudge: LMAO! She boring you rigid?

Fickle: She's telling me about her dog #yaaaaawn#.

Barnaby Rudge: Aw, don't be tight!

Fickle: You wanna talk to her?

Barnaby Rudge: Nah, you're all right.

Fickle: Exactly! Chicken! Wait, I'm gonna tell her someone MUCH more interesting has turned up for me to talk to.

She put a winking sign after that and I felt my heart flip.

Barnaby Rudge: Don't tell her that!

Fickle: I'm kidding ya! But I'm telling her I gotta go.

I waited a while as Fickle did whatever it was she was doing and suddenly found myself bringing up her latest photo on my screen. I thought it would be neat to talk to her and look at her picture at the same time. Kinda bring her closer to me, that sort of thing.

Fickle: K, I'm all yours now, honey.

Barnaby Rudge: Good! Sooooo…You had a good day?

Fickle: Not bad. Better now I'm talking to you.

Barnaby Rudge: You say the sweetest things!

Fickle: Only to you.

My heart thumped. I read her words again, slowly. *Only to you.* I grinned and flicked screens, looking at her lovely face gazing back at me. Damn, she was hot, and damn, how I wanted to tell her that too! Suddenly she wrote:

Fickle: You still with that boyfriend of yours?

Why would she write that? Why?

Barnaby Rudge: Who've you been talking to?

Fickle: No one, why?

Barnaby Rudge: Why would you ask me that?

Fickle: Just making conversation, honey. Keep your hair on!

I paused, my heart still thumping madly away.

Barnaby Rudge: I'm not with him anymore, no.

Fickle: Oh. Hey, I was only kidding before! I didn't know, honest. I'm sorry, Immy!

Barnaby Rudge: Don't be. I'm not.

Fickle: Ouch.

Barnaby Rudge: I had to do it. I was having, uh, issues.

Fickle: With him?

Barnaby Rudge: With me.

I paused again, staring at the screen. I swallowed hard, feeling like I was in some parallel universe or something as I wrote:

Barnaby Rudge: And issues with you.

Fickle: With me, Immy?

Barnaby Rudge: Can we change the subject now? How was college?

Fickle: Again, not bad.

Barnaby Rudge: You got lots of work? I tell you, I've got shitloads. It's gone crazy!

Fickle: Yeah, quite a bit. Can we stop this?

Barnaby Rudge: Stop what?

Fickle: This polite chitchat.

Barnaby Rudge: Oh, K. Have I pissed you off or something?

Fickle: Quite the opposite.

Barnaby Rudge: Well as long as I've not irritated you?

Fickle: No. What issues you got with me, Immy?

Barnaby Rudge: Forget I said it.

Fickle: No. LOL.

Barnaby Rudge: Please?

Fickle: I wanna ask you something.

Barnaby Rudge: Go ahead.

Fickle: Can I ask you if you're...I dunno if I can ask you!

Barnaby Rudge: Ask me what? If I'm what?

Fickle: Immy! If you're confused!

Fickle's abrupt message made the hairs on my arms practically sit up and beg. I paused, staring at the flashing message on the screen, unsure how to answer.

Immy?

Another message flashed up.

Barnaby Rudge: Yeah, I'm confused. I dunno what I am anymore.

Wasn't that the truth?

Fickle: Are you, curious? I mean, you know, bi-curious?

Barnaby Rudge: Why would you say that?

Fickle: I've been getting vibes from you, is all.

Vibes from me?

Barnaby Rudge: I dunno. I suppose, well, I don't really
    know what bi-curious really means.

I added "LMAO" to let Fickle think I was embarrassed.

Fickle: You don't?

Barnaby Rudge: Nope. And if you laugh at me I'll kill you!

Fickle: Hmm. Well I can only equate it to, I dunno…OK,
    say you've never eaten something but one day you
    think you'd like to…

I could feel my face getting redder by the second.

Fickle: OK, maybe eating something ain't such a good
    comparison, LOL, but say you've always wanted to try
    something, yeah?

Barnaby Rudge: Yeah.

Fickle: And you're kinda curious to try it, even if you're not
    sure you'd like it, yeah?

Barnaby Rudge: Yeah, like artichokes?

Fickle: LMAO!!!

*Why were we talking about artichokes? I didn't want to talk
about flipping artichokes!*

Fickle: OK, so you've always wanted to try artichokes but
    you've never had the chance to?

Barnaby Rudge: I s'pose not.

Fickle: Well, just imagine someone put an artichoke in
    front of you? Right there in front of you, so close you
    could touch it. You're not sure what it'll be like, you're
    not sure you'll even like it, but there's something about
    it that makes you wanna try it.

Barnaby Rudge: And if I don't like it?

Fickle: Then you go back to eating boring old cabbage!

Fickle added a winky and I felt my tummy go to mush again for
the second time in about ten minutes.

Barnaby Rudge: LMAO! Sooo, in layman's terms, you mean, do I consider myself straight but curious about what the other side has to offer?

Fickle: Yeah, that's exactly what I mean. Are you curious now, Immy? Have you found yourself an artichoke you wanna try?

I leant forward in my chair and read Fickle's message over three times.

Barnaby Rudge: Why do you wanna know?

Fickle: Just do. Tell me to piss off if you like, I don't mind.

Barnaby Rudge: I don't mind you asking. I'm confused! That much I do know! But lemme put it back to you… are you curious, Fickle?

I sat back in my chair, looking at the screen, chewing at my fingers, not really sure where this conversation was heading, but kinda hoping…

Fickle's answer sprang back at me:

Fickle: The only thing I'm curious about is you.

Chapter Eleven

The skin on the back of my neck prickled. What did she mean, she was curious about me?

Barnaby Rudge: Curious as to whether I'm curious? LOL.

What a dumb reply!

Fickle: No, just curious about you. Are you curious about me?

I sat back in my chair. Was I reading this right?

Barnaby Rudge: Yeah. I am. I'm curious about you, Gemma.

Fickle: Good. That's what I wanted.

She put another wink sign and I felt my breath coming just a bit faster. This sounded to me like it was going somewhere, and it was making my head spin, but in a good way this time. I didn't know what to write, so I waited for Fickle to write something else instead.

Fickle: My hands are a bit clammy all of a sudden. Are yours?

I felt my palms. They were sweaty too. I suppose that's what anticipation does for you.

Barnaby Rudge: They are. And my heart's beating faster.

Fickle: So's mine. That's what you seem to do to me just lately.

I paused, reading her messages again. My mouth felt dry and my pulse raced ten to the dozen in my neck.

Barnaby Rudge: I'm not sure what to say now!

I laughed as I wrote my message.

Fickle: Just tell me you're interested in me

Barnaby Rudge: I am. I'm interested in you, Gem.

Fickle: Good. 'Cos I'm sure as hell interested in you, Immy.

She was interested. She was interested in me!

Barnaby Rudge: What, even after you saw my pictures? LOL!

Fickle: Especially 'cos I've seen your pictures, honey.

So she *did* like my legs! Result!

Fickle: I really like you, Immy. You know what I'm saying here, don't you?

Barnaby Rudge: I think so…I hope so, 'cos I've kinda been thinking about you a lot since we started talking to each other too.

Fickle: I've been thinking about you all the time. You have no idea!

The hairs on my arms stood up again. She'd been thinking about me?

Fickle: Aaaand I've been kinda trying to keep it to myself 'cos I didn't know if you were gay or not, and then you told me you had a boyfriend and…

Barnaby Rudge: But not anymore.

Fickle: Not anymore, no. That's good.

Barnaby Rudge: And that's because of you.

Fickle: Me?

Barnaby Rudge: You. I couldn't concentrate on Matt all the time I was thinking about you. I didn't want to either. All I wanted was you.

I hit the Send button and wondered if I'd gone too far, that she would think I was stupid for finishing with my boyfriend because of her. I started to type a message saying it wasn't just her, that I'd wanted to finish with Matt anyway, that she, Fickle, had been the catalyst to that. Instead she wrote a message back that just said:

Fickle: All I want is you too, Immy. My ex wanted to get back with me the other night but all I could think about when I was out with her was you. I don't want her. I want you! Does that sound crazy?

Barnaby Rudge: No! 'Cos it's just the way I've been thinking lately too! You're all I think about, Gem, nothing else matters, just you. It's madness!

Fickle: It is, isn't it? LOL. I think I've known since the first time I ever spoke to you that I liked you. How can that be?? Something with you just clicked, I dunno.

Barnaby Rudge: And then when you sent me your picture...ohhh boy!

Fickle: And you. OMG, you're sooo hot, Immy. I think I fancied you even more when I first saw you.

I felt like I was floating away and that I'd have to keep a tight grip on the chair to stop me drifting off. I was sooooo happy! This is what I'd wanted to happen for ages, and here it was, right here, right now. This felt right, it felt perfect.

Barnaby Rudge: This feels nice. Weird, but nice.

Fickle: It does. How long have you known?

Barnaby Rudge: Known what?

Fickle: That you liked me, silly! You do fancy me, don't you?

That I liked her. That sounded strange. I've never fancied anyone in my life, apart from a few stupid girl crushes at school. Fancying someone was something different altogether, especially because she was a girl. I fancied a girl. How weird was that?

Barnaby Rudge: A while, I dunno. I s'pose it just kinda crept up on me, you know? That I'd suddenly find myself thinking about you, like, ALL the time and I wanted to talk to you, like, ALL the time, get to know you better. And then, like I said, I saw your picture and it did something to me. It was crazy. And then, ever since then, I haven't been able to get you outta my head.

Fickle: So where do we go from here, Immy?

Barnaby Rudge: I dunno!

Fickle: We should meet up.

Barnaby Rudge: I guess.

Fickle: Don't sound TOO excited will ya?!

Barnaby Rudge: LMAO, sorry. It's just a bit scary, you know?

Fickle: I'm not scary!

Barnaby Rudge: I know that! Not you, just the whole meeting someone new thing.

Fickle: It'll be like a blind date, except that you know what I already look like!

Barnaby Rudge: And I know you're hot, so you won't be a disappointment!

Fickle: Nor you, honey. Nor you. It'll be awesome! There are plenty of trains between Leeds and Oxford, aren't there, FFS?! LOL.

Barnaby Rudge: Totally.

Fickle: So have a think about it, yeah?

I was just typing up a reply when Fickle suddenly said:

Fickle: Shit, have you seen the time? I better go. I don't wanna, but I ought to.

Barnaby Rudge: OK.

Fickle: Can I ring you some time? Tomorrow?

I pulled my hands through my hair. She wanted to ring me? This really was the next stage, wasn't it?

Fickle: Immy?

Barnaby Rudge: 'Course!

Fickle: I wanna hear your voice, Immy. I wanna know what you sound like.

Barnaby Rudge: I wanna hear your voice too, Gem. Sooo much.

Fickle: Kewl! Then I'll call you later, yeah?

Barnaby Rudge: Look forward to it.

Fickle: Me too. Miss you already xxxxx

After she'd logged off I sat back in my chair, leant my head back, and stared up at the ceiling. Had that really just happened?! My face flamed but nothing could burn the enormous grin from my face. I could hardly believe it! In the space of seventy-two hours I'd gone from feeling helplessly stuck in a relationship with Matt, feeling totally confused about Fickle, to being free of Matt and then finally having Fickle finally tell me she fancied me. They say a week's a long time in politics, don't they? Lemme tell you, three days is even longer on the Internet!

❖

I stayed at my computer for ages after Fickle had gone, replaying everything that had just happened. I knew that I wanted to tell the world that I fancied Fickle, then felt an overwhelming feeling of disappointment that only Joey knew about anything. I grabbed my phone and fired a rapid text off to her, telling her everything that had happened, a stupid, soppy grin across my face as I did so. Then I felt bad for not asking her how she was, so I sent her a second one, asking her how Scotland was and whether she'd managed to find anything green and interesting to dissect yet.

I didn't want to go downstairs to my family, worried they'd be able to tell that something had happened. Maybe I was being paranoid, but I kinda thought it would be written across my face. How could I keep something as wonderful as what had just happened a secret? No, I decided to stay in my room and calm down a little before venturing downstairs again.

I looked back at MSN and was pleased to see Twiggy had just signed in and, wanting to talk to her more than I'd ever wanted to talk to her before, sent her a quick message to say hi. Her message came back about a minute later.

Twiggy: Hi yourself! How's you?

Barnaby Rudge: Good! Very good! You?

Twiggy: Glad to be home from work, aaaand I'm off til Friday now.

Barnaby Rudge: Doing anything?

Twiggy: Decorating. LOL. Well, not just me. Husband's helping as well!

I had known that Twiggy was married, for as much as she liked to keep things to herself, she'd let it slip in previous conversations that she'd been married for nearly four years. Trying to get anything else out of her had proved more difficult, though. Knowing she was married also made it harder for me to decide whether to tell her about me and Fickle, so I just decided to see how the conversation panned out.

Twiggy: So what's your week been like so far? Been at college?

Barnaby Rudge: Yeah. It was a bit awkward though 'cos I saw my ex-boyfriend the other day.

Twiggy: The Matt guy you told me about? He an ex now??

Barnaby Rudge: Yeah.

Twiggy: Soz to hear that. Since when?

Barnaby Rudge: Since the other day. LOL.

Twiggy: Yikes! So still raw, huh?

Barnaby Rudge: Not really.

Twiggy: Nah, you don't sound so upset!!

Barnaby Rudge: I'm not. I'm really happy, actually! It's been a really good day today.

Twiggy: Sounds like you've moved on already?!

Barnaby Rudge: I think I have.

Should I tell her? I wanted to talk to someone about Fickle so badly, I thought I would burst. I dare say if Joey had been around, I would have bent her ear back about it, but she wasn't, and in her absence, Twiggy was the only other person I talked to on the board who I knew well enough to talk to about it.

Twiggy: You're a fast mover!

Barnaby Rudge: Yeah!

Twiggy: So is he from your college?

Barnaby Rudge: No.

Twiggy: Jeez, don't give much away, will you?!

Barnaby Rudge: No. LOL.

Twiggy: You don't wanna tell me? It's okay, I understand.

Barnaby Rudge: I do want to tell you, Twigs. I just don't know if you WILL understand.

Twiggy: Sounds intriguing.

Barnaby Rudge: It's someone from the board.

Twiggy: The Lovers and Sinners board?

Barnaby Rudge: Yeah.

Twiggy: Oooh gossip! I love gossip! Who? Speaking of gossip, did you know that Chatte Noire and Josh99 got it together?

Barnaby Rudge: No? Really?

Twiggy: Isn't it cute? Love over the superhighway. Is that what's happened to you?

Barnaby Rudge: I guess. And you don't think it's weird? Falling for someone over the Internet?

Twiggy: No, course not! The Internet's just another way of meeting people, isn't it? Just like you could meet someone down at the supermarket or out walking your dog. No one dictates where you meet someone, it just happens, doesn't it? If it happens over the 'net, so what? Nah, I think it's cute! As long as he's not an axe murderer or anything like that! LOL!

Barnaby Rudge: I never thought it would happen to me.

Twiggy: Well, sounds like it has! So who is he?

Barnaby Rudge: Hmm, that's the thing, Twigs.

Twiggy: Oh God, he's not married, is he?!

Barnaby Rudge: No!

Twiggy: He's not one of the actors from the show, is he? Cos I heard they sometimes post on there, anonymously, you know? Now that REALLY would be mega-cute!

Barnaby Rudge: It's not a bloke.

Twiggy: Oh. I see.

There was a pause as I guessed Twiggy was processing that nugget of information.

Barnaby Rudge: You've gone quiet. I don't like that. LOL.

Twiggy: I didn't know you were gay, thassall.

Barnaby Rudge: Neither did I. Until recently, anyway!

Twiggy: Oh, right.

Another long pause. I desperately thought of something to say to Twiggy, but nothing would come.

Twiggy: So who is it that's stolen your heart?

Barnaby Rudge: Someone called Fickle.

Twiggy: Hmm, all right. Don't think I've ever spoken to her, but I think I've read some of her posts.

Barnaby Rudge: And the good thing is that she feels the same way about me.

Twiggy: I see.

Barnaby Rudge: I'm getting awkward vibes, Twigs. You want me to go?

Twiggy: No, I'm sorry. You'll have to bear with this old, married woman. It's just, I don't know any gay people, you know? It seems a bit strange talking about it.

Barnaby Rudge: You're not old! You're only 24, Twigs!

Twiggy: Yeah, I know. But you'll still have to bear with me. I just don't feel so comfortable talking about it, I'm sorry.

Barnaby Rudge: But, but! You watch Lovers and Sinners, that's got a gay couple in it!

Twiggy: Yeah, but the Ali and Jess stuff is just a small part of the story for me. I'm guessing they're a big part of it for you?

Barnaby Rudge: Yeah. I thought they were for everyone—they are the main characters after all.

Twiggy: Not for me, sorry. I talk about Pete and Sara far more than I do about Ali and Jess.

Barnaby Rudge: Oh. K. I didn't realise.

I looked down at my hands, poised over the keyboard. Any euphoria I'd had earlier seemed to disappear and reality arrived to bite me on the bum. Twiggy wasn't comfortable me talking to her about fancying another girl. I could talk about it with Joey and Fickle quite freely; I s'pose I thought Twiggy liked them as much, but thinking back, we never really ever talked about the story that much, more just about other stuff, like football and stuff.

I felt really deflated. Dirty, even, as though everything me and Twiggy had talked and joked about over the last few weeks counted for nothing. I felt like a stranger to her, and realised that perhaps you sometimes really don't know who you're talking to over the Internet after all.

Barnaby Rudge: Twigs? You still there?

Twiggy: Yeah, still here.

Barnaby Rudge: I wish I hadn't said anything to you now!

Twiggy: I'm sorry, have I upset you? It's not you, BR, it's me. I just don't know any gay people, well, only Joey on here. Not in real life, I mean. It's just not something I feel familiar with!

I read Twiggy's last little bit. *Not in real life.* This wasn't real life, was it?

Barnaby Rudge: And you're not comfortable with it?

Twiggy: I dunno!

Barnaby Rudge: But I'm still me, Twigs. I haven't changed!

Twiggy: I know. I'm sorry. Blame my upbringing, if you like!

Barnaby Rudge: OK, I'm gonna go 'cos this is real awkward.

Twiggy: No, don't go! Please. Tell me about Fickle. I wanna know, really I do. Make me understand? LOL.

Barnaby Rudge: You sure?

Twiggy: Sure, sure. Please.

Barnaby Rudge: I'm not sure I understand myself, Twigs!

Twiggy: Talk to me. It might help?

Barnaby Rudge: OK, well, we kinda got talking a while ago and I dunno, there was something different about her, something that made her stand out from the others. No offence.

Twiggy: None taken! So how did you find out she liked you too?

Barnaby Rudge: She told me tonight.

Twiggy: Just tonight?!

Barnaby Rudge: Yeah.

Twiggy: And you just finished with Matt the other night? Because of Fickle? You must feel real up and down right now.

Barnaby Rudge: Mainly up. Well, I did anyway. LOL!

Twiggy: And I brought you down again? I'm sorry, I never meant to.

Barnaby Rudge: S'OK.

Twiggy: Are you happy?

Barnaby Rudge: Very! I really like her, Twigs.

Twiggy: That's kinda cute!

Barnaby Rudge: #blush#

Twiggy: But you didn't know you were gay until you got talking to Fickle?

Barnaby Rudge: Maybe I thought I might be a bit gay…

Twiggy: LMAO!!! I won't ask which bit!

Barnaby Rudge: And then Fickle appeared in my life and everything got turned on its head. Everything I thought I knew about myself started getting questioned and I couldn't understand what was happening to me. All I knew was that the little part of me that thought I was gay suddenly turned into a big part.

Twiggy: And that's why you finished with Matt?

Barnaby Rudge: Yup. I couldn't carry on seeing him knowing I wasn't into him, could I?

Twiggy: Not when you were so into someone else. No, I s'pose not.

Barnaby Rudge: Do you think I'm a bitch?

Twiggy: God, no! Sounds like you're confused, though.

Barnaby Rudge: But that's just it, Twigs. I WAS confused, horribly confused. But then I broke up with Matt and

Fickle told me she liked me and now…well, everything seems so much clearer.

Twiggy: Until it passes again.

Barnaby Rudge: Until what passes?

Twiggy: Well, what if it's a phase? You just said yourself you didn't know you were gay. What if you're not really gay? What if this really is just a phase? Sounds like Fickle's heaped a whole load of attention on you and you like it. What if you've mistaken her attention for something else?

Barnaby Rudge: Nah, it's more than that. I liked Fickle waaaay before she started coming onto me.

Twiggy: I'm sorry if I sound like an old fuddy-duddy here, BR, but I just don't understand how you can be gay if you've never been with a woman before!

Barnaby Rudge: Of course you can! I fancy women. I don't fancy guys! So it's taken me a while to admit it to myself, but now I have admitted it, it's as clear as crystal to me that that's what I am. Gay.

Twiggy: But you went out with a guy!

Barnaby Rudge: And pretty much hated every second of it, Twigs. Both the dating and the sex! LOL. You gotta try something to know whether you're gonna like it or not, don't you? And I tried dating a guy and I didn't like it. Now I wanna date a girl, see if I like it. And you know what? I reckon I AM gonna like it.

Twiggy: I guess.

Barnaby Rudge: Don't put a downer on it, Twigs.

Twiggy: I'm sorry. It's tricky for me, yeah, 'cos you're talking to someone who's always known she's 100 percent straight.

Barnaby Rudge: And I now know 100 percent that I'm not straight.

Twiggy: Sooooo, you and Fickle, Chatte Noire and Josh99…this message board's becoming quite a hotbed of passion!

Barnaby Rudge: I know! And I'm kinda glad you told me about Chatte Noire and Josh 'cos at least it proves it can happen to anyone, right?

Twiggy: Dead on! I guess you're not going to tell Matt about Fickle, though?

Barnaby Rudge: Shit, no!

Twiggy: Right decision!

Barnaby Rudge: She says she's gonna ring me tomorrow and I'm bricking it already.

Twiggy: What if she's got this awful, squeaky, nasally, heavily accented voice and you go right off her??!

Barnaby Rudge: Shuddup, Twigs!

Twiggy: You'll be fine, BR! Don't stress about speaking to her, it'll be good for you to talk to each other. It'll move things in the right direction for you both as well, if that's what you want?

Barnaby Rudge: It is what I want, yeah. Sooo much! I feel excited and nervous and unsure and happy and scared and giddy and silly all rolled into one!

Twiggy: Ahhh, that's love for ya, BR!

Barnaby Rudge: It feels new to me, but it feels great! I've been walking around with a grin on my face, looks like someone put a coathanger upside down in my mouth!!

Twiggy: I'm pleased for you, I really am. Gah, I'd better go, BR. I've got a stack of ironing waiting for me downstairs. Oh the joy of it!

Barnaby Rudge: K, Twigs. Thanks for listening.

Twiggy: You're welcome. And I'm sorry again I was a bit weird with you earlier, and I'm sorry if it sounds like I don't really understand.

Barnaby Rudge: NP.

Twiggy: You around tomorrow?

Barnaby Rudge: Should be.

Twiggy: Till then, then. Good luck with the phone call!

And then she was gone. I looked down at my phone and saw that Joey had texted me back, telling me some tale of falling into a stream and getting her trousers wet, then having to hold them out of the minibus window all the way back to their hostel so she could dry them off. I laughed out loud and wished, for the umpteenth time, that she were around so I could pour my heart out to her. I was sure about one thing with Joey: she would fully understand.

CHAPTER TWELVE

The shrill ringing of my phone startled me a few hours after I'd finished talking to Twiggy and had finally gone to bed. I was propped up, trying to concentrate on reading a magazine, even though my mind frequently wandered to Fickle, when the tinny shriek of "Dancing Queen" sounding out from my phone made me jump. I looked down at my phone briefly, watching as the light from it reflected on and off my ceiling.

I quickly snatched up the phone, worried that it would wake my parents, only registering Fickle's name flashing on the screen for a split second as I pressed the Answer button and mumbled into it.

"Hey," I said, stretching my legs out under thc duvet.

"Hey yourself." Fickle's voice sounded at the other end. I smiled to myself in the dark, remembering Twiggy's words about hoping Fickle didn't have a squeaky voice. She didn't.

"Do you know how late it is to be ringing?" I propped myself up on one elbow and peered through the darkness at my alarm clock. It was nearly midnight.

"I know, I'm sorry." Fickle spoke softly. "I couldn't sleep."

"I know you said you wanted to ring me, but I didn't think you meant in the dead of night." I laughed quietly, glancing anxiously at the door, hoping that my parents wouldn't be able to hear me talking.

"I didn't mean to disturb you, I'm sorry," Fickle said. "I was lying in bed thinking about you. I thought if I could just talk to you, hear your voice, then I might be able to stop thinking about you for five minutes and actually get some sleep!"

I listened to her voice speaking in hushed tones and felt a million butterflies flutter in my stomach. It was so damned good to hear what she sounded like, after weeks of just communicating with her through typing away on a keyboard or texting her. To finally hear her voice whispering to me down the telephone made me want her now more than I'd ever done.

"You have a lovely voice," I found myself saying.

"So do you," Fickle whispered. "Very sexy, but then I somehow knew you would."

"You think so?" I laughed.

"I do, yeah." Fickle laughed back. "I haven't been able to stop thinking about you, Immy. I can't stop thinking about our conversation tonight."

"You don't regret it, do you?" I felt panic rising.

"God, no!" Fickle said. "Do you?"

"Not a second of it," I replied truthfully.

"Good. 'Cos I meant it, Immy, everything I said." Fickle lowered her voice. "I really fancy you, you know that?"

There went the butterflies inside me again.

"I really fancy you too, Gem." It sounded weird, me telling someone—a girl!—that I fancied her, but it sounded weird-good. I liked it.

"You're sweet and funny and nice, and I never believed I could ever meet someone like you," Fickle whispered. "I feel very lucky."

"Do you believe in fate, Gem?" I asked.

"I hadn't before I met you, but perhaps I should start believing in it," Fickle replied.

"That's what I think," I said, adjusting my position in bed.

"Because if I'd never watched *Lovers and Sinners*, if I'd never found that website, well, then I'd never have met you, would I?"

"And I think meeting you might just about be the best darned thing that's ever happened to me," Fickle said gently.

"You think?" I ran my hand through my hair.

"Yeah, I think." Fickle laughed, adding, "No, I *know*!"

There was a bit of an awkward pause before Fickle then said: "Are you in bed?"

"Yeah." I leant back against my pillow and stared up at the ceiling. "Are you?"

"Yeah." Fickle sighed and paused. "I wish I was with you right now."

"I wish you were here too," I said, thinking how great it would be to have Fickle next to me in my bed, stroking her hair, holding her, talking to her in the dead of night.

"I feel really happy." Fickle laughed. "Happy and relaxed. See? I knew all I needed was to hear you and you'd soothe me. I just needed you, Immy."

"You have me, Gem," I whispered.

"I'll text you in the morning, yeah?" I could hear Fickle stifle a yawn, making me want to yawn too. "Will you be on MSN tomorrow night?"

"Of course!" I said. "I'll be on after dinner, okay?"

"I miss you already and you haven't even gone yet," Fickle said quietly.

"I miss you too, Gem," I replied, closing my eyes and picturing her face.

"G'night, Immy. I'm glad you answered your phone. I'm glad I got to talk to you," Fickle said.

"G'night, Gem," I replied. "I'm dead glad I answered too. Sleep well."

"Until tomorrow, yeah?" Fickle stifled another yawn and then was gone.

I stared at my phone, unable to wipe the stupid grin from my face. If I thought I fancied Fickle before tonight, then just hearing her on the phone had made me fancy her a thousand times more! I switched my phone off and shuffled myself down under the duvet, imagining the sound of her voice in my head over and over again until, at last, my eyes finally closed and I fell into a deep, comfortable sleep.

❖

The next morning I awoke to eight texts from Fickle, all sent one after the other, all saying pretty much the same thing: that she couldn't stop thinking about me and she couldn't wait to speak to me again, and that she'd be thinking about me all day until she got a chance to catch up with me later that evening.

I walked to college feeling so different from all the other times I'd walked to college before. I noticed things: people holding hands, couples in cars together, men, women, wondering if they had someone who was as nuts about them as Fickle seemed to be about me. I grinned, plunging my hands into my jacket pockets, and walked with a dumb, loved-up spring in my step.

I felt very special; the day felt special. Man, LIFE FELT SPECIAL! I was still grinning as I flung open the door to the canteen and heard the muffled ringing of my phone from somewhere deep inside my bag. It was Fickle.

"Hey!" I said happily, wandering over to the coffee machine and fishing in my bag for some loose change so I could buy myself what the machine reliably advertised as being a cappuccino, but which tasted something more like hot chocolate.

"Hey, you." Fickle's voice sounded at the other end. "I just wanted to hear your voice again."

I glanced round the canteen, sure that everyone could hear what I could hear. I shook my head and smiled.

"I woke up thinking about you this morning," I said in hushed tones, looking up and down the list of coffees on the front of the machine.

"Me too. Woke up thinking about you, I mean." Fickle laughed. "What are you doing to me, Immy? You're all I can think about! I've got a shitload of work to get through today and all I can think about is you!"

I bit my lip. Fickle was saying everything I wanted to hear from her. I loved that she couldn't concentrate for thinking about me, I loved that she was making me feel so special. I leaned my head against the glass of the coffee machine.

"It's crazy," I whispered to her down the phone. "Crazy how you make me feel, Gem."

"I've never felt like this about anyone, Immy," Fickle whispered back. She paused. "Ah shit, I'm sorry, I've gotta go. I'm sorry."

"S'ok," I said, leaning back from the machine. "I've gotta go too."

"I just wanted to hear your voice, thassall," Fickle said, "And let you know that I'm counting the hours till I can talk to you again later."

"Me too," I said, tracing my finger up and down the glass of the coffee machine. "It's gonna be a long day," I added, groaning.

"I'll speak to you later, yeah?" Fickle said. I could hear the sound of a door opening at the other end of the phone followed by the muffled noise of voices.

"Laters," I said, snapping my phone shut and staring at it for a second, a stupid smile on my face.

"Someone looks happy." A voice sounded next to me and I jumped as I felt an arm being casually flung round my shoulders.

I turned my head and saw Beth peering in through the glass of the coffee machine, then watched as she screwed up her nose and pulled a face.

"All tastes like shit but they still charge you two quid for it." She glanced over to the bar and grabbed my hand. "For an extra 50p we might as well have something that tastes like it's had a coffee bean run through it. Come on. I'll buy you a latte if you tell me who or what's put that stupid grin on your face."

Before I could answer, she'd dragged me over to the counter and had ordered us two skinny lattes, fishing a five pound note out of her bag and hungrily eyeing up the cakes.

"D'you s'pose eight in the morning's too early for a doughnut or two?" she asked, more to herself than to me.

"Nah, just the lattes, please, mate." She jerked her head at the spotty guy serving behind the counter, her decision made, and handed him the fiver.

We turned away from the counter and she slung her arm round my shoulder again, pulling me in to her, making me spill a drop of my coffee on the linoleum floor.

"I don't have a stupid grin on my face," I said as we sat down at a table near the door.

"You so did, though." Beth grabbed a sachet of sugar from a cup on the table and opened it.

"So maybe I'm in a good mood?" I said, kinda defensively.

"Did you get back with Matt, then?" Beth's voice was high, almost anxious.

I snorted.

"News *does* travel fast, doesn't it?" I gave her a wry look.

"Emily wasn't gossiping, honest!" Beth put her hands up in the air. "She just happened to mention it. I suppose she kinda thought you might have told me too."

"It's no biggie." I stirred my coffee, then tapped the spoon on the side of the cup. "I only told Emily 'cos I saw her the day after it'd happened and I was still feeling a bit weird about it all."

"I wasn't surprised, I have to say." Beth studied me over the top of her cup, the steam from her coffee masking her face slightly.

"No?" I cupped my mug with both hands and blew gently into it, making the liquid inside ripple.

"Nope." Beth sipped her coffee. "I always figured he was way more into you than you were him."

"You were right."

"Although I did find it strange 'cos he seems like the ideal guy, but I guess we're all different, huh?"

"There was nothing wrong with Matt," I said slowly. "It was me, not him."

"That's what they all say!" Beth laughed.

"But it really was all me, nothing to do with him," I persisted, part of me wanting Beth to push me further. She didn't.

"I heard on the grapevine that Sarah Burgess has been sniffing round him already." Beth studied my face carefully.

"Then she'll be a lucky girl if she gets him," I replied truthfully.

"You wouldn't be hurt if he moved on so quickly?" Beth raised her eyebrow.

"No," I replied. "I wouldn't. In fact, I'd be pleased for him."

"Yeah, right!" Beth turned and looked away briefly before turning back to me. "You only say that to make yourself feel better for dumping a prize guy!"

"No, really." I put my coffee cup down and leant back in my chair, folding my arms across my chest. "In fact, I'd actively encourage him to find someone who would be better for him than I was. He deserves someone nicer than me."

"That sounds a little self-pitying, don't you think?" Beth placed her coffee down in front of her and gave it another quick stir.

"I was a bit shit to him, to be honest." I shrugged. "Could have been more enthusiastic than I was, I s'pose."

"I'm sure you did your best." Beth picked her coffee cup up again. "No point in flogging a dead donkey, though, was there, as my old gran used to say."

"No, not when it wasn't him I wanted," I found myself saying.

"You wanted someone else?" Beth put her cup down again and leaned over the table. "You dark horse! You never said!"

"I didn't dump him for someone else, though," I said. "Well, not technically."

"Technically, shmechnically!" Beth scoffed. "You gave him the old heave-ho 'cos you've got your eye on someone else, didn't you?"

"Mmm," I mumbled.

"Mmm?" Beth made big eyes.

"Mmmm!" I mumbled again, more exaggeratedly this time.

Could I tell Beth? I so wanted to talk to her about it, but a part of me was terrified she'd have the same reaction as Twiggy the night before. That was the thing about telling people you're gay, I supposed. The danger was that everything they ever thought about you, or felt for you, could change in the blink of an eye and they might not ever think about you or treat you in the same way ever again. Why was that? Why did people automatically think you different just because you tell them you're gay? You're still the same person underneath, right? Still the same person who laughed and joked with them the day before. Still the same person whom they know and love.

I looked at Beth. I'd known her most of my life. We'd been at school together since year 11; we'd been told off by Mr Plummer for chatting in class together, we'd stood outside the headteacher's door together for various misdemeanours, we'd taken exams together and now here we were, both eighteen, helping each other through our tough college years together.

"So you're seeing someone else?" Beth's eyebrows were practically touching her hairline by now. I looked at her in amusement.

"Sort of," I replied.

"Sort of?" Beth repeated. "Surely you either are or you aren't?"

"It's complicated." I shrugged.

"Isn't it always with guys?" Beth laughed ironically.

"Yeah." I laughed too.

I didn't elaborate; after all, why should I? I decided there and then that I wouldn't tell Beth about Fickle; I was absolutely sure she wouldn't understand, and I didn't want to risk alienating her over it. With Twiggy last night it had been different; the anonymity of the Internet made me feel braver, somehow. Typing it out to someone who was essentially still a stranger to me was a darned sight easier than telling someone face-to-face—especially one of my older friends. In that split second I decided that if Beth wanted to think it was a guy, then I'd let her. After all, I hadn't even met Fickle yet. What exactly could I tell Beth about her? She'd think I was crazy, dumping a perfectly good boyfriend for a girl I barely knew. Even as I was telling myself this in my head, I could see it was ludicrous.

I felt deflated. I drained the last of my coffee and gathered up my bag, making some big show of looking at my watch and pretending I was late for my first lesson. "Well, much as I'd like to sit talking all day," I said, scraping back my chair and stepping away from the table, "I gotta go."

"See you later?" Beth looked up at me from her chair. "I'll ask Emily over too. We can grill you about your new paramour." She winked at me.

"Maybe," I lied, knowing full well I'd do everything in my power to avoid them for the rest of the day.

I walked from the canteen and hurried up the stairs towards the college's library, flipping open my phone as I did so. There was another text from Fickle, telling me she was at college and that she couldn't concentrate on her work 'cos she was thinking about me, and what was it I was doing to her? She'd put a winking sign after it and, like, a thousand kisses and I wondered if I was doing the right thing, getting carried away with Fickle. Maybe Twiggy had been right? Maybe I just liked the attention Fickle was giving me and I was using her as an excuse to get away from Matt. But I'd gotten away from Matt, hadn't I? I'd taken the plunge and finished things with him, and I was still crazy about Fickle. That wasn't using her, was it?

I flipped my phone shut again, turning the corner just in time to see Matt walking down the corridor towards me. It was too late to turn and walk away as it was obvious by the look on his face that he'd seen me, so I carried on walking towards him, smiling warmly at him. It felt forced.

"Hey," I started as we finally stopped in front of each other, but my voice sounded strangled. I cleared my throat and said, "Hey," again, louder this time.

"Hey." Matt gazed down. He stood awkwardly in front of me, hands dug deep in his pockets, college bag slung diagonally over his shoulders. His hair, as always, was just so, his skinny jeans slightly ripped, tight T-shirt with the name of some band I'd never heard of before written across the front. It was Matt, just like he'd always been.

"How're you?" I asked, kinda weakly.

"Yeah, good." He looked down at his feet. "You?"

"I'm good too, yeah." I nodded.

There was an awkward silence as we both stood facing each other, neither sure what to say.

"So what've you been up to lately?" I asked, not particularly caring, just asking for want of something to say to break the deafening silence.

"What, since you dumped me?" Matt twisted his mouth to the side.

"Yeah, about that," I started.

"It's cool." Matt adjusted his bag and stared down at his feet again. "It happens, yeah?"

"I'm sorry," I said, truthfully. "I really am."

"I know." Matt looked straight at me. "Like I said, it happens, and I still feel like shit about it right now, and I wish we were still together, but I'll get over it."

"Sarah Burgess has been asking questions," I said casually. "She could help you get over it." I pulled a face and he laughed.

"I know, I heard." Matt rolled his eyes exaggeratedly.

I put my hands in my jeans pockets and scuffed my foot back and forth on the floor, shifting my glance from Matt's face down to my feet.

"But I am sorry, Matt. You gotta believe that. We just, I dunno, we just weren't right for each other." I thought about taking his hand, then thought against it, instead keeping both hands firmly in my pockets.

"I guess." Matt shrugged. "And I know you're sorry 'cos if you say something then I know you really mean it, and I appreciate that. Doesn't mean I understand why you did it, though…" His voice trailed off.

I nodded, unsure how to answer that, and automatically glanced down at my bag as I heard my phone beep from somewhere deep inside it.

"I better go," I said, moving away. "I'm glad you're doing well."

Matt nodded.

"Yeah." He paused, and I wondered for a minute if he was going to say something else. "Well, I'll see ya, yeah?" he said, before brushing past me and wandering off down the corridor.

I watched his retreating back and felt, well, nothing again, just like I'd felt nothing that night at the café. I *was* glad, though, that I'd seen him so soon after finishing with him, and that I'd had a chance to tell him again how sorry I was. Maybe it made me feel less guilty, more able to move on. I don't know. All I did know was that now I'd spoken to him I really could move on and concentrate more on Fickle without feeling so bad about it all. I fished my phone out of my bag to see who'd texted me and, half-expecting to see a message from Fickle, instead saw it was from Joey.

Hey trouble, it said, *Back from Scottyland. U around 18r? Wd b gd 2 talk.*

I texted her back, secretly glad that Joey wanted to talk to me. *Wanna Skype 18r?* I wrote. *We can talk in hushed tones. Parents have ears LOL.*

Joey answered pretty much straight away.

Sure thing! Got heaps to tell you!

I was dying to tell her about Fickle; Joey would understand far more than Twiggy, Beth, or Emily about it all. With another grin I snapped my phone shut and finally headed off to the library, my mind now set towards the work I knew would be waiting for me there.

CHAPTER THIRTEEN

Later that night, after a day more gruelling than I thought it would have been, with lessons and meetings with course leaders about forthcoming work and such, I finally arrived home just desperate to be able to switch off and indulge in a few hours' fun on the message board.

I called out around the house, standing in the hall listening for a reply from anyone. There was silence, so, knowing I could talk to Fickle safe in the knowledge no one would eavesdrop on us, I flipped open my phone and dialled her number. I felt the familiar squidgy feeling in my stomach when, after a couple of rings, she answered.

"Hey, gorgeous," she said. "How was your day?"

"All the better for speaking to you," I replied, shrugging my jacket off and flinging it onto the stairs. I wandered into the kitchen and heaved the fridge door open, peering inside searching for something to eat.

"I was thinking today," Fickle said. "About us meeting up, you know, like I said before?"

I put the piece of cheese that I'd found lurking in the back of the fridge and that had been en route to my mouth down on the sideboard, suddenly nervous.

"Yeah?" I said, kinda unconvincingly.

"Yeah," Fickle replied. "After all, we wanna get to know each other better, don't we?"

"Well, yeah," I said, again without much enthusiasm.

"You don't sound keen." Fickle sounded hurt.

"Oh I am, I am," I replied truthfully. "I s'pose, I dunno, I s'pose I'm just kinda nervous at the thought, thassall."

"What's there to be nervous about?" Fickle laughed. "It's cool! I really like you, Immy, I wanna meet you."

"I really like you too, Gems," I replied. "And of course I wanna meet you, you know I do."

I swallowed hard.

"Good," Fickle said. "So go get your arse on the Internet and look up some trains. We can find somewhere halfway and meet there, yeah?"

"When?" I said, "I mean, when do you wanna meet?" I climbed the stairs to my room and sat myself down in front of my computer.

"This weekend?" Fickle replied. "I think I'll burst if I don't get to see you soon."

I stared at the computer screen as it kicked into life and eased out a breath, trying to quell the shakiness in my voice. This was real. This was happening. Me and Fickle were going to meet and I wasn't sure it was what I wanted.

Wait, who was I kidding? It was *exactly* what I wanted, but I was crapping myself at the thought of moving things with Fickle to another stage.

"Saturday?" I ventured. "I could look up trains for next Saturday."

"Saturday sounds good," Fickle said. "Wait, I'm putting on my laptop. Lemme see what trains I can find too."

"Wanna Skype?" I asked, typing the URL of a train company into the computer with one hand. "You have Skype, don't you?"

"I can't." Fickle lowered her voice. "Mum's downstairs and, well, you know."

I laughed.

"Yeah, I know. It's all very clandestine, isn't it?" I said, watching as the page on the screen started to download.

"I love it," Fickle whispered, "I get a real buzz from it, don't you? All this secrecy. I always do."

"I guess," I replied. Truth was, I hadn't really thought of it that way. I was just happy that me and Fickle had admitted that we fancied each other. Anything else hadn't really occurred to me.

After ten or so minutes looking at trains, we each both chose and paid for a train from our respective cities that would mean we would both arrive at Birmingham railway station, which was halfway between us, mid-morning on the following Saturday. I chose a mid-afternoon train home, telling Fickle I would need to get back early evening so that I could have a lift back from the station. It was a lie, albeit a white one. In reality, I was shit-scared that me and Fickle wouldn't hit it off and worried that we'd spend the whole day in silence, each of us wishing to God we'd booked an earlier train home. I figured if we did get on, there would be plenty of other times to meet, right? Best play it safe for this first one.

"So we're done," Fickle said. "Saturday eleven a.m., Birmingham New Street station."

"No finer station in the country." I giggled.

"I really can't wait to meet you, Immy," Fickle said. "It's gonna be sooooo good."

I sat back in my chair and puffed out my cheeks. *Please, God*, I thought, *let her be right. Let it be good.*

❖

After we'd both said good-bye and I'd logged off again, I spent the next hour kinda just walking round the house in a daze, wondering just what the hell I was doing. It was madness; it was weird; it was like nothing I'd ever done before and a million questions kept creeping into my head, like, was it safe? Was it right? Was it what ordinary people did, meeting a total stranger at Birmingham New Street railway station on a Saturday morning?

I rubbed my eyes impatiently. I wanted to meet her, I really did. I mean, how would I ever know if what Fickle and I had been telling each other could ever be true unless I did meet her? How would I know if my feelings were real if all I ever did forever more was just to talk to her on the phone, or on MSN? I snatched up my phone and, knowing the one person who could make all this seem sane was back home from Scotland, wanting to talk to me, sent a text with a plea of help to her. Joey was going to be my voice of reason tonight.

❖

Joey: Hey chickeroo!

I calmed down the minute I saw Joey's name appear on MSN. She was like, oh I dunno, like a favourite cardigan that you couldn't wait to put on, and wrap round yourself, knowing that she would be comfortable and safe and relaxing straight away.

Barnaby Rudge: All right, Joe? How was Scotland?

Joey: Cold. And wet, but then I kinda expected that it would be! How are you?

Barnaby Rudge: I'm great, yeah. When did you get back?

Joey: Just this morning. Nine-hour overnight coach journey last night. Guh!

Barnaby Rudge: And did you get lots of work done?

Joey: Kinda, but I had the shittiest time ever when I was there.

Barnaby Rudge: Erk. Why?

Joey: Claire finished with me while I was away.

Barnaby Rudge: Oh Joe, that's awful!!

Joey: Tell me about it. I've felt like crap since she told me.

Barnaby Rudge: She told you while you were in Scotland??

Joey: Yeah. LOL. Nice, huh?

Barnaby Rudge: Nasty. I feel for ya, I really do. Did she say why?

Joey: She met someone else, apparently.

Barnaby Rudge: While you were away?? You were only gone a few days!!

Joey: Nah, it'd been going on for a while I think. Someone down at her gym, apparently. Just me being away gave her the time to think about stuff, I guess, and decide who she wanted to be with. It obviously wasn't me.

Barnaby Rudge: I'm sorry, really I am.

Joey: She's bisexual, right? So you'd kinda think she might go off with a guy but noooooo! She met another woman. Ain't that the ultimate insult? LMAO.

Barnaby Rudge: Yikes. Are you all right?

Joey: Not really, but I guess I'll get over it. I always do, sooner or later. Aaaand, there's plenty more trout in the river, as my old gran used to say.

There was a pause as I sat and looked at her last message, not sure what to write next.

Joey: Anyway, kiddo, enough about me! How're you??

Barnaby Rudge: I'm very good, yeah!

Joey: You still stressing over that Fickle girl from the message board?

Barnaby Rudge: Yeah, stressing a bit, but for a different reason now! Things have, uh, how can I put it? Things have moved on a bit since we last spoke!

Joey: Ooooh do tell! I got your text about finishing with your boyfriend. That was very brave. Soz I didn't text you back more about it all, but I was probably up to my armpits in green water.

Barnaby Rudge: No worries. It was tough to do but I felt relieved after doing it. Does that make me sound like a bitch?

Joey: No, LOL! It just means you did what you had to do. I'm sure he'll live!

Barnaby Rudge: I saw him at college today and he seemed normal.

Joey: Well then, there you go! See? Aren't I always right?!

Barnaby Rudge: And things have changed with me and Fickle.

Joey: Go on…

Barnaby Rudge: She told me she liked me the other night.

Joey: Reeeeesult!!! And you told her you liked her??

Barnaby Rudge: Yup!

Joey: All that stressing over whether she fancied you, and here you are now, telling me you've both told each other how you feel. It's too cute, it really is! Are you happy?

Barnaby Rudge: Very. I feel like things are starting to slot into place, you know?

Joey: I'm pleased for ya!

Barnaby Rudge: We're meeting up next Saturday.

Joey: Blimey! You don't let the grass grow, do you?!

Barnaby Rudge: You think it's too soon??

Joey: Not if it's what you both want.

Barnaby Rudge: We do. Fickle suggested it. I suppose I'd have been happy just to take things slowly, let it sink in, but she seems dead keen. And I figured the only way I'll know if she's the one for me is if I actually go meet her. I might not get on with her, you never know.

Joey: True. Where are you meeting?

Barnaby Rudge: Birmingham.

Joey: Well, if you can get on with each other in Birmingham you can get on anywhere!

Barnaby Rudge: But I'm real scared.

Joey: Understandable. I was nervous the first time I met Claire, 'cos it's kinda like going on a blind date, isn't it?

Barnaby Rudge: I booked a mid-afternoon train just in case we don't get on. At least that way I can make an early escape!

Joey: Good idea. Well, I'll be texting you throughout the day, wanting updates. You do realise that, don't you?!

Barnaby Rudge: I'll give you a running commentary! Do you think I'm doing the right thing? The other night I was lying in bed at night worrying that I'm having a mid-life crisis or something, and I'm only eighteen!

Joey: I guess only you know whether what you're doing is the right thing, but if you want my opinion then I say just go for it. Why waste your life wondering what if? You only get one shot at life. You gotta grab it by the balls, kiddo!

Barnaby Rudge: It's just, this isn't me, you know? I'm a sensible, smart, rational girl! None of this seems rational at the moment. It's like my life's been tipped upside down.

Joey: So what would you rather? That you just carried on being what everyone expects you to be? That you carry on pretending everything's okay when all you wanna do is follow your heart? Don't wake up in, like, a year's time or two years' time, Imms, and wish to God you'd done this while you had the chance. Life's not about having regrets; it's about living and being who you want to be.

Barnaby Rudge: Thanks, Joe. I mean it.

Joey: I like it when you call me Joe!

Barnaby Rudge: I like it when you call me Imms!

Joey: Nice isn't it?

Barnaby Rudge: We're all so anonymous on here, aren't we? It's nice sometimes to have a bit of reality, I guess.

I looked at the yellow clock on my bedroom wall. It was gone six.

Barnaby Rudge: Listen Joe, I better go. I can hear my parents downstairs so I guess I better go show my face, let them know I'm still alive.

Joey: K, kiddo.

Barnaby Rudge: I'm real sorry about you and Claire.

Joey: Pff, I'll live! And it means I'll have more time now to concentrate on college work. There's some slimy, green samples awaiting my attention in the labs at college. Every cloud, huh? LMAO.

Barnaby Rudge: LMAO! K, speak to you later maybe.

Joey: Sure. Mind how you go.

I quickly checked my e-mails, trying to ignore the brief, fleeting sense of disappointment that Fickle had neither logged on nor e-mailed me.

CHAPTER FOURTEEN

The time leading up to the Saturday when I'd see Fickle was hellish. All I could think about was meeting her and how it would be, playing scenarios over and over again in my head of the moment when I would see her. Where would she be exactly? What would she be wearing? Would she be there at all? I just kept turning things over and over in my head, unable to concentrate on college work, unable to even take in properly what my parents were saying to me, let alone the teachers at college.

Finally, I awoke on that Saturday with a mixture of excitement, nervousness, and dread all rolled into one. I lay in bed, awake before my alarm clock had even had its chance to wake me, all manner of negative thoughts running through my head at about 100 miles per hour. I kept wondering if I was doing the right thing in meeting Fickle, bearing in mind I hadn't really known her that long and couldn't absolutely say that I really knew her at all. A voice in my head, though, constantly counteracted the negative thoughts with just the one, important thought:

This was meant to be.

I rolled over in bed and switched my mobile on, listening to the familiar beep of an incoming text and knew, instinctively, that it was from Fickle.

Soooooooo can't w8 2 c u 18r, it said, followed by her usual winking sign. *Be gentle with me, yeah?!*

Grinning, I sent her a message back, saying I couldn't wait to meet her and that I'd be gentle with her, of course I would.

After making up some total lie to my parents about being out for the whole day with Beth to look for something for her sister's wedding, I finally found myself on the train taking me ever closer to what I hoped would be the next stage of my life.

The train journey up to Birmingham seemed to stretch on forever. I sat watching the English countryside roll past me out of the window, taking me ever closer to Fickle. This was it; too late to back out. Any reservations I might have had about meeting her, wondering if it was the right thing to do, were immaterial now. This was happening, and I was determined to make a good impression.

I'd chosen my clothes carefully, not wanting to look too dressed up, but not wanting to look like some scruff-pot (like I sometimes do) either. I was careful not to wear the one low-cut top I owned either, for whatever weird reason. I supposed a part of me didn't want Fickle to think I was wearing something revealing for her, didn't want to embarrass either her or me. I plumped instead for my favourite pair of faded boyfriend jeans, black tee, oversized black cardigan, and the only pair of Airwalks I had that weren't scuffed beyond recognition. I'd piled my hair up on my head and slapped a bit of mascara onto my already dark eyes, hoping that Fickle would like it. I was kitted out, in short, in just the kind of gear I wore every day and, yeah, not the most exciting thing to wear on a first date, but it was what I felt safe and comfortable in, and I reckoned that counted for a lot.

A text from Fickle about an hour into my journey told me that she was about forty-five minutes into her journey and that she *Can't w8 2 c* me. I read her message and looked down at my own hands, holding my phone tightly, realising that they were trembling. I sent her a quick text telling her I couldn't wait to see her either, but that I was *shaking with nerves*, and she sent me one back about ten minutes later asking why I was so nervous. *You dope! There's nothing to b scared of!! xxx*, she wrote. I wished I could have believed her...

I looked at my watch and figured that if Fickle wasn't due in for another forty minutes or so, then I would arrive at Birmingham around ten minutes before she did. I felt this ridiculous overwhelming feeling of relief that I would be the first to arrive and wouldn't have to get off the train knowing she was waiting for me. I dunno why.

My train finally pulled into the station around twenty-five minutes after Fickle had texted me, and as I stepped from it into the hubbub of New Street with what seemed like a million people milling around or running for their trains, my heartbeat quickened. I wandered aimlessly around the concourse, ambling past the various shop windows, trying desperately to quell the panic that threatened to rise up and propel me onto the next train home, Fickle or no Fickle. To take my mind off the waves of nausea, I peered into one of the book shops' windows, surreptitiously looked at my reflection in the glass, checking that my hair was passable, that I hadn't any dirty smudges on my face, spinach in my teeth, stupid things like that.

Finally, after what seemed like hours, Fickle texted me to tell me she'd arrived too and was waiting for me under the neon sign for platform 12. I looked over and counted down the platforms, standing as I was close to platform 8, and finally caught sight of her waiting, just as she'd said, under the sign for platform 12. I held back a while and took in the sight of her, standing there with a rucksack slung over one shoulder, her hands in her jeans pockets, leaning idly against a post, gazing round the station.

She looked, well, just like her pictures had. I don't know what I was expecting—that she'd be somehow different in the flesh? She wasn't, and I felt that familiar mushiness in my stomach. Bracing myself with a strong inhale, I tucked my chin and strode towards her, heart pumping ten to the dozen, making the blood rush in my ears until it almost deafened me.

"You planning on running away, then?" I stopped just in front of her and grinned, nodding at the rucksack on her shoulder.

"What?" Fickle jerked her head up and looked cross for a second before realising it was me. A broad grin spread across her face. "Heyyyyyyyy!" She flung her arms around me, and I jumped, stiffening.

She pulled away and stood back, looking me up and down and whistling softly.

"Niiiiiiice," she said with approval, one eyebrow arched.

My face flamed. I stood stock still, unsure what to say next. What an idiot. "You been waiting long?" I finally managed to blurt out.

"Just arrived. You?" Fickle countered.

"'Bout ten minutes ago." I tried to relax some but failed miserably.

"Wanna coffee?" Fickle jerked her head over towards a Costa Coffee across the concourse.

"Sure." I was stiff with nerves and hoped a coffee might calm me down.

We walked to the coffee place, with me being careful not to edge too close for fear of touching her. It was nuts, I thought to myself, that I could be telling her how crazy I was about her just twenty-four hours earlier, and yet here I was, totally terrified in case—horror of horrors—I should do something as terrible as actually touch her.

We sat in Costa Coffee, me slurping on a cappuccino, Fickle on a mocha that smelt fabulous, and kinda just stared at each other shyly to begin with.

"How was your journey?" I asked, licking cappuccino froth from my top lip with my tongue.

"You look cute when you do that." Fickle winked at me.

"Do what?" I frowned.

"Lick your lips. I like it." She arched an eyebrow.

"Oh." I ducked my chin and hastily wiped my lips. Fickle laughed.

"My journey was uneventful," Fickle went on. "But let's talk about you, yeah?"

"What do you wanna know?" I self-consciously tucked a stray bit of hair behind my ear.

"Everything." Fickle leaned across the table. "I wanna know everything about you, Immy."

"Gemma, we've been talking for ages! You know everything you possibly could about me!" I laughed.

"Humour me." Fickle flicked an empty sugar packet across the table towards me.

"Well," I began, "Okay, uh, I have size five feet, my favourite takeaway is Chinese, and I cried when they showed the final episode of season three of *Skins* on Channel 4. How's that?"

"It's a start." Fickle dipped her spoon into her mocha, then licked it slowly.

"What about you?"

"Did I cry when season three of *Skins* finished? Nah!" Fickle poked her tongue out.

"Nooo." I rolled my eyes. "What can you tell me about yourself?"

"Other than what you already know? Hmm, only that I'm allergic to peanuts and that I have a dog called Sid, and that I fancy the arse off you, but then you already know that last bit." She looked at me mischievously, making me dart my gaze round at the other tables, worried that other customers might have heard what she'd said.

"I knew you had a dog called Sid." I poked my tongue out at her. "You told me that aaaages ago."

"Do you fancy me?" Fickle asked, the mischievous look on her face still there.

"You know I do," I said, lowering my voice.

"When did you first know?" Fickle lowered her voice too. "'Cos I knew pretty much straight away with you."

"Did you?" My coffee cup paused mid-way to my mouth.

"Yeah! Couldn't you tell?"

"I knew I liked you early on, but I ignored what I was feeling 'cos, I dunno, I was a bit freaked out by it, I s'pose," I said. "And I s'pose it felt weird 'cos I don't think I've ever fancied a girl before you. Well, not many anyway." I laughed, thinking how strange it was telling her all this. I'd been fine telling Joey certain things over the Internet, but telling Fickle face-to-face that I fancied her? That was a whole different thing, and it felt weird.

"You intrigued me from the off," Fickle said. "I knew you had something about you just by the way you used to talk on the message board, and I kinda knew I wanted to get to know you better."

"You used to flirt with me, didn't you?" I asked, remembering our very first MSN conversations when I wasn't sure if I was reading too much into her messages.

Fickle laughed. "Hell, yeah! But you liked it, didn't you?" She leant across and briefly linked her fingers in mine, making about a million butterflies release themselves from whatever net they were hiding in and flutter about inside me.

"I liked it a lot," I said, truthfully.

"You finished that?" Fickle jerked her head towards my cup.

"Yeah."

"Good, let's get out of here, then." Fickle stepped down from her stool and waited, holding the door open as we returned to the station concourse and headed for the exit. Once outside on the street she took my hand, bold as day. I flinched.

"Relax." She bumped her arm playfully against mine. "Birmingham's a busy place; we'll just blend in with the crowd."

I clasped her hand more firmly and enjoyed the feel of it in mine, warm and soft, occasionally gripping mine more tightly, occasionally linking fingers. We walked close to each other this time too, our arms frequently brushing as we strolled through the centre of Birmingham, not knowing, not caring where we were heading, just walking.

We ate lunch in Pizza Hut, sharing an oversized pizza between us. Fickle repeatedly cut slices or forked up bits of salad and offered them to me without any hint of self-consciousness. I even allowed her to place the last slice of pizza directly in my mouth. As I chewed, I watched her lick her fingers slowly, watching me carefully, apparently not caring if any of the other diners saw us. I warmed with embarrassment but it kinda turned me on at the same time.

It was, I figured, the ease of someone who was intimately used to another woman's company and who didn't give a shit about who saw them. And even though I had bouts of self-consciousness, I was blown away at how happy I felt in Fickle's company, and how normal and natural it felt to be with her, far more normal than it ever had with Matt. If Matt had ever tried to feed me pizza, I would have recoiled and felt so awkward, it would have been impossible to hide it.

This was how it was meant to feel to be on a date. Happy, relaxed, and, shit yeah, turned on in the company of someone whom you genuinely fancied. I thought of all the stilted conversations I'd had with Matt in the past, how pretty much every date we'd been on had dragged on, how I'd always been desperate to go home.

Not now.

This was what I'd waited my whole eighteen years for: to be with someone because I actually wanted to be with them, not because it was what I thought was expected of me. I loved being with Fickle; I wanted to be with her for as long as I could, to take in every single detail of her, to touch her, to hold her, to tell her how much I wanted her.

Because, hell, I did want her. So, so much.

❖

I couldn't believe it when it was finally time for me to leave for my train. I could have kicked myself for booking such an early train, regretting that I'd ever considered that me and Fickle wouldn't have got on, on our first meeting. I mean, how could I have ever doubted it?

She walked with me back to the station and managed to book herself on an earlier train home too, probably thinking me a complete dumbass for booking myself a mid-afternoon train. She stood with me at my platform as we waited for my train to allow loading, standing opposite me, holding both my hands in hers, gazing directly into my eyes.

"So," she looked kinda sexily down at her feet, then slowly back up at me, "you wanna do this again, or now you've met me, are you gonna head for the hills?"

"I wanna do it again," I said, squeezing her hands slightly. "I definitely wanna do it again."

"Good." Fickle chewed on her bottom lip. "I think you're neat, Immy. I think I could fall for you in a big way."

The butterflies fluttered again as I stared into her eyes while time stood still. We were the only two people left in the world right at that moment.

"I think I've already fallen for you in a big way," I said, willing the train doors to stay shut so that I didn't have to get on it, away from her.

"I'll text you later, yeah?" Fickle pulled me towards her and for a fleeting moment I thought she was going to kiss me. Instead, she wrapped her arms tight around me in a hug, pressing her body hard against mine. We remained like that for a few seconds, me enjoying the feel of her soft body against mine, savouring the musty smell of her leather jacket.

Finally I pulled away and reluctantly headed towards my train, turning to wave as I reached the train door, feeling like my heart would break at the sight of her, so small and lovely, waving good-bye from beyond the platform's barrier. I sat heavily in my seat and stared unseeing out the window as the train pulled away from the platform. Away from Fickle. How it was possible that our date could be over so soon?

I flipped open my phone and saw that I'd had a text from Joey, sent earlier that day. It just said: *Good luck today, chickeroo. I'll b thinking of u.*

I smiled to myself and sent her one back. It said: *Just had the best day of my life. Think I'm in love!!!!*

I held my phone in my hand a while, lost in my own thoughts, and had just placed it back in my bag when it beeped at me again. Thinking it would be Joey replying, I couldn't help the soppy grin that spread across my face when I opened it and saw that it was from Fickle.

I love you, it simply said.

I stared at the words over and over again, thinking hard about the word "love" in my head, shaping each letter as if to try and etch its image into my brain. I read the message as a whole again.

I love you.

She loved me, and I realised that until that moment I hadn't actually figured out that I really did love her too, that I'd never felt that way about anyone before, so happy, so complete. I sent her one back, telling her I loved her too, and she replied, like, thirty seconds later asking me when we could see each other again.

I settled back in my seat and rested my head against the window, enjoying the cool of the glass against my forehead. Content.

She loved me.

❖

I arrived home shortly after six p.m., floating on air. Fickle and I had texted each other a few more times on the journey home, telling one another what an awesome time we'd had and how neither of us could believe we could be so lucky to have met someone as perfect as each other. I told Fickle that never in my wildest dreams did I ever think I could fall for someone so hard and so quickly over such a short space of time as I had done with her and that I had to pinch myself in case I was dreaming it all.

"Someone's had a good day." Mum smiled at me as I came into the kitchen, dumping my bag down on the kitchen table and opening up cupboard doors in search of something to eat.

"Yeah, s'been good," I replied cryptically. "What's for dinner?"

"Spaghetti carbonara. How was Beth?" Mum was stirring something bubbling in a saucepan.

"Yeah, good." I crossed my fingers briefly to ease the guilt of lying.

Beth. Suddenly I felt like I wanted to tell her about Fickle, tell her that her fears about meeting someone from the Internet were unfounded. Tell her I'd just had the best day of my life and that, in my opinion, my life was about to get a hell of a lot better.

"How long till dinner?" I jerked my head towards the stove.

"Twenty minutes."

"Where is everyone?" I asked, craning my neck to peer out the kitchen door and into the lounge.

"Your dad's slumped in there in front of the twenty-four-hour news." Mum lifted her chin in the direction of the lounge. "And your sister's eating over at Melissa's tonight."

I nodded, figuring it would be safe to talk on my phone or on Skype up in my room without being interrupted by Sophie, and left the kitchen heading straight up to my room. I shut the door tight, flung myself down onto my bed, and rang Joey. I wanted to tell her about my day, talk to her about Fickle, tell her every minute detail of what happened.

"All right, trouble?" Joey's cheery voice sounded at the other end.

"Whatcha, Joe," I said happily, lying back on my pillow.

"I take it it went well, then, judging by your texts?" Joey laughed.

"More than well!" I kicked off my Airwalks, which clattered onto the floor.

"And you got on?" Joey asked.

"Yeah. We couldn't stop talking, it was brilliant," I said. "Just wished the day had been longer, thassall."

"So you're seeing her again, then?"

"She's already said she wants to see me again."

"And it feels right?"

"It feels perfect, Joe."

"That's good."

Good? It was bloody fantastic!

"You had a good day, Joe?" I asked, staring up at the ceiling.

"Not bad, yeah. Not bad," Joey replied, kinda stilted.

"You sound tired," I said, meaning it. She sounded weary, kinda flat. I hadn't ever heard her like that before.

"Do I?" Joey sounded surprised. "I've just had a long day, thassall."

"Up to much?"

"Just thinking 'bout stuff, really."

"About Claire?" I immediately felt guilty for being so cheerful about Fickle when Joey'd only recently been dumped. I didn't want her thinking I was rubbing salt into wounds.

"Yeah, about Claire." Joey paused. "And other stuff."

"Oh," I said. "Wanna offload?"

Joey laughed.

"Nah, thanks. I'm heading out into town in a minute anyway. That'll take my mind off things."

"Anywhere nice?" I asked, absentmindedly, my thoughts already heading to Fickle later.

"Just out for a few beers. I think I need to get out." Joey laughed, kinda hollowly.

"Beer drinker, huh?" I said, tucking a hand behind my head.

"Every time, kiddo." Joey paused. "Now, can you imagine me drinking cocktails?"

"Hmm, nah!" I imagined the priceless look on Joey's face if anyone ever presented her with blue drink with an umbrella sticking out of it.

A brief silence ensued, and I was just about to break it when Mum called up the stairs, telling me dinner would be ready in five.

"Ah, gotta go Joe," I said, hauling my legs over the side of the bed and wriggling my feet into slippers that were waiting conveniently just next to me on the floor.

"No worries, chick," Joey said. "I'm glad you had a nice day with Fickle. Now you've met her for the first time, it'll just get easier and easier."

"Yeah, I reckon it will," I said, standing up and making for my bedroom door.

"I won't be back late tonight, it's just a quick drink. So, you wanna Skype later?" Joey asked.

"Sure!" I replied, wanting to talk to Fickle on MSN as well, but figuring I could do both. "My bratty sister's out and my 'rents'll be downstairs for the duration 'cos there's some programme on the telly tonight that they both watch, so I should be okay to talk."

We said our good-byes and I headed downstairs again, jerked back into the reality of my sensible life by the sight of my parents sitting at the table, sucking up bowls of stringy pasta.

Dinner dragged on for what seemed like forever. I was desperate to go back to the sanctuary of my room where, I dunno, where everything seemed to make sense right now. I knew Fickle would probably be waiting for me on MSN, wanting to talk to me about our day, probably desperate to arrange another meeting. I certainly was. I'd only left her a few hours ago but I missed her like crazy already. Hell, I'd been texting her telling her that since I left her.

After I'd helped with the dishes, talking to Mum about nothing in particular, I finally managed to escape back upstairs again, switching my computer on eagerly, excitement and anticipation building inside me, which rose the second I saw Fickle's name appear on MSN.

Barnaby Rudge: Hey!

Fickle: Hey, sexy!!

Barnaby Rudge: You good?

Fickle: Never been better, thanks to you!

Barnaby Rudge: Flatterer.

Fickle: I mean it. Haven't stopped thinking about you since I got home.

Barnaby Rudge: Me neither. About you, I mean.

Fickle: I need to see you again, Immy. Sooo much.

Barnaby Rudge: When? I so wanna see you again too.

Fickle: Saturday after next? Give me a chance to save up
for the train fare!

Barnaby Rudge: Sounds good to me.

A rush of butterflies took flight inside me. She wanted to see
me again. She was desperate to see me again.

Fickle: I'll ring you about it later, yeah? I'm going out
tonight so won't be on here.

Barnaby Rudge: Oh, right. You never said.

I felt deflated. Why? I guess I kinda thought she'd want to
stick around and chat with me all night, like I wanted to with her.

Fickle: Last minute thing. Soz. You don't mind, do you?

Barnaby Rudge: Why would I mind? LOL! You going
anywhere nice?

Fickle: Just out with mates. I can stay if you want?

Barnaby Rudge: Don't be daft!

I willed her to say she'd stay, that she'd changed her mind. But,
instead:

Fickle: Kewl! I won't be back till late so won't ring you till
tommoz, yeah?

Barnaby Rudge: No worries.

Fickle: I meant it when I said I loved you, Immy.

Butterflies again. Millions of the little blighters.

Barnaby Rudge: I meant it too.

Fickle: I'm dead glad we met today.

Barnaby Rudge: Yeah, me too. Even if I was as nervous
as hell.

Fickle: You're cute when you're nervous.

Barnaby Rudge: I'm daft when I'm nervous.

Fickle: You're not daft. You're lovely. When you walked
towards me in the station today…WOW!

Barnaby Rudge: Shuddup!

Fickle: I mean it. I thought you were fit in your pictures but...whoa!

Barnaby Rudge: You're well fit too.

Fickle: So they say.

She put a winking sign next to that, which made me feel dead flushed. I imagined her winking at me, like she'd done in Costa Coffee that morning, and suddenly wanted to see her again more than I'd ever wanted to see anyone in my life.

Fickle: I better go.

Barnaby Rudge: So soon?

Fickle: Soz. I'll text you later, yeah?

Barnaby Rudge: K. Have a good evening.

Fickle: You too. I love you.

Barnaby Rudge: I love you too.

And then she was gone, and I was left staring at the screen, lost in thought and incredibly lonely.

Not wanting to be alone up in my room anymore, I went downstairs and chatted to Mum and Dad for a couple of hours before returning to my room once their TV programme started, kinda hoping that someone would be online to talk to. I wandered round various websites for a while, posting a few funny comments on the *Lovers and Sinners* website, saying hi to a few people on there that I knew, but all the while I was doing that, all I could think about was Fickle. Sighing, I was about to log off when I heard the familiar singsong ringing of Skype calling me. Joey.

"Hey, you!" I leaned in towards the screen, more from habit than from necessity. "That was quick! You back already?"

I looked at the yellow clock on my wall. It was just past nine p.m.

"Evening," Joey replied in a daft voice, which made me giggle. "Yeah, I said it would just be a quick one tonight."

"I didn't know you were around. You're not on MSN." I looked at MSN and saw that Joey was showing up as offline to me.

"I set my status to offline, thassall," I heard Joey say.

"You can do that?" I frowned, just as Joey's webcammed face finally flickered into life and appeared on my screen. She was poking her tongue out at me.

"'Course you can, you clot!" Joey snorted. "You don't know much about MSN, do you?"

I poked my tongue back out at her.

"'K, so I'm not so hot on technology." I shrugged. "I just talk on it, I didn't bloody well design it!"

"It's a handy little thing, actually." Joey nodded. "Especially when you're on the net to work. It stops people bothering you."

"Am I bothering you now?" I narrowed my eyes at Joey on the screen and she rolled her eyes.

"Who rang who, durr?! Nah, you're all right!" Joey looked at me. "Anyway, I thought you'd be all loved up with Fickle on here tonight." Joey spoke in lowered tones.

"She's gone out." I pulled a sad face.

"Right." Joey nodded. She paused. "I had a text off Claire today."

"Oh yeah?" I looked hopefully at the screen. "What did it say?"

"Just said sorry for being a wanker but she hoped I understood." Joey shrugged.

"And do you? Understand, I mean," I asked.

"Suppose, yeah." Joey looked thoughtful. "At least she had the grace to text me and say sorry. I'm grateful for that."

I watched Joey carefully. "You always see the positives in people, don't you?" I asked.

"You have to, kiddo." Joey rolled her eyes. "No point in being bitter. Move on, that's what I say."

I looked at Joey and thought just what a nice person she was. I know that the word "nice" is sometimes pooh-poohed by English language groupies as being, I dunno, insipid and non-descriptive. But I figured in Joey's case it summed her up perfectly. She was just…well…*nice*. She always seemed cheerful and saw the good in everything and everyone.

"So when are you seeing Fickle again?" Joey peered at me on the screen, one eyebrow mischievously arched.

"Shh!" I said, glancing over my shoulder, half-expecting to see Mum or Dad standing there. "We have to use hushed tones when I talk about her."

"Of course." Joey pulled a sorry face. "I forgot, sorry!"

"It's fine. It's just, well, I don't want them to know anything. Not just yet."

"Totally understand."

"Do your family know about you?" I asked, hoping I hadn't overstepped the boundary.

"God, no!" She pulled a horrified face, adding, "And I want it to stay that way."

"And in reply to your question earlier, we're supposed to be hooking up again in two weeks' time, just as soon as Fickle finds enough for her train fare," I whispered.

Joey gave me the thumbs up on the screen, then made a zipping action with her hand across her mouth, making me laugh.

We chatted on for a good hour afterwards, Joey mainly telling me about her trip to Scotland and how she had so much work on at college in the coming weeks, it was unreal. I listened to her talking away but my mind kept wandering to Fickle, wondering where she was, and kinda wishing I'd asked her more about where she was going and who with. I periodically looked down at my phone, knowing darned well that if she'd texted then I would have heard it beep, but kinda hoping that I might've not heard it. You know how you do?

As it was, Fickle didn't text me back until way gone midnight. I'd long since finished talking to Joey and had gone to bed, trying desperately to stem the feelings of jealousy inside me when, finally, I heard my phone beep in the darkness and there she was.

Soz, honey, it said. *Didn't realise the time. U had a gd night?*

I texted her back, just kinda saying I'd had an okay night and hoped she had too, even though I didn't really mean it, and that was about it. She sent one back saying she missed me and I sent her one saying the same thing, and then asked her where she'd gone, but she didn't reply again. It was dead late, I figured, to be sending texts back and forth, but it still didn't stop me from missing her like crazy and having, like, a million questions in my head.

CHAPTER FIFTEEN

Sunday, as it turned out, was a bit dreary after my totally brilliant Saturday with Fickle. She never did answer my question about who she'd gone out with, so I figured it was better not to push it with her, instead just sending her a few texts asking her if she was having as crap a Sunday as I was. We didn't even get a chance to talk on MSN much that day, either, just catching a few moments here and there, but it wasn't nearly as much or as intense as I'd wanted it to be.

Now here I was, back in the college canteen on Monday morning, feeling, well, just a bit flat, really. It was back to the reality of a heavy week of work after such a fantastic weekend. It was shortly after ten and I'd just plonked myself down at a table when I spotted Emily coming in through the door, phone in hand, deep in thought as she punched away at its keyboard. She looked up and spotted me as I waved at her, then picked her way through the maze of tables and chairs to reach me.

"My mother texting me," she said, waving her mobile at me. "Why does she do it? I mean, whose mother ever texts them? Does yours text you?"

"Er, no," I said, amused, as Emily tutted loudly at her phone and flung it into her bag.

"Exactly! So why does mine feel the need to text me?" Emily looked horrified. "And as for using text-speak. Guh! I mean, she's forty, for crap's sake!"

"Good weekend?" I asked.

"Not bad, yeah," Emily said, finally seeming to relax a little. "You?"

"Great, yeah," I replied, looking down at my hands.

"I'm glad I caught you, Immy," Emily said. "I wanted to run something past you."

"Oh yeah?"

"About Matt."

"Oh." I wondered how I should react. "Okay."

"The thing is—and I don't know how you're going to take this—but the thing is that, well." Emily pulled a face.

"That?" I raised my eyebrows.

"That Beth's, well, Beth's kinda seeing him."

"Is that it?" I laughed.

"You're not bothered?" Emily stared at me.

"God, no!" I replied truthfully.

"Well, Beth'll be relieved!" Emily laughed. "She's been dreading telling you."

"She didn't let the grass grow much, did she?" I said.

"She liked him when you were seeing him, you know that, don't you?" Emily looked embarrassed.

"I didn't, no. But it doesn't bother me if she did," I said. I meant it too. "Anyway, I thought Sarah Burgess was hunting him down? That's the last I heard, anyway."

"I think Beth got in there first." Emily winked at me. "But she did wait a decent amount of time to start talking to him and, well, he kinda asked her out, so it's not really her fault."

"But I'm so not bothered. Honest!" I shrugged.

I looked carefully at Emily.

"Anyway, I'm seeing someone else now," I said slowly.

Emily perked up.

"Beth mentioned you'd said something about some guy to her," Emily said.

"Did I?" I said, playing dumb.

"Yeah. Someone you met off the Internet?" Emily said. "Beth said you said it was complicated."

"It might have been complicated once, but it's all okay now," I said, smiling.

"So have you met him yet?" Emily leaned in closer, her eyes widening.

"Yeah. On Saturday," I said, choosing my words carefully.

"Ooooh!" Emily clapped her hands. "First Beth and Matt, now you and your mystery man. It's all happening, isn't it?"

"Seems to be, yeah," I said, nodding.

"So what's his name? Where does he live? What does he do for a living? C'mon, spill!" Emily looked at me in rapt attention.

"It's tricky," I said. "I mean, it's tricky to explain. Could be tricky to explain."

"God, he's not out on bail or something, is he?" Emily pulled a horrified face.

I laughed and looked down at my fingers, inspecting them as if my life depended on it. "No, nothing like that."

"If you don't want to tell me, it's cool," Emily said, raising her eyebrows, obviously not meaning it.

I fixed my gaze down at my coffee and my throat began to tighten.

"I just don't know how you're going to react, thassall," I said, swallowing hard.

Emily took a sip from her coffee and, grimacing, opened another sugar packet and sprinkled it in.

"So, what? Is he married? Bald? Bald and married?" Emily

frowned, stirring her coffee. "Oh crap, he's not a Young Conservative, is he?"

"Nothing as bad as that!"

"So try me, Immy," she said. "I'm your mate. I love the bones of you. Whatever you tell me, it'll be cool, I promise."

"I've been so confused lately," I began, staring back down at my fingers. "And then this person came along and everything suddenly seemed so much clearer."

"Okay…"

"She's called Gemma, you see?" I looked up at Emily, trying to gauge her reaction. "Aaaaand we got talking and I realised that everything I was doing, or had been doing for the last God knows how many years, had been a lie."

Emily nodded. I carried on.

"And we talked a lot for like, jeez, three or four weeks and then, well, we kinda realised we both liked each other and, uh, we met up on Saturday and now we know we definitely like each other," I said, looking at Emily. "And suddenly my life makes sense."

"Did you like girls before you met her?" Emily asked carefully.

"Yeah, I think I did," I replied. "But I guess I'd ignored those feelings, you know? Meeting Gemma hit me like a thunderbolt, and I guess it's hard to ignore a thunderbolt when it comes and smacks you in the face."

"So Matt was…?" Emily asked, her voice trailing off.

"I think Matt was supposed to be my 'cure'," I replied. "I s'pose, I dunno, I s'pose I thought if I dated a guy, all my feelings towards women would disappear, that it would prove that they'd all just been phases."

"But they weren't?"

"No." Tears welled in my eyes and I clenched my jaw tightly. "And it's been so hard, you know?" I continued, my brow crumpling.

"So hard living a lie, not being who I wanted to be because I didn't think it was right. And then Gemma came along and I got even more confused and unhappy, especially 'cos I was still seeing Matt at the time."

"If I'm honest, Immy, I did kinda wonder once or twice," Emily said, smiling.

"Really?" I wiped at my nose.

"Yuh-huh. I always kinda knew you weren't into the whole Matt idea." Emily twiddled her empty sugar packet in her fingers. She paused. "It must have been awkward."

"It was." I nodded. "And I feel such a cow for stringing Matt along when I had no feelings for him."

"At least you did the right thing with him, though," Emily said. "And it looks like he's got over it, doesn't it? I'm sure Beth's more than helping him with that." She winked at me and I laughed.

"I'm glad I told you," I said, tears pricking at my eyes again. "It's crap keeping stuff from friends."

"I'm glad you told me." Emily reached over and grabbed my hands. "I don't like to think you've been so unhappy."

"And you're okay about it?" I asked. "'Cos I know people can go a bit weird on you when you mention the gay word."

"I'm fine with it," Emily said. "This is the twenty-first century, Immy. Perhaps if we'd known each other, like, fifty years ago it might have been different, but thank God we've moved on from there, huh?"

I sniffed back tears.

"You can't help who you are or who you fall in love with, can you?" Emily carried on. "It's not as if you just woke up one day and decided to be gay just for the hell of it, is it?"

"No." I sighed, rubbing my eyes with the balls of my palms.

"And you're still you." Emily smiled. "You're still our lovely, sweet, silly, funny Immy. That'll never change."

"Silly?" I wiped my eyes.

"Sometimes." Emily shrugged. "And that's why we love you, you dope."

We sat in silence for a few moments, both of us processing what the other had been saying.

"So tell me about Gemma," Emily suddenly said.

I immediately pictured Fickle in my head.

"She's, well, she's just lovely," I said. "She's the same age as we all are, lives up in Leeds, uh, goes to college there too, and she's just the nicest person."

"Is she hot?" Emily whispered, leaning in closer.

"Yeah," I said, feeling my face redden slightly. "She is."

"You seeing her again soon?" Emily asked.

"Saturday after next, if all goes to plan." I drained my coffee cup. "I'm gonna be spending a fortune on train tickets!"

"But it'll be worth it, I bet." Emily squeezed my hands.

"Worth every penny." I sighed happily.

❖

The week dragged on forever, seeming to know somehow that I couldn't wait for the weekend to come, so that I could have Fickle all to myself without any parental or college work interruptions. It was as if time deliberately went even slower just to piss me off, making me wait for my Fickle fix just that little bit longer.

We'd texted and spoken to each other pretty much every day, just fleeting moments throughout the week, but nothing was ever as good as when the weekends came and we could MSN long into the night.

I had been glad I'd been able to speak to Emily about Fickle, and even more glad that her reaction hadn't been the same as Twiggy's. It felt good to finally tell a "real" person about what had been going on inside my head for so long, and it felt as if a burden had been lifted from my shoulders.

A couple of days after my heart-to-heart with Emily, I found myself on MSN with Joey. She was online on the pretext of doing follow-up work from her Scotland trip, but I was soon telling her all about my chat with Emily.

Barnaby Rudge: It's like, I dunno, Joe, like I'm free for the first time in my life. Telling Emily the other day felt liberating.

Joey: Yeah, it's good to be able to tell someone. Sometimes being gay feels like a weight you gotta carry around with you all the time.

Barnaby Rudge: Cos, like, I told Twiggy and she was a bit off.

Joey: Off?

Barnaby Rudge: Yeah. She said she didn't come across many lesbians in her daily life and I think I weirded her out a bit.

Joey: You know what Twiggy's like. She doesn't like me talking about me being gay either so I figure if it makes her uncomfortable then just don't talk to her about it. I guess if she feels like she can't handle it, then why make her?

Barnaby Rudge: You think I embarrassed her?

Joey: Maybe. But that's for her to deal with, not you. Twiggy's just a bit old-fashioned, I think, even if she is only 24. Knowing her, she probably wears bloomers and rides around on a bloody penny farthing, but if she's led a sheltered life then she's not going to be 100 percent comfortable talking about something which, to you and me, is perfectly normal.

Barnaby Rudge: But it IS normal, Joe!

Joey: But it's OUR normal, not hers, Immy. Deal with it. You gotta accept that there's a small percentage of people that still don't think it's "right". Whatever the heck "right" is!

I looked at Joey's messages to me and sensed a kind of, I dunno, a kind of off-ishness with me. I frowned, wondering if my twittering on about Fickle recently had been getting on her nerves. Understandable, I supposed, considering all the shit she'd been going through with Claire.

Barnaby Rudge: I hope you don't mind me talking about Fickle all the time. I'm sorry if I do.

There was a long pause. I stared and stared at my screen, waiting for Joey to reply.

Joey: Nah, you're in love! What you gonna do? You're gonna wanna talk about her.

Barnaby Rudge: It's not pissing you off? I'm just glad I can talk to you as well as Emily about her.

Joey: It's what I'm here for, kiddo.

Just at that moment, Twiggy logged on, making Joey immediately send me a winking sign.

Joey: Remember, if she asks you how you are, don't tell her you're happy and gay. LOL!!!

Barnaby Rudge: LMAO, you neither, if she asks you!

Joey: That won't be difficult. Can't say I feel too happy ATM.

Barnaby Rudge: Oh? You okay?

Joey: Ach, I've been better. Never mind. Hang on, Twiggy's talking to me. BRB.

I sat back in my chair feeling, well, just a bit pissed off really. This was the second time recently Joey had snubbed me the second Twiggy had logged on, 'cos she'd done it, like, about a week before when I'd been chatting to her on MSN as well, and I didn't much like it. I hoped Joey wasn't bitching about me, about how fed up she was with me banging on about Fickle, then crossly told myself off. Joey wasn't like that. I might not know her as well as, say, Emily or Beth, but I'd been talking and texting her enough over the last month to know she wasn't like that.

I told myself not to be so damn paranoid and instead idly flicked my phone open, writing out a quick text to Fickle, just to say hi and to tell her I was thinking of her, and asking her if she'd be on MSN 'cos I was on there now. I glanced back at my screen, seeing Joey's last message to me there, and guessed she was still deep in conversation with Twiggy. Thinking that I really should start doing some college work rather than chatting, I brought up Google and starting typing some key words about the boring British bloody economy in, sighing as I remembered an assignment that needed finishing by the end of the month.

I was only five or so minutes into my research when boredom set in and the fancy of a chat set in again. I've never had much of an attention span; I figured I could add it to my list of faults.

Barnaby Rudge: Hey Twigs! How's you tonight?

I flicked back to Google and scribbled down some notes from a page that I'd found, then grinned as I saw my MSN conversation tag light up.

Twiggy: Hey BR! Long time, no speak! I'm good, yeah. You?

Barnaby Rudge: I'm good too! Glad for a distraction from work!

Twiggy: I'm talking to Joey. She told me you and Fickle met up then?

I read Twiggy's message and felt briefly taken aback at that. Twiggy and Joey were talking about me?

Barnaby Rudge: Yeah. Joey told you?

There was a long pause.

Twiggy: Oh, she wasn't gossiping! Just mentioned it in
passing.

Barnaby Rudge: Right.

Why were they talking about me?

Twiggy: And it went okay then?

Barnaby Rudge: Yeah, real well.

Twiggy: And you both got on?

Barnaby Rudge: More than. Went better than I could ever
have imagined.

A beep at my side drew my eyes away from the screen and
to my phone. It was Fickle. I grinned, feeling the familiar soppy
feeling I saw whenever I saw her name.

Hey u! it said. *Soz, won't be on MSN 2night. Bit busy. Catch u
2moz, yeh? Love youuu xxxx*

My grin faded but I told myself not to be stupid. So Fickle
was busy. Deal with it. She was at college just like I was; and if her
course was anything like mine was, she'd be up to ears in work as
well. I looked down at my assignment notes, all three lines of them,
and sighed.

Twiggy: That's fab! So you're gonna see her again?

I looked back at my computer screen.

Barnaby Rudge: Yeah, Saturday after next. Hey Twigs,
are you still talking to Joey? We were talking just now
but she's gone quiet.

Another long pause.

Twiggy: Yeah, I'm talking to her now.

Barnaby Rudge: Is she doing well? She said she wasn't
happy just now.

Twiggy: Seems to be, yeah.

I stared at the screen again, thinking for the hundredth time that I ought to kill this conversation and carry on with some work. A rumble in my stomach, however, told me it was nearly dinner time. I glanced up at the yellow clock on my wall; 6.30 p.m.

Barnaby Rudge: Twigs, I'm gonna go get something to eat.

Twiggy: Sure. Be back later?

Barnaby Rudge: Try and stop me!

Twiggy: You know we ain't done any virtual karate for a while. Fancy an arse-kicking later?

Barnaby Rudge: You're on!

I sent a quick message to Joey to tell her I was leaving and she sent me one back, her message littered with apologies 'cos she'd gone quiet on me. I grinned and told her it was fine, then said good-bye to her and Twiggy, not waiting for a reply this time. Instead I logged off and headed downstairs where I was greeted by the sound of pots and pans being clattered about by Mum and a smell of something spicy in the kitchen that made my mouth water and suddenly made me realise just how hungry I was.

❖

I got kinda caught up in college work for the next few days, only managing to text Fickle a few times throughout the day rather than our usual twenty or so daily texts to each other. I'd done nothing all week but think about her and think about seeing her on the following Saturday, and not being able to catch up with her properly had nearly killed me. Finally, on Friday, I decided I'd done enough college work all week to warrant being allowed a night in front of the computer without feeling guilty for neglecting work.

I brought up a train website on the screen and started looking for trains for the following Saturday, to Birmingham again. Feeling a warm glow of contentment inside me, happy that it was only eight days until I'd see Fickle again, I grabbed my bank card and booked the same 10.00 a.m. train that I'd caught last week. This time, though, I booked an open return, thinking with a kinda smug satisfaction that there was *no* way I'd be bailing out on her early again this time.

I snatched up my phone and instinctively rang Fickle to tell her I'd booked, and that she should get her arse moving and book her train too. She picked up within two rings and I felt, as I always did when I heard her voice, my heart quicken slightly.

"Hey," she said, in her gorgeous, soft voice.

"Hey you," I replied. "So, I've booked my train for next Saturday. Just thought I'd ring you and tell you."

"Oh right," Fickle said, kinda slowly, I thought. "Okay."

"For Birmingham, of course." I carried on, idly flicking screens on my computer. "Same time as last time?"

"Perfect," Fickle replied.

"You not booked yours yet, I take it?" I asked.

"No." Fickle paused. "To be honest, Immy, funds are a little, uh, a little tight at the moment."

"Oh." I suddenly felt a bit deflated. "Right."

"But I'm sure it'll be okay to book next week," Fickle went on.

"They're not much," I persisted. "I just got mine for £20 return. If you book today you might get it at the same rate?"

"I can't book it today, Im," Fickle said. "I'm down to my last few quid."

"I could pay for it and you pay me back?" I said, hoping I didn't sound too desperate.

Fickle laughed.

"No, Immy, you don't need to do that. I'll book something nearer the day."

"I don't mind, honest," I persisted again, thinking that the fares would rocket next week.

"No," Fickle said, kinda impatiently, I thought. "But I appreciate the offer, honey."

There was a bit of a silence. I wasn't sure what to say and, if I'm honest, I was kinda embarrassed at having apparently pushed it with Fickle. She spoke first.

"Have you had a good day? I've been thinking about you loads."

I perked up a bit, hearing that she'd been thinking of me.

"Yeah, it's been fine," I said, watching the computer screen as I saw Joey logging onto MSN. "Just shitloads of work at college at the mo. I mean, my exams aren't for, like, ages yet, so what's the deal with all the work?"

A message flashed up from Joey, just kinda saying hi and asking how I was. I nestled my phone in the crook of my neck and tapped out a quick message back to her.

Barnaby Rudge: Hey Joe! Just on the phone to Fickle. Howz you?

"Tell me about it," Fickle was now saying to me on the phone. "Get this, right, I was given a fifteen-hundred-word essay to write about—in *French*, mind you—the rising fuel prices affecting Western Europe."

"Jeez, Gemma!" I whistled under my breath. "That's a bit heavy going, isn't it?"

"That's what I said to my teacher," Fickle said. "Not that he took a scrap of notice of me."

"And I thought my piddling little assignment was tough going." I laughed.

"So it kinda means I'm not going to be around much this weekend…" Fickle's voice trailed off.

"You're kidding me?" I felt my heart sink. "When's it gotta be done by?"

"Monday," Fickle said.

"And when did he give it to you to do?"

"Today," Fickle replied. "Uh, no, uh yesterday. Yeah, yesterday. Shit, isn't it?"

"You're telling me!" I glanced at the computer screen and saw Joey had replied.

Joey: K, kiddo. I won't disturb. Catch you later maybe?

Barnaby Rudge: No, stay Joe! Be good to talk!

I meant it. I'd missed talking to her for the last few days. And if, as it seemed she wouldn't be, Fickle wasn't going to be around, then who better to have a laugh and a chat with but Joey?

Joey: OK! I'll sit here and paint me nails or whatever while you finish with Fickle!

I grinned. Joey painting her nails wasn't an image I thought I'd ever have in my head.

"I'm sorry I won't be able to speak to you so much, Immy," Fickle was now saying. "I'll miss you."

"I'll miss you too," I said truthfully.

"I better go. Mum needs me downstairs for something," Fickle said, sighing.

"Will you be back later tonight?" I asked, trying to keep my voice casual.

"Doubt it, hun," Fickle said, adding, "Sorry."

"S'okay. I understand. I'll text you later, yeah?"

"Yeah, sure."

"I love you, Gem."

"Catch you later, Immy. Miss you already."

And then she was gone. I held my phone, still warm, in my hand for a while, thinking about what she'd said, and tried to stop the feelings of complete disappointment inside me. All my excitement of booking my train and thinking that I would have Fickle all to myself all weekend had completely disappeared. I looked back at my computer.

Barnaby Rudge: Hey.

Joey: Hey! Fickle gone?

Barnaby Rudge: Yeah. #Sigh#

Joey: Aw! You got it bad, ain't you?

Barnaby Rudge: Yeah. #Sigh#

Joey: LOL.

Barnaby Rudge: And the pisser is that she's not going to be around so much all weekend 'cos she's got so much work on at college.

Joey: That's a bastard.

Barnaby Rudge: Tell me about it! I was sooooo looking forward to having her to myself all weekend.

Joey: Are you still seeing her next week?

I grinned.

Barnaby Rudge: Yeah. Just booked my train tickets today too. Can't wait.

There was a long pause.

Barnaby Rudge: Joe?

Joey: I'm here.

Barnaby Rudge: Ah. You went quiet.

Joey: Did I? Soz.

Barnaby Rudge: S'OK.

There was another long pause, longer this time. Then:

Joey: Is she around tonight? Perhaps if you can't talk to her over the weekend you can at least have some time with her tonight.

Barnaby Rudge: No. She said she doubts she'll be

around. She's gone now anyway, said her mum
needed her or something.

Joey: Right.

Barnaby Rudge: What's going on, Joe? You seem awful
quiet tonight.

Joey: I've kinda got a lot on my mind at the moment. Soz.

Barnaby Rudge: Claire?

Joey: Sorry?

Barnaby Rudge: Are you thinking about Claire?

Joey: Oh! Sorry! No, not thinking about Claire.

Barnaby Rudge: Oh, right. Just checking.

Yet another long pause ensued. After staring at my computer
screen for what seemed like ages, I decided I'd had enough of trying
to get anything resembling conversation out of Joey and told her I
was going.

Barnaby Rudge: It's a bit like pulling teeth with you
tonight, Joe!

Joey: Thanks.

Barnaby Rudge: So I'm gonna go.

Joey: Wait. Don't. I'm sorry.

Barnaby Rudge: I really ought to go, anyway. My parents
haven't seen me for days. For all they know, I could be
covered in dust and cobwebs up here!

Joey: I have a dilemma, Imms, and I dunno what to do
about it. That's why I've been quiet.

Barnaby Rudge: Oh right. Well, maybe I can help? I like a
nice dilemma! Go on, spill!

Joey: But I don't quite know where to start!

Barnaby Rudge: At the beginning? It's a very good place
to start. Did okay for Julie Andrews, didn't it?

Joey: LOL. Yeah, I guess.

Barnaby Rudge: Try me. I'm very good at dilemmas. Well, usually.

Joey: I found something out about someone and I don't know what to do about it.

Barnaby Rudge: Well, share! I'll help you decide what to do. Well, hopefully!

Joey: You might not like this, though. It's about you and Fickle.

I frowned at the computer screen. Me and Fickle?

Barnaby Rudge: Go on.

Joey: More specifically Fickle.

Barnaby Rudge: Fickle? What about Fickle?

Joey: And I don't really know how to tell you about what I found out about her.

Barnaby Rudge: I'm listening.

Joey: It's difficult…

Barnaby Rudge: Jeez, Joe! Just cut to the chase, will you?

Joey: Fickle. I think she's cheating on you, Imms.

CHAPTER SIXTEEN

I stared at Joey's words in front of me, my mouth slightly open, my heart caught well and truly in my throat. Fickle, cheating on me?

Barnaby Rudge: What are you talking about, Joe?

Joey: Don't get angry with me. Promise you won't get angry with me?

Barnaby Rudge: I can't promise anything.

Joey: Then I won't tell you.

Barnaby Rudge: Oh, you will! You can't tell me you think Fickle's cheating on me then not tell me anything about it.

Joey: I don't want to upset you.

Barnaby Rudge: Then why bring it up in the first place??

Joey: 'Cos I've been wrestling with it for days and I know things and I think you should know them too. Specially 'cos you like Fickle so much. It's only fair.

Like Fickle? I *loved* Fickle. At least I thought I did.

Barnaby Rudge: So tell me what you've "found out" then.

Joey: I post on another website as well as the L&S one. Another one dedicated to Jess and Ali from Lovers and Sinners, you knew that, yeah?

Barnaby Rudge: OK.

Joey: And they have a message board there as well, kinda like the one we all post on.

Barnaby Rudge: OK.

Joey: And last week I saw Fickle's name on there.

I laughed.

Barnaby Rudge: She's allowed to, you know! And, y'know, it could have been another Fickle.

Joey: I know, but it wasn't, I checked. It was her. Same e-mail address, same location, same date of birth, everything.

Barnaby Rudge: Why did you check?

Joey: Because she was flirting on there like there was no tomorrow.

Barnaby Rudge: So she likes to flirt! I knew that when I hooked up with her! That's what made me fall for her in the first place, Joe!

Joey: But she was flirting with one girl on there in particular. Like, PROPER flirting.

A whooshing sound enveloped me and I realised it was blood pumping furiously in my head. I stared at Joey's words.

Barnaby Rudge: What a crock of shit! I don't believe you.

Joey: Why would I lie? I'm not doing this to hurt you!

Barnaby Rudge: I dunno. 'Cos you're sore about Claire? 'Cos you think everyone's like Claire and cheats? You tell me.

Joey: Don't be like this, Imms. I'm telling you 'cos I don't want you getting hurt.

Barnaby Rudge: Even though you're talking bollocks? Fickle wouldn't do that to me. She loves me, she told me.

I looked down and saw that my hands were shaking. My breath

was getting faster and faster and I suddenly felt like the room was going round. Without waiting for Joey to reply, I quickly typed:

Barnaby Rudge: So what was it that Fickle was supposedly saying to this other girl? I assume it was a girl?

Joey: Yeah, it was a girl. It was just dead flirty, very sexual, you know? She was telling her she missed her and couldn't stop thinking about her. You want me to show you the link, if you don't believe me?

Barnaby Rudge: Why not? It'll all be a mistake so I'm not bothered what you do.

The truth was, I felt sick. Staring dumbly at the screen, I suddenly said to Joey:

Barnaby Rudge: Still could have been someone pretending to be Fickle. Why would Fickle go onto another board and start flirting with someone else when she knows I could see it? It's a bit public, isn't it?

Yeah, I know. It was desperate, but what was I supposed to do? I was clasping at straws right now.

Joey: I don't know, Imms! Maybe she just doesn't care? Who knows what goes on inside her head?

I watched as Joey posted the link to the website and read her last message again. *Who knows what goes on inside her head?* Not me, obviously.

Barnaby Rudge: If it's her, then that would show I don't know her as well as I thought I did, huh?

Joey: Go read it, Imms. It's deffo her. I got chatting to someone who knew the girl that Fickle was flirting with on MSN and asked her if she knew what Fickle's real name was. She told me it was Gemma. That's Fickle's real name, isn't it?

I paused.

Barnaby Rudge: Yeah.

Joey: I'm sorry, Imms. Seems Fickle ain't what you think she is.

I thought for a minute.

Barnaby Rudge: Yeah. Listen, Joe, I'm gonna go. See ya.

Without waiting for a reply, I minimised MSN and walked slowly to my bed, kinda in a daze. My phone rang pretty much immediately, but when I saw it was Joey ringing me, I cancelled the call and switched the phone off, flinging myself down onto my bed, and my phone to the floor. I lay there for a while, hands folded behind my head, just staring up at the ceiling, my mind blank. Finally I closed my eyes and let the tears that had been threatening for the last ten minutes come streaming down my cheeks.

❖

After an hour of just lying there, turning things over and over in my head until I was beginning to think I was incapable of rational thoughts anymore, I suddenly got back up and went over to my computer, which was still switched on. I maximised MSN again and found the link that Joey had sent me, directing me straight to the *Ali and Jess* website's message board.

Joey had made a mistake, that was all there was to it. Fickle wouldn't do this—not to me. Not wanting to, but knowing that I had to, I scrolled down the numerous threads and messages until I found what I was looking for:

Username = Fickle.

There she was. Attached to her name were, like, about thirty or so threads and messages; it looked like she'd been busy over the past few days. Almost as if I was on autopilot, I clicked on some of her messages and read them, my heart racing, my hands shaking.

There were messages, dozens of them, to someone called LisaD, and as I read them in silence, I could feel the tears that had only just dried up ten minutes before start to fall down my cheeks again.

There was no mistaking that it was Fickle. I recognised the words, the style of writing, the flirting, the winking signs—everything she'd been doing to me over the last month, she was now doing to LisaD. I couldn't stop reading their messages to each other, almost as if I wanted to punish myself, like I wanted to prove to myself what an idiot I'd been. Then I saw that she'd posted a message only about a few hours ago—when she'd told me she had been too busy to talk to me on MSN.

A message from Twiggy flashing in the corner of my screen suddenly caught my eye. I'd been so engrossed in what I'd been reading I hadn't even noticed that she'd logged on. I didn't want to speak to her and really wished I'd killed MSN or set my status to Away, or whatever. But it was too late. Her message was there waiting for me.

Twiggy: Hey, BR! How are you?

Did she know? Did Twiggy know? I was being paranoid! How could she know?

Barnaby Rudge: Twiggy.

Twiggy: How's your day been?

Barnaby Rudge: OK till now. Now it's shit.

I carried on reading Fickle's messages to LisaD, not wanting to, but unable to stop myself. It was like torture, but something seemed to force me to keep reading.

Twiggy: Wassup?

How would Twiggy understand? She always thought it was wrong anyway, me and Fickle. Just how the hell would she understand?

Barnaby Rudge: Nothing. S'OK.

Twiggy: I'm here if you wanna talk?

Barnaby Rudge: Have you seen Joey on here in the last hour?

Twiggy: No, but then I only logged on five minutes ago.

Barnaby Rudge: Yeah, course. Sorry.

Twiggy: You got a message for her, in case I see her later?

I frowned, suddenly angry.

Barnaby Rudge: Yeah, tell her from me that in the future she needs to butt out of my business.

There was a long pause.

Twiggy: Erk! Everything okay with you guys?

Barnaby Rudge: Not now, no.

There was a long pause, then suddenly:

Twiggy: How's Fickle?

WTF?? Why was she asking me that? We were talking about Joey and now she was asking me about Fickle. Why? Because she knew.

Barnaby Rudge: Why you asking?

Twiggy: Just am.

Barnaby Rudge: Joey's told you, then?

There was another pause. Real long this time.

Twiggy: Yeah.

Barnaby Rudge: Why did she have to tell people? I suppose you're all laughing at me now, aren't you? Stupid, dumb Imogen gets taken in by a girl she'd never even fucking-well met and then meets her, falls for her, hook, line, and sinker, and then finds out a week later the girl's doing the same thing to someone else. Brilliant! Couldn't make it up, that one.

Twiggy: It wasn't just you that Fickle did it to, if that's any consolation.

Barnaby Rudge: What?? Ohhh it just gets better! Do tell!

Twiggy: And no one's laughing at you, BR.

Barnaby Rudge: So, what? Fickle's a serial adulterer? Is that it?

Twiggy: She has a, uh, a reputation, let's just say that.

Barnaby Rudge: And on what basis are you telling me this?

Twiggy: Joey said she found a nasty message from someone to Fickle on that Jess and Ali website as well.

Barnaby Rudge: So?

Twiggy: So she e-mailed this girl and asked her what it was all about.

Barnaby Rudge: And the girl said?

Twiggy: That about a couple of months ago Fickle had been coming on to her, like, dead strong and had been telling her all these things she wanted to hear, had been bombarding her with texts, e-mails, phone calls.

Barnaby Rudge: And?

Twiggy: And then this girl said she met her, they got on real well, the girl thought Fickle was "the one," then she suddenly went cold on her. She said Fickle got arsey with her whenever she asked her stuff and then not long after she found out that Fickle had been coming on to someone else on another board.

Barnaby Rudge: Please tell me it wasn't me?

Twiggy: Sorry, yeah. It was you. This girl found your messages to each other on the L&S board.

I looked at Twiggy's words. *It was you.* I rubbed at my eyes angrily, eyes that were already red and dry from crying, and sat back in my chair, breathing out slowly, trying to control the wild thumping of my heart.

Twiggy: Joey didn't know what to do.

Barnaby Rudge: She talked to you about it?

Twiggy: Yeah, just after she found out. She's been in pieces about it, wondering whether to tell you.

I closed my eyes. So that's why Joey kept disappearing every time Twiggy logged on. She was talking to her about me! It would go a long way towards explaining why Joey hadn't been her normal self lately as well.

Barnaby Rudge: Fickle told me she was busy tonight. I s'pose that was a lie too?

Twiggy: It's possible. I dunno, BR.

Barnaby Rudge: And she told me she had college work to do all weekend. Another lie.

Twiggy: Who knows? All I do know is that this Fickle girl sounds like she gets a kick out of coming on to people over the 'net.

Barnaby Rudge: And then when the people respond, she gets bored, backs off and finds someone else.

Twiggy: It's the classic cliché of the thrill of the chase, by the sounds of it.

Barnaby Rudge: No matter who she hurts?

Twiggy: So it would seem.

I knew I had to speak to Fickle. She'd have an explanation for me, I was sure of that. Who knows? Maybe I was the one she really wanted. Maybe she was just trying the others out—*is trying the others out*—until she found the real deal. Me.

I switched my phone on and, ignoring Joey's three texts and voicemail message, all left within the last hour and a bit, scrolled down to Fickle's number, knowing that the second I heard her voice, everything would be normal, that she'd tell me it was all a huge mistake, it wasn't her, and she loved me and would never do anything like that to me.

It rang through, four, five rings then, surprisingly, the phone went dead. I cursed under my breath and dialled again, thinking my reception had disappeared or that I'd pressed a wrong button. That happens sometimes, right? Again, it rang a few times, but this time, the familiar, husky voice of Fickle answered.

"Hey," she said.

I took a deep breath.

Chapter Seventeen

H ey," I said, trying to control the wobble in my voice.
"You all right?" Fickle said, kinda automatically.

"Yeah. You?" Just the sound of her voice made my stomach turn to mush and my heart beat faster. Nothing had changed. Why would it?

"Yeah." Fickle paused. "Good."

I could practically sense she was thinking of things to say to me. I heard her quietly tap something into her computer and felt my jaw clench.

"How's your work going?" I asked lamely.

"Work?" Fickle seemed distracted.

"Yeah. You had work to do tonight, remember?" I spoke slowly.

"Oh yeah, right!" Fickle laughed. "Of course, yeah. Yeah, it's going good."

"'Cos, like, I can hear you tapping on your keyboard there," I said, my voice steadier now. "Wondered if you were online? We could chat?"

"I'm not online, no." Fickle sounded impatient. Maybe I was imagining it? "Sorry."

There was a long pause as I tried to think of what to say to her next. I wanted to ask her about LisaD, but I didn't know what to ask. What *could* I ask? I frowned, a feeling of frustration welling inside of me.

"You okay?" Fickle was now asking.

I jolted myself back to the present.

"Yeah, fine," I lied. "I just wanted to say hi, thassall."

"I miss you," Fickle said, but I sensed there was something missing in the way she said it. There was no feeling, but, again, was that just my imagination?

"I miss you too," I said. I at least meant it.

"I've really gotta get on, Immy," Fickle said. "I don't mean to cut you short, but, y'know."

"Yeah, I know," I said. "Maybe catch you later?"

"Yeah."

Then she was gone. I didn't know whether I felt better for talking to her or not. She'd said she missed me, but then she might not necessarily have meant it. Maybe she just said that to get me off the phone so that I wouldn't ask her too many questions?

Frowning, I went back onto the computer, bringing up the Jess and Ali website's message board again. I found Fickle's messages to LisaD and started reading back through them, trying to create a timeline in my head, trying to figure out when it was she first started talking to her.

I read every single one of their messages, each one feeling like a steel blade being pushed into my heart, but I read on. The messages went back just four days, to the Monday after I'd met Fickle on the Saturday. In just two days she'd gone from telling me she loved me and couldn't wait to see me again to trying it on with another girl, on another site.

I refreshed the page, bringing me back to the most recent page, and felt my jaw pretty much literally drop open as I saw a message from Fickle on there, timed at 8.56 p.m. Right now. Her message was to LisaD and just said: *Shall we MSN, babe? I think I'm being watched.* She put a winking sign next to it and I felt sick, remembering how that winking sign used to make me feel, and thought that LisaD, whoever she was, and wherever she was, was probably feeling exactly as I used to feel.

Except that Fickle still had the power to make me feel it, even now, even after all this.

❖

I spent the rest of the evening in bed, my mobile switched off, telling Mum I was sick and didn't want any dinner, and asked her not to disturb me 'cos I was going to try and sleep. I didn't want to hear, speak, or have to think about anyone. Except it wasn't that easy. All I could think about was Fickle and what she'd done. How could she have done that to me? Hadn't I meant anything to her?

I woke up the next morning, Saturday, after a fitful night filled with images of Fickle, winking signs, and me crying, and knew that I had to speak to her again. I had to hear it from her, had to know why she was doing this. I switched on my phone and expected to have some overnight texts from her, telling me she loved me, that she missed me.

There was nothing. It was as if she'd moved on already and everything we'd said to each other over the last month had never been said. I read through messages from Joey and Twiggy, plus a message from Emily asking me if I wanted to meet her in town later. I didn't. I read Joey's message three times. It just said: *I'm here if u need me, chickeroo. Any time. Just call me and I'll be here.*

Joey.

I'd been such a shit to her the night before when all she'd wanted to do was help me. I sent her a message back just saying thanks, and kinda apologising for not believing her and for being so nasty. Then I said I still needed to hear it from Fickle herself, 'cos a part of me still refused to believe it was true. I felt a small crumb of comfort when I heard my phone beep almost immediately and saw it was from Joey. It just said, *Of course. I understand. And thanks for ur apologies but totes understand why u reacted how u did.*

I read Joey's message again, still feeling comforted by it, then, my heart beginning to pound, for whatever ridiculous reason it had decided to pound, I sent a message to Fickle telling her I needed to speak to her urgently. I knew by now I probably wouldn't get a reply, but sent it just the same. I knew none of this would make any sense until Fickle explained it to me, and even then, I wasn't convinced I'd still fully understand.

As it was, Fickle called me back, around three hours after I'd sent her the message. I was still in bed, propped up with pillows, staring vacantly out of the window, my mind numb and apparently immune to anything going on around me, nursing my fourth cup of coffee of the morning when she rang. I stared down at my phone, ringing away, flashing her name on and off at me, kinda like it was mocking me. Almost in a daze, I answered and spoke to her.

"Hello," I said, as curtly as I could.

"Hey," she replied, a bit robotically, I thought. "You all right?"

Was I all right? Was she kidding me?

"No, Gem, I'm not all right," I said, trying to sound as pissed off as I could.

"Oh," she said, sounding surprised.

What kind of game was she playing here? I took a deep breath, trying to control the thumping of my heart.

"Who's LisaD?" I said bluntly.

"LisaD?" she replied, kinda airily, I thought.

"Yeah, LisaD." I spat the words out. "The girl you've been chatting up online?"

Fickle sighed, short and sharp, kinda like your dad does when he's just been asked to put the bins out.

"She's a friend," she said shortly.

"Good friend, huh?" I said.

"Yeah, a good friend," Fickle repeated. "Listen, Immy, what is this?"

"This is me trying to work out just what the fuck you've been up to last week," I said, trying to keep my voice down.

"What are you, my mother?" Fickle laughed sharply.

I was stung by her tone and felt my face begin to crumple.

"I thought I was your girlfriend?" I said quietly.

There was silence. How can a silence sometimes be so deafening? A silence where no words are said, but a thousand are spoken?

"It was a bit of fun, me and you." Fickle laughed lightly. "I thought you knew the deal."

"I'm sorry?" My voice rose with incredulity.

"You and me," Fickle repeated. "I thought you realised it was just a bit of fun?"

I squeezed my eyes tight shut, pinching the bridge of my nose with the finger and thumb of the hand that wasn't holding the phone and exhaled slowly, not quite believing what I was hearing.

"Was that what it was to you, then?" I asked wearily. "Just a bit of fun? 'Cos it was more than just fun to me."

Fickle paused.

"I do like you, Immy," she said. "But I thought it was always clear it was just a bit of harmless flirting, thassall."

"Are you kidding me?" I hissed. I looked at the door, making sure it was tight shut. "You came on to me like there was no tomorrow. You sucked me in with all your flirty messages, all your come-ons, telling me you loved me, that you missed me, and now you tell me it was only a bit of fun? Are you crazy?"

"I didn't think you'd see it as anything other than a laugh, Immy," Fickle said.

"Just what kind of head-fuck are you, Gemma?" I said through clenched teeth. "You knew my situation, you knew I had a boyfriend, that I was confused. You must have known that I would have taken in all your flirting and acted on it. How could you have been so cruel?"

"Cruel?" Fickle sounded amused. "What's cruel about a bit of excitement? You enjoyed it, didn't you? You got off on it, all my late-night messages, didn't you? That made you feel good about yourself, made you laugh, made you happy? What's cruel about that?"

"Didn't you know how I felt about you?" I said, feeling tears welling in my throat. "You told me you loved me, for crap's sake!"

"People say that all the time." Fickle sighed. "It's just a turn of phrase, Immy!"

I couldn't believe what I was hearing. I squeezed my eyes tight shut again, determined not to cry, determined not to let Fickle have the satisfaction of knowing she'd crushed me.

"Are you kidding me here? What is it with you, Gem?" I said, suddenly feeling drained of all my energy. "Do you get off on this sort of thing? How does it work, huh? You find some sucker on the Internet, come on to them, then when they fall for all your crap, then what? You get bored? Is that it? You get bored and then move on to the next one?"

Fickle paused.

"Yeah, something like that," she said, and for the first time in our conversation, she actually had the grace to sound slightly sheepish.

"You're a head case," I said, not caring what I said to her anymore.

"Yeah, maybe I am," Fickle said. "Clue was in the name, though, Immy. Fickle? Er, hello? So I'm fickle—what can I do?"

"You can go fuck yourself," I said, pressing the Cancel button on my phone and sliding back down under the duvet, pulled the covers high over my head, and then just sobbed and sobbed until there were no more tears left to cry.

CHAPTER EIGHTEEN

I didn't hear much from Fickle after that. It was as if the last month had never happened; like I'd never known her, or that it had all been a dream. I'd gone from feeling like the happiest girl in the world to one who couldn't face the world ever again in just a few short days. She sent me a few texts, spaced out over the days, and even had the grace to send me an e-mail, trying to explain herself, trying to justify what she'd done, but by that point I was past caring. She'd made it bluntly clear in her texts and e-mails that whatever we'd "shared" had just been a bit of fun and now she'd moved on, but that she "hoped we could still be friends".

Priceless, huh?

I pretty much just shut myself away in my room all week, telling Mum and Dad I was ill. And I *was* ill; my heart was well and truly broken, but more than that, I felt sick to my stomach over how stupid I'd been and I just couldn't face them. I couldn't hide my pain, my hurt, my anger—and the last thing I needed was to get the third degree from them about what was up with me. I felt eaten up with grief—that was the only word I could use to describe it—grief at losing her, almost like she'd died. I missed her dreadfully, crying myself to sleep with the realisation that I'd probably never speak to her ever again.

I couldn't face college either, and I sure as hell couldn't face

Emily or Beth. The truth was, I felt like a complete idiot. I felt so stupid and annoyed with myself for letting my feelings run away with me over a girl whom, as it turned out, I never knew at all. Everyone had been right all along; everyone had said it was dumb to get carried away with the attention Fickle had been heaping on me. Maybe they hadn't said it, but they'd all thought it. I could tell.

I spent my time lying in bed, almost in a daze, numb with hurt, only leaving my room once I knew everyone had left for school or work. Then I'd go to the kitchen with the intention of making myself something to eat, but just the smell and sight of food made me want to throw up. I sat in the lounge looking at the walls or paced the house, trying to shake thoughts of Fickle from my head. I left my phone off all day and couldn't bring myself to go anywhere near the computer, almost as if Fickle was physically inside it. I didn't want to risk seeing her name anywhere on my screen; not on any message board, not on MSN, and certainly not on Skype. Quite simply, I just went to ground to lick my wounds and try and heal myself the only way I knew how.

Finally, nearly a week after I'd last spoken to Fickle, I woke up and didn't feel like I wanted to cry anymore. My pain and grief had turned to silent fury, literally overnight, it seemed, and I didn't want to feel like shit anymore, didn't want to waste another second of my life hurting over Fickle and what she'd done to me. I missed being human; missed talking to Mum and Dad, missed being at college, missed Beth and Emily, and missed chatting to Joey, Twiggy, and all the other friends I'd made on the message board. They were the ones that mattered now; they were my real friends.

I switched on my phone for the first time in ages and listened guiltily as it beeped with loads of texts and voicemail alerts. There were some from Beth and Emily, just saying hi and asking me where I'd been, with a few from Twiggy too, asking me if I'd be on MSN and stuff like that. Most were from Joey, though, telling me she was worried about me and begging me to let her know I was okay. There were none from Fickle, but then I hadn't really expected any more from her.

Instinctively, I dialled Joey's number, listening to it ring as I pulled a brush through my hair and peered at myself in the mirror. It wasn't pretty.

"Imms?" Joey's voice sounded at the end of the phone.

"Hey Joe." I looked at myself in the mirror.

"Oh thank God," Joey breathed out. "I've been worried sick about you, after everything that's happened."

"Yeah, I went a bit crazy for a while, Joe." I tried to make my voice sound light. "But I'm okay now, I think."

"Everyone's been asking about you on the message board," Joey went on. "Twiggy's been worrying herself silly as well."

"I'm sorry I didn't get in touch," I said truthfully. "I just didn't wanna know anyone for a while, you know?"

"Yeah, I understand," Joey said. "I'm just glad you're…you know…okay."

"I'll live." I laughed. "Mind you, I wasn't so sure about that a few days ago, but that was then."

"Good on you, kiddo," Joey said, with more sincerity in her voice than I think I've ever heard.

She paused.

"So you spoke to Fickle, then?" she asked, kinda tentatively.

"Yeah. On Saturday. Exactly a week after we first met and she's telling me it's over. How about that?" I laughed, but the laugh was laden with irony.

"I don't know what to say, Imms," Joey said. "I'm so sorry."

"Better to know now, I guess," I said, "than later, when I was in deeper than I already was."

"I could wring the little cow's neck, I really could," Joey said savagely. "What she did to you was just downright brutal. I tell you what, Imms, if I ever see her name on any message board anywhere, I'll kill her. I mean it."

"You can't kill someone over the Internet." I laughed. "But I appreciate the offer anyway."

"I had to tell you, Imms," Joey said. "I couldn't let her do it to you."

"I'm glad you told me," I said honestly. "Imagine how awful we'd both have felt further down the line? Like I said, best to nip it in the bud early."

I felt my voice wobble at those words, and cleared my throat quickly, hoping that Joey hadn't noticed.

"Did she tell you why she did it?" Joey asked.

I thought for a second.

"No, not really," I replied. "She just said that me and her was just a bit of fun and that it was never going to go anywhere, and that she couldn't help but flirt with other girls. It was in her nature to do it, she said."

"For crap's sake…" Joey gasped.

"I know," I said. "I just wish she'd made that clear from the start. That it was a game, you know?"

My voice threatened to crack again.

"Silly little girl playing with people's emotions," Joey said bitterly. "What a selfish idiot she is."

"She told me she loved me, Joey," I said simply. "That's not a game, is it?"

"It's not, Imms," Joey said gently. "That's just darned cruel."

"I really liked her—*loved her*, I think—Joey," I said, still looking at myself in the mirror, watching my face crumple slightly.

"I know, kiddo, I know," Joey said. "But you have to find some positives in amongst all the negatives, if you can."

"Like what?" I said. I found it impossible at that moment to think there was anything positive about the whole sorry mess.

"Well, it allowed you to be true to yourself," Joey said. "It confirmed what you'd suspected for a while—that you like girls."

"You're right." I nodded to myself in the mirror. "And I s'pose it got me out of a dead-end relationship with Matt."

"See? Another positive. You might still be with him now if you hadn't met Fickle."

I thought about that for a second. Joey was right; Fickle might not have been the cause of my deciding to finish with Matt, but she'd sure been the catalyst.

"I guess she gave me the guts to finally get round to doing something about it," I said. "He's seeing my mate, Beth, now. Did I tell you?"

Joey laughed.

"You didn't, no. And you don't sound down about it, so I'm guessing you're cool with it?"

"Oh, totally!" I said, laughing as well. "If anything, it's a relief to know he's with someone who wants to be with him, 'cos by all accounts, Beth's crazy about him."

"See? Another positive!" Joey giggled. "And let's face it, kiddo, he's probably getting a helluva lot more action in the sack with her than he was with you. No offence, like."

I laughed out loud.

"None taken, you cheeky bugger!"

I looked at my reflection and saw that I was actually smiling, seeing life in my eyes for the first time in days. Joey was good for me, I decided. She was saying everything I needed to hear, and I figured in that moment that I needed Joey in my life, probably more than I'd ever needed anyone before, and I needed her to keep telling me the things I wanted to hear. Maybe that way Fickle would eventually fade from my memory.

"Wanna Skype later?" Joey's voice jolted me back to reality. "I'll wear a silly hat, make you laugh?"

"Sure," I said. "It'll be nice to see a friendly face after hiding myself away in my room for nearly a week!"

"I'm glad you're doing better," Joey said. "I missed seeing you around. I only had Twiggy for company last night, and she's lovely and all, but, well, you know!" She laughed.

"Argh, Twiggy!" I sighed. "I s'pose I'll have to face her at some point as well."

"You don't have to face anyone you don't want to," Joey said kindly. "But she's been worried about you too. Just send her a text, tell her you're alive?"

"I will," I said. "And Joey, thanks. Thanks for listening and not judging. I'm sorry if I was rude to you last week when you told me about Fickle."

"Ah, pff!" Joey laughed. "It's water under the bridge now, Imms."

She hesitated.

"Not everyone's like Fickle, you know," she said. "Not everyone you meet online is a total shit. Don't let what happened with her cloud your opinions of others 'cos there are some great people out there—people who care about you. Just 'cos we're a face that talks to you through a computer screen doesn't mean we don't care, okay?"

I nodded to my reflection. "Thanks, Joey."

"No problem, kiddo," Joey said. "Speak to you later."

And with that, she was gone. I sat down on my bed and thought about everything Joey had just said to me, and finally felt a pinprick of something that resembled optimism.

❖

A hot shower and my first proper food in days made me feel 100 percent better. Mum and Dad had come back from work, and

Sophie was lurking somewhere in her bedroom, on the pretext of doing homework, which meant she was probably either texting, Tweeting, or on Facebook.

I smiled as Mum came into the lounge just as I was finishing off my second bacon sandwich. She ruffled my hair as she sat down next to me and looked across to me.

"You feeling better, my love?" she said, picking up a magazine and flicking through it.

"I am, yeah." I nodded, wiping my mouth with the back of my hand. "Some sort of nasty bug got me, but I think it's gone now." I smiled at her.

"That's all it was?" Mum cocked her head and gave me a look that only mothers can give you. "Nothing else?"

"Nothing else, Mum." I nodded. "I'm much better now. I'll go back to college tomorrow, I think."

I picked up my phone, not wanting to talk any more about it with Mum. I sent Twiggy a text, just telling her I was okay and that I'd be on MSN later if she fancied a chat. I started deleting some messages from my in-box and saw some of Fickle's texts to me from the week before, and felt my heart momentarily drop. Without another thought, I pressed Select and deleted them all before going to my contacts box and deleting her name as well.

Perhaps I was finally beginning to get rid of the bug, once and for all.

CHAPTER NINETEEN

As the weeks passed, I managed to clear myself of every trace of Fickle that had ever existed in my life. I removed her from my MSN buddy list, deleted every fake e-mail she'd ever sent me with all its fake words within, removed her from Skype, and deleted all the photos she'd sent me of herself.

It was only after I'd done that, that I felt, I dunno, sort of cleansed, like I was starting over again.

I still missed Fickle like crazy, but Joey's words to me from before kept swimming into my head, about how Fickle had at least given me the courage to stop denying to myself that I was gay and to start believing in myself more. I took Joey's words on board and got used to being, well, *me*, and stopped beating myself up about being gay, telling myself that, for the first time ever, I could live my life the way I wanted to live it, not the way I thought people expected me to. I figured by being true to myself, at least everything I'd shared with Fickle, and all the shit afterwards, wouldn't have been for nothing.

I finally started to feel happy once more, happy with who I was, something I'd not ever really experienced before. I'd come out to Beth too, in an extremely frank and funny conversation one day over a few beers in the pub, the beer having loosened my tongue and my anxieties, and it had been another huge weight off my shoulders. Of course, I'd been vague with Emily when she'd asked me questions about Fickle, just telling her that things hadn't turned out as I'd hoped and that my experience with Fickle had been just that—an experience.

"There's plenty more girls out there, Ems," I'd said to her. "And I plan on having fun finding them!"

To my relief, both Beth and Emily were totally cool about me being gay, and to my complete amusement, took it upon themselves to embrace it as enthusiastically as I had, and I began to think that I'd finally turned a corner. In fact, their enthusiasm towards my new life extended way beyond the call of duty, which is how we found ourselves, one Friday night around three weeks after Fickle had dumped me, sitting in a gay bar called the Porter in town, chatting over drinks while Emily and Beth eyed up potential new girlfriends for me.

"It's buzzing in here, isn't it?" Beth had to shout to be heard over the sound of the music. "Who knew this place even existed?"

"Not the sort of place you'd normally come to." I laughed. "Nor me, for that matter!"

I looked round the room, thinking that even six weeks ago I would never have dared come to a gay bar. Times were changing for me.

"What about her?" Emily leant over and nodded towards a girl standing at the bar.

I looked at her. She looked to be in her early twenties, shortish hair, cool clothes. She looked nice, and I watched as she gazed around the room, kinda hoping she'd look over my way.

"She looks cute," I half shouted back to Emily, dissolving into a fit of giggles with her as we watched another girl come join the girl at the bar and put her arm around her waist.

"Ah well, there'll be others!" Beth laughed.

I stared around the room, watching in, well, awe really—there's no other word to describe it—as women danced with other women, women kissed other women, and women arrived and left with women. What struck me was how normal it all was. And why not? I thought back to the conversation I'd had with Joey when she'd told me being gay was nothing to be ashamed of, that it was totally normal and if people couldn't hack that, then it was their problem, not mine.

Looking round the place now, I felt, I dunno, at home. Like I'd waited all my teenage life for this moment; like anything that had gone on before was immaterial. This was a new chapter in my life, and I was going to grab it with both hands, not do what I'd done in the past and stick to doing something just because it was considered the "right thing to do."

"She's cute as well," Emily leant over and said in my ear, jerking her head towards another girl leaning on the bar, drink in hand.

I looked at the girl. Emily was right; she *was* kinda cute.

"You should go talk to her." Emily jerked her head back to the girl at the bar. "She's well hot. If I weren't straight, I'd have a crack at her."

Beth and I collapsed into giggles.

"Do you *know* what you sound like?" Beth playfully punched Emily on the arm.

I looked back at the girl. Yeah, she *was* hot, and if I didn't make a move now, I never would. I drained my glass and rose from my chair.

"Wish me luck!" I grinned down to Emily and Beth before wandering over in the direction of the girl, just in time to see her finish her drink and walk onto the dance floor. Within seconds she'd disappeared into the crowd and I was left standing next to the bar like a spare piece. I turned and looked back at Emily and Beth, shrugging then frowning in mock fury as they both collapsed into a fit of giggles again.

"Guess this whole 'picking up a girl in a bar' stuff isn't so easy," I said with a sigh as I sat back down.

"Maybe wait to be picked up, rather than doing the picking up," Beth said. "It'll happen when it happens, Immy."

"Yeah, that's just what Joey said to me," I said absent-mindedly.

"Who?" Emily looked at Beth and winked.

"No one," I replied. "Right, I'm gonna call it a night, girls. I'm not sure if this is me after all."

"You give up too easily," Emily said. "But yeah, I'll agree we should call it a night now."

"Until the next time," Beth said, finishing her drink.

A thought struck me as we all three walked home together, all arm in arm, giggling like a bunch of schoolkids. I figured that in the weeks since all the shit with Fickle, I'd become closer to Beth and Emily—closer to them than I had been in years. It was almost like me coming out to the pair of them had changed something, but it had changed it for the better. I was no longer a closed book to them, like when I'd been with Matt and hadn't wanted to talk about him, like, ever.

In the past I'd found it so difficult going out with them, having to endure the torture of a night of eyeing up boys, or talking about boys, or chatting with boys I really didn't want to chat with. Now I was happier because, I guessed, I was freer. I didn't have to pretend to be something I wasn't with them; I could actually be me, Immy Summers, and our friendship had blossomed because of it. Now I could open up to them, tell them what I was really thinking and feeling, and it felt great.

We said our good-byes and headed in our separate directions, with me arriving home shortly after eleven p.m. After passing the time of day with Mum and Dad, fending off questions about where I'd been, I took myself off up to my room and, on a whim, switched on the computer, happy once more to chat on the message board and on MSN. Fickle hadn't been seen or heard anywhere on the *Lovers and Sinners* message board for weeks, and I assumed she'd now taken up residence on the *Ali and Jess* website instead. Making a promise to myself that I would never, *ever* go on there to see what she was up to, or who she was talking to, I found I could cope with life back on the *L&S* message board. People knew, of course, that Fickle and I had become close, and then people knew, of course, that we were no longer together. I'd had the odd message of support on the board, and a few personal e-mails telling me to "keep my chin up", but soon my news became old news and everything quickly got back to normal again. Such is the life on an Internet message board.

I grinned as I saw Twiggy and Joey were online, and joined into their MSN conversation so that we were soon having a three-way chat, bouncing thoughts and ideas off each other and generally taking the piss out of one or the other. I saw a new message from Joey appear next to our three-way conversation box, and figured she wanted to talk to me alone, without Twiggy seeing.

Joey: You okay? It's fun talking to Twiggy but she does tend to just piss about a lot, LOL.

Barnaby Rudge: I'm good, thanks, yeah. You?

Joey: Yeah. You sound happy! What you been up to this evening?

Barnaby Rudge: I went to a gay club with my friends! It was the best! Such a laugh!

Joey: A gay club??? You ARE getting more confident, aren't you?!

Barnaby Rudge: I know! I surprised myself! Girls' only night. It was wicked.

There was a bit of a pause, so I went back to Twiggy's conversation, thinking that Joey was writing there. She wasn't.

Joey: Did you pull?

Barnaby Rudge: LMAO, no!

Joey: Any hawt girls there?

Barnaby Rudge: Hah, hah! Yeah, a few.

I put a winking sign next to that, just to kinda let Joey know I'd seen some girls I liked.

Joey: Cool.

Barnaby Rudge: It was, yeah. I felt a bit like a kid in a sweet shop, to be honest. So much choice! I bet half of them were straight, though; I mean, I was there with my two straight mates, after all.

Joey: LMAO.

There was another, longer pause. Then:

Joey: Are you looking for someone, then?

Barnaby Rudge: Yeah, I s'pose I am. I guess I want to feel what I felt with Fickle again; those butterflies when you think about them, that rush of excitement when you know you're gonna see them, you know?

Joey: Yeah, I know! Listen, you wanna Skype?

Barnaby Rudge: Yeah, but I'll have to keep my voice down. Mum and Dad are in bed.

Joey: Mine too! We'll whisper.

We said our good nights to Twiggy and logged off from MSN, bringing up Skype, poking our tongues out at each other, like we always did when our videos flickered into life and our grainy webcam faces peered at each other.

"You've got eyeliner on!" Joey exclaimed, pointing at my face. "I don't think I've ever seen you with eyeliner on!"

"Well, I've been out, haven't I?" I did a silly pose, like a model pouting, and she laughed.

"You look nice." Joey nodded, smiling.

"Thanks! Are you saying I don't normally look nice?" I carried on pouting at her.

"Of course not!" Joey laughed.

"Meaning, of course not, I don't usually look nice?" I raised my eyebrows.

"You know what I mean," Joey said. "You always look nice." She looked away from the webcam briefly.

"So what have you been up to tonight?" I asked.

"I spoke to Claire earlier." Joey smiled tightly.

"Great!" I said, meaning it. "And?"

"And nothing." Joey smiled again. "She was just on MSN and we had a quick chat, that was all."

"And, uh, is she still with whatserface?" I asked.

"Anna? Yeah, she's still with Anna. And very much in love, apparently." Joey nodded.

"Nice of her to tell you that," I said sarcastically.

"I can totally handle it," Joey said. "Maybe not six weeks ago, but I'm so over her now."

"And you know what?" I smiled at Joey. "I think I'm over Fickle at long last too."

"That's what we like to hear." Joey smiled back.

"I certainly think about her a lot less now," I said.

"Sounds like we're both getting there, then," Joey said.

"I finally figured I'd wasted enough tears and enough of my life on her," I said. "I deserve someone better than that."

"You do," Joey said.

"And my mates have been great about it all, and they said they'll come out to some bars with me, so maybe I'll strike lucky soon," I said, grinning at Joey.

Joey looked at her watch.

"Have you seen the time?" she gasped. "Gone midnight! I

better go; I'm getting dragged into town tomorrow by Mum to buy my dad a birthday present." Joey mock yawned, fanning her mouth with her hand.

"'K," I said. "I need some beauty sleep as well."

"Yeah, you do!" Joey blew a raspberry at me.

"Cheek!" I blew one back.

"It's good to see you looking so happy, Imms," she said, smiling warmly.

"It's good to feel so happy," I replied, meaning it.

We said our good nights and I logged off, heading straight for bed. I lay in bed awhile, thinking about gay bars, girls, and Joey and had just started thinking that Claire must have been absolutely crazy to dump her, when tiredness overcame me and I fell fast asleep.

CHAPTER TWENTY

I woke up the next morning to a text from Twiggy, telling me she had a day off from the supermarket and did I fancy some cyber-karate on MSN later? I giggled as I read her text through bleary eyes.

It'll b like the old days, she wrote. *B good 2 just piss about, just me and u, like we used to.*

I sent her one back, telling her the challenge was on and that I'd see her online later in the afternoon. I spent the morning knuckling down to some college work, work that had been put on the back burner over recent weeks, primarily because I'd been too depressed over Fickle to even think about stupid studying.

I thought about Joey too, being dragged round the shops by her mum, and smiled to myself. Joey didn't really strike me as the shopping kind, certainly not if the numerous photos I'd seen of her were anything to go by. She was a lot like me, I thought; not really into fancy clothes, just the sort of gear you feel comfortable in and that you know will suit your style; bit of Jack Wills, bit of Superdry—jeans, oversized jumpers, Converse trainers, Airwalks, nothing too snazzy.

By lunchtime I figured I'd done enough work for a Saturday and texted Twiggy, telling her to get her arse onto MSN so I could kick it into touch. She arrived around ten minutes later, full of her usual corny jokes and tales of her lazy husband. I suddenly realised what fun I'd missed out on during those weeks when I was so wrapped up in Fickle that I seemed to forget about everything and everyone around me.

Barnaby Rudge: I just wanna say that I'm sorry if I got so caught up with all that Fickle business that I neglected you, Twigs.

Twiggy: LMAO, that's okay! I'm a big girl, I don't ever feel neglected.

Barnaby Rudge: Yeah, but you know what I mean.

Twiggy: I do. And thanks.

Twiggy paused.

Twiggy: And I'm sorry if I didn't fully understand what you were going through with Fickle, both when you were seeing her and when you weren't.

Barnaby Rudge: S'OK, Twigs.

Twiggy: And I know Joey feels bad about being the one to have to tell you about Fickle.

Barnaby Rudge: I know she does, but I had to know, didn't I?

Twiggy: She had her reasons for telling you.

Barnaby Rudge: I know, she told me. She didn't want me to get hurt. I understand.

Twiggy: Yeah, 'cos, like, if she ever thought she'd hurt you, she'd be devastated.

Barnaby Rudge: Okay, devastated is a bit OTT, Twigs, but I see where you're coming from. LOL.

Twiggy: Yeah, okay. LOL!

Barnaby Rudge: Anyway, perhaps she did me a favour in the long run.

Twiggy: Yeah? How?

Barnaby Rudge: I dunno, I guess all that shit with Fickle has kinda jerked me into action. I'm on the lookout for a new girlfriend now.

Twiggy: You told Joey that?

Barnaby Rudge: LMAO, kinda. She seemed fairly interested in it.

Twiggy: I'll bet! She'll be well pleased! That's what she wants! It's what she's wanted for ages!

Barnaby Rudge: Eh?

Twiggy: Ah. Just read your message just now again and read it wrong first time! Soz.

Barnaby Rudge: About me looking for a new girlfriend?

Twiggy: Yeah.

Barnaby Rudge: So why does Joey want me to get a new girlfriend?

Twiggy: She doesn't.

Barnaby Rudge: Yes she does. You just said.

Twiggy: Did I? Well, ignore that. I didn't mean it. I just read it wrong.

Barnaby Rudge: Eh? I don't understand, Twigs!

Twiggy: Forget it. My mistake.

Barnaby Rudge: No! Tell me!

Twiggy: There's nothing to tell you, BR!

Barnaby Rudge: You said, she'll be pleased. That's what she wants.

Twiggy: Yeah, she does.

Barnaby Rudge: I still don't understand!!

Twiggy: She wants YOU, BR. Joey wants you. She likes you.

Barnaby Rudge: I like her too, Twigs. She's kewl.

Twiggy: No, I mean, she LIKES you, you twit!! She'll never tell you, so I'm telling you for her.

I stared at the screen, my eyebrows sky high.

Barnaby Rudge: Likes as in…likes??

Twiggy: Yeah, you clot!

Barnaby Rudge: Wants as in…wants??

Twiggy: Yes!

Barnaby Rudge: How do you know?

Twiggy: She told me, idiot!

Barnaby Rudge: When?

Twiggy: When you were still with Fickle. She said she hated that you were with her, but she had to sit and watch it all unfold. Said it was awful.

Barnaby Rudge: And then she went out of her way to dig up some dirt on Fickle so that I'd finish with her? Is that it?

Twiggy: No!! It wasn't like that. She stepped back when you were with Fickle, let you get on with it. But when she saw that Fickle was making a fool of you, she said she had to step in.

Barnaby Rudge: That was big of her.

Twiggy: Don't be like that, BR. If you only knew the nights she's poured her heart out to me over you, you wouldn't be saying that. She likes you, BR, and she couldn't sit back and watch you get hurt.

Barnaby Rudge: That's crap. I don't believe you.

Twiggy: Believe it, BR.

Barnaby Rudge: The only reason Joey told me about Fickle is 'cos she'd been dumped by Claire and couldn't stand to see me happy. And now she's telling you she likes me to, shit, I dunno, to justify it.

Twiggy: That's bollocks and you know it.

There was a pause. Then:

Twiggy: I got something for you, gonna e-mail it to you, okay?

I waited while Twiggy went quiet, then flicked up my e-mail in-box and opened a message that she'd just sent me. It was dated from around six weeks ago; the time when she first told me about Fickle. My eyes flickered over the message, picking out certain sentences:

> *I really like her, Twiggy. Have done for a while but I gotta keep it to myself 'cos she's so wrapped up with this Fickle kid that if I start declaring words of love to her now it's gonna totally pickle her head, isn't it? And I figure Immy's head's pickled enough already without me jumping in with my bloody great size nine feet (except that I'm only size six LOL). So what can I do? Just say nothing to Immy about the fact I think she's the best thing since sliced bread and that I can't stop thinking about her, and let her figure things out with Fickle for herself? I just dunno, Twiggy, and it's doing my bloody head in!*

Then another one, dated a bit later:

> *So, I dunno what to do, Twiggy. It's like, she's with this girl and this girl's making an idiot of her with some other chick, and do I tell Immy or not? And I've, like, spent sleepless nights wondering just what the hell to do and the only thing I can come up with is to tell Immy, however much it's gonna crush her.*

Barnaby Rudge: So?

Twiggy: All the times you were busy with Fickle, Joey would be telling me on MSN how much it hurt her, but that she was happy as long as you were happy. She left you to it, BR. She could have made something up about Fickle if she'd wanted to break you two up, but Joey's not like that. Even you know that.

I suddenly felt like I'd been stung. The thing was, I did know that. The one thing that was a dead certainty was that Joey wasn't devious. She was wise, she was sensible, she was nice; she certainly wasn't sly or malicious in any way.

Barnaby Rudge: I know that, yeah.

Twiggy: But then when Fickle started all this up with this LisaD person, Joey said she couldn't sit back and ignore things any more.

Barnaby Rudge: Sounds like Joe.

Twiggy: You know as well as I do that Joey's nice to the core. She isn't Fickle, BR. Don't tar her with the same brush 'cos Joey's a million times nicer and better than Fickle.

Barnaby Rudge: I know.

I did. I knew.

Twiggy: So, BR, you see as one door shuts, another one opens. Must be nice to be so popular!!

Barnaby Rudge: But I've never thought of Joey as anything more than a friend, Twigs. It'd be too weird— it'd be, I dunno, like shagging my own sister! LOL.

Twiggy: Oh right! Well, uh, don't go telling Joey that, will you? In fact, in hindsight, probably best not to say anything at all to her, yeah?

Barnaby Rudge: I kinda wish you hadn't told me, Twigs.

Twiggy: I s'pose I just wanted you to know that Joey had her reasons for doing what she did.

Barnaby Rudge: I hope this won't make things awkward with me and her now.

Twiggy: It doesn't have to, BR. Just carry on as you were and pretend I never said anything.

Barnaby Rudge: I think I'm gonna go now, Twigs. I think I need to process all this!

Twiggy: Sure thing. Hey, BR, just don't say anything to Joey. I don't know whether she wants you to know she likes you. She figures you're still raw over Fickle and you don't need any more hassle.

Barnaby Rudge: I won't tell her, I promise! See ya.

Twiggy: Cya, BR.

I logged off and headed downstairs, kinda in a daze. Joey was nice, yeah, and I liked her—I liked her a lot—but she was, well, she was Joey. Funny, silly, dependable Joey. Always there for me with her gags and wise words and chickeroos…but she was Joey! I knew I could never go there! Why did life have to be so bloody complicated sometimes?

❖

I managed to avoid speaking to Joey for the next few days, in part because of the amount of work I'd been given from college, but primarily because I didn't really know what to say to her. Twiggy blurting out to me that Joey liked me had thrown me into a bit of a spin and I figured the best way out of it was to do what any other pickle-headed person would do—ignore it and hope that it went away.

I met Beth and Emily most days either in the college canteen or in the pub across from the college, Beth always careful to not come with Matt because, as she told me, "It would be, like, toooo weird, don't you think?"

I had to agree. Matt, of course, never knew anything about Fickle or my coming out to Beth and Emily, and I'd been eternally grateful to Beth in particular for never telling him. I'd asked her specifically once I'd come out to her not to tell him. I figured the guy had had enough shit from me without finding out that he'd been dating a gay girl once.

"Now, this we have to go to!" Emily said one particularly noisy Friday lunchtime in the pub, which was crammed to the rafters with students, giddy with excitement that the weekend had finally arrived.

She pushed the free paper she'd been reading across the table to me and tapped her finger on an advert in the bottom right hand corner of the page.

Singles Night at The Porter, the advert read. *Get your glad rags on, boys and girls, and come and meet the person of your dreams.*

"The Porter's where we were the other week, isn't it?" I looked up at Emily.

"Sure is." Emily grinned back. "You up for it?"

I thought for a second.

"Could meet the woman of your dreams, Immy," Beth said. "Says so in the advert, right there."

"I'm too shy to go on my own!" I laughed, picking up my glass and taking a large slug from it.

"We'll come with you, won't we, Em?" Beth winked mischievously at Emily.

"Try and stop us!" Emily giggled.

"But you two'll be like a pair of wallflowers all night," I said.

"Ah, but we can also check out the talent for you," Beth replied, picking up her glass and taking a drink, looking playfully at me over the rim.

"I dunno…" I started.

"Don't give me 'I dunno', missy!" Emily interrupted. "You're never going to find Miss Right just sitting at home night after night, are you?"

"S'pose not," I said, trying not to sound too sullen.

"And you want to get this Gemma girl out of your system once and for all, don't you?" Beth nudged me playfully.

"She's already out of my system," I said, suddenly thinking of Joey, for some bizarre reason.

"Then it's decided." Emily clapped her hands. "Next Saturday, the Porter, you, me, and Beth, deal?"

I nodded reluctantly. Did I have any choice in the matter?

❖

It was all very well, me ignoring Joey, but of course, she had no idea that I knew she fancied me, and as far as she was concerned, things were just as they'd always been between us. She carried on texting me and e-mailing me, even though I didn't always reply, and although I felt like a complete cow ignoring her, the truth was, I didn't know how else to handle it. Looking back, yeah, I handled it badly, but at the time, it seemed the only thing to do.

By the fourth night of blocking her out, she finally rang me. I was up in my room, my head stuck in one of my maths textbooks, trying to work out some stupid formula that, no matter how many times I looked at it, just refused to make sense. I saw her name flashing up on my mobile and my finger hovered over the Off button, but something inside me told me I couldn't ignore her forever.

"Hi, Joey," I said, speaking kinda warily, which was dumb. This was Joey, after all.

"Hey, chick," Joey's familiar cheery voice sounded. "You okay?"

"Oh you know," I said, "same old. How about you?"

"Yeah, not bad." Joey paused. "You've been quiet lately. Everything all right?"

"Just busy, thassall," I said, and it was kinda the truth. "College work, stuff like that."

"Right…" Joey's voice trailed off.

"Up to my eyes in it," I said, trying to justify myself.

"Not out on the pull every night, then?" Joey laughed.

"No." I laughed back. Then: "Going this weekend, though."

I winced after I'd said it. Why had I told Joey that? There was silence on the end of the phone.

"Oh, right," Joey finally said, sounding quieter than before.

I didn't really know what to say to Joey after that, which was ridiculous. In the time that I'd known her, I'd never been short of anything to say to her, but here I was now, struggling to find two words to say.

"Is everything all right?" Joey finally spoke again. "You're very quiet."

"Yeah, everything's fine," I replied.

"And you kinda haven't been replying to some of my texts or e-mails," she carried on. "Have I done something to piss you off?"

"No, Joe, you haven't, honest," I said. "I…"

I paused. Did I want to bring this up now? Part of me didn't, but another, bigger part of me wanted to, if only to clear the air, which was as thick as a foggy day in November right now.

"I…I haven't known what to say to you, if I'm honest," I kinda mumbled.

Joey stayed silent.

"And I s'pose a part of me needed to process something," I wittered on. "Something that I heard."

Still Joey stayed silent.

"Say something, Joe!" I laughed.

There was a long pause, then Joey finally spoke.

"Have you spoken to Twiggy, by any chance?" she said.

I breathed out slowly.

"Yeah," I said. "She told me you and her had a heart-to-heart about me."

"I could bloody kill her," Joey said, kinda savagely.

"Don't," I said. "I'm glad she told me."

"And?" Joey asked. "What did you think about what she told you?"

"And, um, I dunno," I mumbled.

"That tells me pretty much all I needed to know." Joey laughed ironically.

"I do really like you, Joe, honest, it's just that it's too soon after Fickle and everything, and you know?" I stuttered slightly.

"And you don't feel the same way as I do?" Joey said.

I bit my lip.

"Not really," I said, truthfully. "I mean, I really do think you're great and everything, and I like you as a friend, but…"

"But no more than that?" Joey asked.

"I don't know," I replied. "I don't think so. I just think it'd be a bit strange, don't you? You feel more like my sister."

"Yikes!" Joey chuckled.

"You're brilliant, Joe," I said. "But I really do think it'd just be too weird, you and me. I'm sorry."

Joey paused. I heard her breathe in and out slowly, presumably choosing her next words.

"It's fine," she finally said, taking me slightly aback. "I have a bit of a track record when it comes to liking people who don't feel the same way back. I guess I'll get used to the idea of you as a friend, no more."

"Do you think we can still be friends?" I asked.

"Of course!" Joey laughed. "I'm happy as long as you're happy, Imms. You deserve it, all the shit you've been through lately."

"Thanks," I said, meaning it.

"And if you want me to back off for a bit, then I'm happy to do it," Joey added.

"Don't back off, Joe," I said softly. "I like talking to you. I'd miss you."

"You soft git." Joey giggled. "I'd miss you too, so looks like you're stuck with me!"

"Good," I said, hesitating slightly. "You'll find someone far better than me, Joe. Someone who deserves you. I don't."

"I doubt that very much." Joey laughed. "But never mind. Just forget I said anything, yeah?"

"Can we start again?" I said, feeling kinda awkward. "Tell me what sort of day you've had?"

We chattered on for about the next ten minutes about nothing in particular. I was half-pleased that we'd at least managed to get over any awkwardness, but still a bit upset that our conversation seemed a little, I dunno, a little bit stilted. When we'd finally finished talking, and promised that we'd catch up on MSN later, I returned to my impossible maths task, but my mind constantly drifted to Joey, and a nagging thought that just wouldn't go.

CHAPTER TWENTY-ONE

Luckily for me, and certainly luckily for my feelings of total confusion over everything that had happened lately, I didn't have time to either worry about or speak to Joey for the rest of that week, thanks mainly to four new assignments given to me at college.

I spent each night that week hidden away in my room, working out ridiculously difficult maths equations while at the same time trying to find out economic production possibility curves. I know. I didn't have a clue either, but at least it kept me away from Skype, MSN, and the *Lovers and Sinners* message board for a few nights. I did miss speaking to Joey dreadfully, but figured that all the studying I had to do was not only good for my college work, but even better for my sanity.

Saturday finally arrived like a welcome breath of fresh air. I'd kinda hoped that Beth and Emily would have forgotten about our plans to go to the Porter for their singles night, and that I could slip away from college on the Friday without them seeing me, then kinda just hibernate for the rest of the weekend. Not a bit of it. Beth rang me first thing Saturday morning, full of enthusiasm for the evening.

"I told Matt I was having a night out with the girls." She giggled. "Well, I am sort of, aren't I?"

"I guess so, Beth," I sighed. "You know it's not my sort of thing, though."

"Oh have some enthusiasm, Immy, puh-lease," Beth chastised. "It's going to be brilliant. All that totty."

"All that totty?" I scoffed. "Have you been reading the tabloids again?"

"Oh, you know what I mean." Beth brushed me off. "I just think it'll be brilliant for you."

"Well, as long as you two don't show me up," I said, trying to keep the whiney sound from my voice.

"Have we ever?" Beth sounded indignant.

"Do you want me to answer that?" I laughed.

"Pff! Right, well we'll see you outside the post office at seven," Beth said. "We can all walk from there."

I put the phone down and returned to my room from the kitchen where I'd been speaking to Beth. Mum and Dad were out, having gone to some garden centre about twenty miles away, as parents like to do, and Sophie was in town with her bunch of friends, no doubt all hanging around the shopping centre making nuisances of themselves. I was bored. Seven o'clock seemed like a long way off. I didn't want to go to town as well, and I sure as hell didn't want to do any more college work.

Sighing, I switched my computer on, kinda hoping that Twiggy might be around and we could have a game of virtual karate, or at least talk about that afternoon's football games. Failing that, I thought, I could post some comments on the *L&S* message board. The last episode of the programme had been weeks ago, but people were still discussing the whole series and wondering if there was to be another series later in the year.

There was just one person around on MSN—a girl I'd spoken to quite a few times called Betty Blue Rinse, who had a wicked sense of humour and who never failed to make me laugh. Neither

Twiggy or Joey were anywhere to be seen, so I spent a funny hour or so talking to Betty, periodically flicking back and forth to the *L&S* message board. I looked at all the day's messages on there, then went back a little further, to the previous night, and was kinda surprised to see Joey had posted on there.

Me, Joey, and Twiggy only ever posted on there once in a blue moon these days, preferring to chat amongst ourselves away from the board. It had become like that for quite a few other people on the board too; friendships had been forged, relationships started and ended, and a lot of people had ended up doing what we had done and gradually drifted away from the board to more personal, intimate surroundings to chat in.

But there was Joey's name, on the board. She'd been posting the previous night, and had been busy, from what I could see. I read through her posts, and saw that she'd been chatting mainly to one person, a new arrival on the board, someone called Willow. A strange mixture of emotions went through me as I read their messages to each other; a combination of curiosity, intrigue and another emotion that I tried to ignore but which just wouldn't go away—a pricking of jealousy.

❖

Seven o'clock finally arrived, and I'd never been so glad to get out of the house, regardless of the fact I wasn't keen on the idea of sitting in a bar all night while Beth and Emily picked out a new girlfriend for me. But anything had to be better than reading and rereading Joey's messages to Willow, as I had been doing all afternoon.

I didn't know why I felt I had to do it, but something kept pulling me back to their conversations, started earlier the previous evening and running right through to the early hours of Saturday morning. Joey had never spoken to me much past midnight, in all the time we'd been chatting, always telling me she was tired and needed her bed—so what was it about Willow that made Joey want to stay? Okay, that was a ridiculous thing to be thinking about, but it was the way my brain was working right now, you know?

I'd spent the rest of the afternoon not only reading Joey and Willow's chats, but also rereading some of Joey's e-mails that she'd sent to me over the past months, and which I'd never got round to deleting. They were funny, they were kind, they were wise; and as I read through them in chronological order, it became glaringly obvious that we'd become extremely close, especially in the last few weeks, apparently without me even realising it.

I thought back to the messages Joey had been exchanging with Willow and wondered why they made me feel so, I dunno, so insecure. Was it because I was frightened that Joey would move away from me now that she knew I didn't like her in the same way that she liked me? Or was it just that I couldn't stand the thought that Joey had found someone else, another friend, and I was now surplus to requirements? That was ridiculous. There was one thing I knew about Joey, and that was she wasn't fickle. And no pun intended there. Joey wasn't like that. Joey was kind and caring and she'd never just walk away just because she couldn't handle something.

A text from Beth stirred me from my thoughts. I looked at my watch and saw that it was 6.30 p.m. Muttering under my breath, I threw on some fresh clothes, put a bit of makeup on, and bundled my hair up on top of my head so that a few strands just fell about my face. I peered at myself in the mirror, adding some mascara for good measure, even though my eyes didn't need it, and a pale lipstick, which always somehow managed to bring out the blueness of my eyes more, then pouted a little, and nodded. I'd do.

Flinging my jacket on and wrapping a scarf around my neck against the chill wind outside, I hollered a good-bye to no one in particular and set off into town, hitching my bag across my shoulder as I walked off down the road. Beth and Emily were waiting for me outside the post office when I eventually arrived, slightly out of breath, slightly late.

"Jeans?" Emily raised her eyebrow at me and waved a dismissive hand in the direction of my legs.

I looked down.

"They're my best ones," I said feebly.

"And…Vans?" Beth sniffed, looking down at my feet.

"Will you two give me a break?" I laughed. "It's what I'm comfortable wearing. If no one likes it, then tough."

I opened my jacket up.

"Anyway, I'm wearing a tight top, look." I grinned. "Shows everything it needs to show. Girls'll be looking up here, not down at my feet."

"You hope," said Beth, linking her arm in mine and setting off with me.

"It used to work on Gemma," I said airily. "She liked me in this top when we Skyped."

"Will you quit talking about Gemma?" Emily playfully punched my arm. "Do that all evening and you'll get nowhere."

"But it's a good top. It's my best one," I protested.

"I'm backing up Emily here." Beth tutted loudly. "You're here to find yourself a new girl, right?"

"Okaaay," I said, with mock grumpiness.

The bar was already heaving by the time we arrived, just after seven. It seemed half the city, plus half the population of at least a dozen other towns around us, had decided to come along. The music was pumping, the dance floor was packed, and the bar was just a sea of heads. I didn't much care for it, if I was honest, but I meekly followed Beth and Emily to the bar, ordered some drinks, then sat down at one of the few available tables left in the place.

"Who knew a gay singles night could be so popular?" Emily shouted to me over the sound of the music. "Place is crammed tight!"

I looked around the bar and felt a bit out of place, every inch of me urging me to get the hell out of there and go home. I watched as girls chatted up girls, guys chatted up guys, and the drinks just kept flowing. All the while me, Beth, and Emily sat huddled at our table, not quite sure what to do, looking uncertainly at each other and making silly jokes to lighten the mood.

We'd been sitting there for around ten minutes when a tall, thin girl approached our table, asking if she could sit with us, as there were no other tables left in the place. Beth gestured to a spare chair and the girl sat down, leaning over towards Emily to shout something in her ear, which I couldn't hear. Emily shook her head and smiled at her, self-consciously taking a gulp of her drink, then gazed out to the dance floor.

"I think she just asked Emily to dance," Beth whispered excitedly in my ear. "Why don't you ask her what her name is? She might wanna dance with you instead."

"Thanks!" I hissed back. "What am I? Seconds?"

"Just ask her!" Beth hissed back.

I didn't want to. A girl standing at the bar had caught my eye while Beth had been whispering to me and was still staring at me. I looked away briefly, taking a sip from my drink, then looked back. She was still looking at me. I smiled at her and she smiled back, and I wondered what my next move should be.

"There's a girl at the bar," I whispered to Beth. Emily and the girl that had joined us were now deep in conversation, talking loudly about some soap opera they both watched on TV.

"Where?" Beth spun round in her chair.

"Don't look!" I hissed, embarrassed.

"The girl over there?" Beth whispered breathlessly.

"That's her." I slapped her leg. "Quit staring at her, will you?"

"Well go on, then," Beth said, louder now. "Go and speak to her! She keeps looking over. She wants you to go talk to her."

I looked closely over to the girl again. She was about my age, I'd guess, longish hair, slim but still nicely curvy. She had nice eyes too—as far as I could see in the gloom of the bar—framed with long, dark eyelashes and probably the most expressive face I'd ever seen, reminding me straightaway of Joey.

"She looks just like someone I know." I laughed, peering. "But Joey would never wear something like that! She's more of a jeans and hoodie kinda girl…" My voice trailed off.

"Who's Joey?" Emily leant in closer. "You've never mentioned a Joey to us, has she, Beth?"

"No, no Joey." Beth's eyes twinkled mischievously.

"Oh God, no!" I laughed again. "Joey's a mate. Someone I talk to online."

I saw Emily and Beth look at each other.

"Seriously, no!" I raised an eyebrow at them. "Joey's a mate. So's Twiggy, she's another one I talk to online."

"Joey *and* Twiggy, huh?" Beth nudged Emily.

"And Betty Blue Rinse, and SpyderWoman, and Chatte Noire, and HoBo…" I paused, looking in amusement at them both. "Do you want me to go on?"

"No." Emily grinned. "I want you to go and talk to that girl!"

"I can't," I said. "I dunno what to say to her."

"Well, durr, start by asking her if she wants a drink," Beth said, nudging me in the ribs.

I guessed it was pretty pointless coming to a singles night if I wasn't going to at least make the effort to try and meet someone. Reluctantly I got up and made my way over to where the girl was still standing, holding her drink and surreptitiously watching me.

"Hi." I nodded nervously, a bit like those nodding toy dogs that you see in the back of cars.

"Hi." The girl smiled at me. She looked as nervous as I felt.

"Busy here, isn't it?" I said, jerking my head in the direction of the dance floor.

"Yeah, yeah it is." The girl nodded.

"I'm Imogen," I said, just stopping short of offering her my hand. "Immy."

"Nic," the girl said.

"You want another of those?" I pointed vaguely at her glass.

"Thanks," Nic said, turning to face the bar. "You get this one, then I'll get the next one."

"Sure," I grinned, now standing next to her at the bar.

I ordered us two more drinks then, seeing a table become free, followed her over to it, briefly looking over my shoulder to see Emily, Beth, and the girl who had been sitting with us, all grinning and giving me the thumbs up. Suddenly embarrassed, I wandered over to the table and sat down opposite Nic.

"Have you been here before?" Nic asked, taking a large gulp from her drink. "Dutch courage," she said by way of explanation.

I laughed.

"Need some of that myself," I said. "Yeah, been here once before, few weeks back. But never to a singles night."

"Me neither," Nic groaned. "It's a bit like a cattle market, isn't it?"

"A bit," I agreed. "You here alone?"

"No, my ex-girlfriend's here somewhere." Nic smiled sheepishly. "Yeah, I know it's weird, but we're still friends."

"I'm here with my friends." I jabbed my thumb behind me in the direction of Beth and Emily and laughed as Nic looked past my shoulder to them and raised her glass.

"So how long have you been single, Immy?" Nic asked.

I thought back to Fickle.

"Not long." I laughed. "Last girlfriend did the dirty on me, so I'm cautious now, to say the least."

I figured it wasn't a lie calling Fickle my girlfriend. I thought that's what she'd been, anyway.

"That's rough." Nic pulled a face.

"Yeah." I sipped at my drink and looked at her. "I'm ready to meet another girl, but I'm not desperate, you know?"

"Yeah, I know." Nic smiled at me.

"It's like my mate Joey says, it'll happen when it happens." I nodded.

"Is Joey one of your mates over there?" Nic jerked her head over to Beth and Emily.

"Oh no." I leant back in my chair. "She doesn't live in Oxford. Anyway, I don't really think this is her sort of thing. Not one for dancing, is Joey…" My voice trailed off.

Nic nodded. "I see."

We chatted for a while longer, and over another round of drinks, Nic started telling me about her previous girlfriend, about her job and a little bit about her family. She was nice, kinda quirky, and all the time I was talking to her, I could practically feel Beth and Emily egging me on from behind me.

I told her some more stuff about Fickle, and about how she'd been the first girl I'd properly fallen for, and how she'd broken my heart. I didn't tell her I'd met her online; I guessed I thought she might be a bit weirded out by that, I dunno.

"But I'm totally over her now," I said hastily. "Joey, she's been brilliant through it all, helping me get over her…" My voice trailed off.

"Do you want another?" I pointed to her glass, which was now empty.

"Dance first, then a drink, yeah?" Nic asked.

I didn't want to dance one little bit, me being the sort of person who has two left feet and feels dead self-conscious when I get anywhere near a dance floor, but before I'd had a chance to protest, Nic had pulled me to my feet and had practically dragged me into the crowd of people already dancing.

"I'm a crap dancer," I shouted in her ear, kinda feebly.

"Me too." Nic winked. "We'll have fun!"

We danced a bit and, yeah, I felt awkward, gawky and shy, but Nic's enthusiastic dancing, if not always conventional, at least made it difficult for me to feel too uncomfortable. By the third song I was out of breath and dying for a sit down, but just as the music stopped, a slower track came on.

"I'm done!" I laughed, mock fanning my face and turning to go.

"I'm not," Nic said, reaching out and grabbing my hand, pulling me towards her. She pulled me in close to her so that I could feel the heat from her body, and wrapped her arms round my shoulders, starting to move against me as the music played on.

I put my arms round her waist, feeling her hips moving against me, and tried to stop feeling so nervous. The music and the heat and the noise were swirling round my head, and all I was aware of was Nic, pressed up against me, her brown eyes gazing into mine.

She suddenly looped her hand behind my head and pulled me in to kiss her, her lips feeling warm and soft against mine. It didn't feel like kissing Matt; this felt different. She was soft and tender, allowing her lips to gently brush against mine, making me tingle. I liked the feeling of it, far more than I had ever done with Matt. I kissed her back, enjoying the taste of her, loving the feeling of the warmth and softness of her body pressed against mine, so much nicer than the hardness of Matt's body that I had only ever been used to before.

Finally she pulled away and grinned at me.

"You're a good kisser!" she whispered in my ear before kissing me again.

I felt like my head might explode, like it was filled with a million party poppers all going off at once. So this was what kissing was supposed to feel like! This was how good it was supposed to make me feel!

We pulled away from our kiss again. Grinning, I took her by the hand and led her back to the bar, holding her hand all the while as we negotiated our way through the other dancers and away from the dance floor.

"Now for that drink." Nic laughed, fishing a £10 note out of her pocket and waggling it at me.

I turned and looked over to Emily and Beth, both still sitting at the same table as they were before, both with grins on their faces like a pair of Cheshire cats. I noticed the girl who'd been with them had now gone, so I jerked my head at them both, as if to say, "You two all right?"

Still grinning, they nodded in unison, Beth raising her eyebrows in Nic's direction, a playful look on her face.

"Beer please, mate," Nic was now saying to the bar guy. "I'm parched," she said, turning to me, as if to explain.

I nodded.

"Joey's choice of drink, like, *always*." I laughed, then stopped myself. "So she says," I added, kinda weakly.

"Joey, huh?" Nic winked.

"I'm sorry?" I looked sheepishly at Nic.

"No matter." Nic laughed. "You still on the vodka?"

"Yeah, thanks." I glanced at her from the corner of my eye, taking in details of her.

Nic handed me my vodka, watching me closely as she did so. We were still at the bar, the table that we'd been sitting at before our dance now taken by a group of four or five women, all chattering and laughing excitedly.

"Avanti!" Nic laughed, raising her glass to me and taking a large gulp of her beer.

She placed her glass back down on the bar and looked at me.

"You talk about this Joey girl quite a bit," she said. "Did you know that?"

"Do I?" I said, kinda airily. "I didn't know I did."

"Uh-huh." Nic nodded, smiling. "You like her, don't you?"

I took a sip of my vodka, looking at Nic as I did so.

"Yeah," I said. "She's a mate."

"Is that all?" Nic asked.

"Oh God yeah, I…" I stopped myself. "I…"

I was stuttering. An image of Joey swam into my head; an image of Joey as I'd seen her dozens of times before on Skype, pulling faces at me, larking around, poking her tongue out at me, sitting with a baseball cap on back to front or something, just 'cos she knew it looked daft and it would make me laugh. I could see her face, her eyes, her hair cascading down round her shoulders. I could hear her soft voice talking to me, giving me advice, making me laugh, calling me "chickeroo, kiddo, chick", all the things she called me which, unbeknown to me until now, had made me feel something. It had made me feel safe and wanted. Joey made me feel safe and wanted.

I looked back at Nic and guessed the expression on my face told her everything she needed to know. She smiled at me and suddenly drained her drink.

"I think I'm gonna go." she said, touching my arm.

I shook my head.

"No, wait," I said. "I thought we were getting on well?"

"We are," Nic grinned. "But I'm still gonna go."

"Oh," I said, feebly. "Why?"

"I think you like this Joey girl more than you'll admit," Nic said. "But I *do* have to go, honest. I have a seven a.m. start tomorrow."

"Can I see you again?" I asked halfheartedly.

"Get this shiz sorted out with Joey first, then call me, yeah?" Nic said.

"There's no shiz, as you call it, to sort out with Joey," I said, taking her hand in mine. "Now, gimme your phone number." I grinned at her.

I took out my mobile and put her number into it as she was reading it out to me, telling her I'd call her in the week, if she wanted me to? She smiled at me, then suddenly leant in to me and kissed me quickly on the lips before turning and making her way around the tables in the bar and out of the door.

I stood at the bar, kinda numb, a tingle still on my lips from where she'd just kissed me. I wanted to touch my lips, you know, like they always do in the movies? But then I figured Emily and Beth were still watching me, and thought again. Sure enough, the pair of them was still seated at the table, deep in conversation over something. I wandered over to them and plonked myself down on the chair next to Beth.

"That was quite a show, wasn't it?" She grinned at me.

I felt my face start to go red.

"Come on, then," Beth added. "Spill. Name? Age?"

"Nic," I said, looking at the door that Nic had just gone out of. "Oh, age? I dunno, I never asked her."

"So, did you get her number?" Emily leant across the table to me.

"Yeah," I said, waving my phone in the air as if to confirm it.

"And you're going to call her, right?" Beth asked. "You seemed to, uh, you seemed to be getting on well."

Emily looked in amusement at Beth.

"Yeah, of course I'll call her," I said truthfully.

I would call her too. I knew I would.

"Try to at least look a bit happier about it then, Immy!" Emily frowned at me. "Aren't you pleased? I thought this was what you wanted?"

I looked at Emily.

"I am pleased, 'course I am," I smiled. "Nic's wicked. I really like her."

I looked at Beth and Emily.

"And thanks for coming with me tonight, you've both been great too," I added.

"Thass all right." Beth grinned.

"We told you you'd find someone here, didn't we?" Emily high-fived Beth. "We're always right!"

They were always right, yeah. But was Nic right about what she'd said to me about Joey?

CHAPTER TWENTY-TWO

Try as I might, it was difficult to forget about what Nic had said. I'd really liked Nic, I mean, proper liked, and kissing her had been perfect—there was no other word to describe it that could do it justice. It had been just, well, magical and perfect.

And, okay, so I'd only ever kissed Matt before, so I couldn't exactly say I was an expert in it, but the fact that kissing Nic had made me feel like my head was spinning and I was floating in the air had to mean it was having some sort of effect on me, right? Kissing Matt had only ever felt, I dunno, strained, forced and, well, dull, really.

But the more I thought about what had happened, and what Nic had said to me about Joey, the more it made sense. I tried to replay the evening over in my head, trying to remember what had happened, what I'd said to her and whether, as she'd suggested, I'd mentioned Joey's name more times than I should have done. When I thought back, I came to the conclusion that Nic was probably right. Subconsciously Joey had been with me every step of the way. Everything I'd done, seen, spoken about, I'd had Joey on my mind.

I'd thought about what it would have been like if she'd been there with me. What would she have worn? What would she have drunk? She wouldn't have danced, that much I was sure of, because she'd told me in previous conversations that she had two left feet and did everything possible to avoid dancing. We would have sat together at a table, I thought, and watched other people dancing, both of us grateful that the other didn't want to dance. I was sure we'd have had a giggle at some of the people there too, and would have dissolved into a heap of sniggers at the first person we'd seen funny dancing, or dressed silly.

Me, Beth, and Emily shared a taxi home from the club that night. I sat in the back of the taxi with them, travelling the whole way home in virtual silence as they both chattered away to one another, me lost in my own thoughts. After I'd been dropped off at home and had said my good-byes, I headed straight to my room, got undressed, and crawled into bed. I lay on my back, fingers linked behind my head, and stared up at the ceiling. It was, after all, the place where I did my best thinking, and I needed to think about things now more than I had done in a long, long time, certainly since all that shit with Fickle.

I realised that I knew Joey like she'd been my friend all my life. Even though we'd been talking to each other for just over two months, I felt like I knew her better than anyone else in the world, family aside. But possibly without me actually realising it, she'd become more than a friend, and I suddenly thought I didn't know what I'd do if she wasn't in my life anymore.

I thought back to Joey's messages to Willow online and wondered if they had shaken me up more than I'd realised. Maybe seeing those had been just the kick up the arse I'd needed to make me realise that I'd started to think of Joey as being more than just a friend. I mean, she *was* a friend to me, and in my own way I loved her for that. But those messages seemed to have stirred something deeper inside me, something that went deeper than just friendship.

I replayed the conversation I'd had with Joey when I'd told her she was more like a sister to me in my head, and cringed. I remembered how I'd told Twiggy that the idea of me and Joey would have been too weird, and wondered why on earth I would have said that. Maybe because me finding out that Joey liked me had kinda come out of the blue? Maybe it was some sort of innate defence mechanism I'd developed since Fickle, one that made me cautious when another person online said they liked me. I hadn't been cautious with Nic, but perhaps that was because, subconsciously, I didn't really care whether I saw her again or not.

But I cared about Joey, and the more I thought about it, the more obvious it became. She'd told me that she liked me, and I'd practically thrown it back in her face and now it was too late.

She'd moved on and I only had myself to blame.

❖

I woke up the next day, Sunday, with a feeling of, I dunno, melancholy. I had a feeling that I might have dreamt about Joey, but you know how it is when you think you've dreamt something, and at the time you dreamt it, it was wonderful and fabulous, but when you try and recall it the next morning, you can't, no matter how hard you try? That was what was happening to me that Sunday morning.

I wanted to talk to Joey, not to make any declarations of love or anything daft like that, but just to hear her voice, to let me know she was still around, and that she hadn't disappeared from my life. I picked up my phone from the bedside cabinet and, through sleepy eyes, sent her a text asking her if she'd be online later. I kinda hoped that just one word from her would take this heavy feeling of downheartedness that seemed to be weighing heavily on my chest, almost like someone was sitting on me, away. One word from Joey and everything would be all right.

I scrolled down my list of contacts, finally stopping on Nic's name. I looked at her name, remembering her face, her laugh, her kiss, and how she'd made me feel last night. I started writing a message to her:

Hey Nic, it's Immy LOL...

I snapped my phone shut again, not sending the message, not saving it either, thinking I'd send her something later, but knowing deep down I probably wouldn't. Instead, I quickly got up, showered and dressed, and headed downstairs, pulling my jumper over my head as I did so. Dad was in the kitchen, trying to scrape burnt bits from toast and make coffee at the same time.

"Your mother's having a lie-in," he said, rolling his eyes and grinning as he buttered some toast. "And put in a request for breakfast in bed."

"Nice," I said, opening a bottle of milk from the fridge and sniffing it.

"You have a good time last night?" Dad rubbed his hand affectionately up and down my back. "We didn't hear you come in."

"Yeah, it was okay," I replied, smiling at him. "I wasn't late. Midnight or so."

"And you got a taxi home?" It was more of a statement than a question.

"Of course, Dad!" I puffed out my cheeks in mock exasperation. "Shared one with Beth and Emily."

"Good." Dad leant over and kissed the top of my head.

He picked up the tray with coffee and toast on and headed for the door.

"Best get this to your mother before she starts ringing a bell, huh?" He winked at me.

"You're soooo under the thumb, Dad!" I laughed, shaking my head.

"I am to all of you girls," Dad winked again before hooking the kitchen door open with his foot and heading out of the door. "And I wouldn't have it any other way!" he called as he headed off up the stairs again.

My phone beeping from inside my jeans pocket made me put down my coffee and fish it out, flipping it open. It was from Joey, telling me she'd be online later that afternoon if I fancied a chat.

My immediate thought was that she was putting me off until later in the day because she wanted to talk to Willow first, but then I shook my head angrily and frowned. Joey would never do that; if Joey said she wouldn't be around until later, that meant she really wouldn't be around until later.

I spent the morning deep in thought, while at the same time fielding a barrage of questions from Beth, who had been texting me all morning, like someone possessed, about Nic:

But ur going 2 call her, aren't u?

She was well in2 u, Immy!

Don't let her slip away...

These were just three of the approximately twelve texts she managed to send me up until lunchtime when she finally stopped—and that was only because she said Matt was taking her out for lunch.

Matt.

She mentioned him so casually that I barely even noticed, but the mention of his name seemed to plunge me even deeper into thought. Beth had been seeing him for a good few weeks now and they seemed blissfully happy. I thought back to the night a couple of months ago when I'd been to see Anathema play at the Metro and Ryan had given us all lifts home. Ryan and his girlfriend Lou had been so happy, and I remembered how I'd wanted to be as blissfully in love as they had been—and still were.

I hoped that Matt would find the love I never had for him with Beth, and sent her a text pretty much saying that. I suddenly somehow knew that the only person who could make me blissfully happy and in love was Joey, not Nic, not anyone else.

I just had to tell her that before it really was too late.

CHAPTER TWENTY-THREE

I had just finished my lunch, a not altogether inspiring concoction of lamb chops and limp vegetables, when Joey sent me a text asking me if I'd be online soon.

I managed to make my excuses to Mum and Dad, quickly helping to clear plates from the table before heading up to my room, two stairs at a time, trying to think about what I'd say to Joey. If I'd say anything at all, that was.

She was already on MSN when I logged on, and a brief ripple of jealousy spread through me as I wondered if she was talking to Willow. I opened up the *Lovers and Sinners* message board, looking to see if she'd been talking to Willow on there, and felt ludicrously relieved when I saw that they'd not posted any messages to each other since the Friday night when I'd first seen them. But, I guessed, that wouldn't necessarily have stopped them MSNing each other, would it?

I frowned, cross with myself for getting jealous and ratty with Joey for talking to someone else. She could do what she liked—who was I to tell her or want her to do otherwise?

Joey: You all right?

I looked at her message. Was I all right? Who knew?

Barnaby Rudge: Yeah, not bad. You?

Joey: Fair to middling LOL.

Barnaby Rudge: What you been up to today?

Joey: This and that. You?

Barnaby Rudge: Same.

There was a long silence. I sat at my desk, wondering what I could say to her next. I wanted to ask her about Willow, wanted to tell her reading their messages had stirred up feelings of jealousy, but how could I?

Joey: What about last night? You have a good time?

Barnaby Rudge: Ah yeah, it was fine.

Joey: Oh, right.

There was another long silence.

Joey: So did you go anywhere nice?

Barnaby Rudge: The Porter in town. You know it?

Joey: The gay place? Yeah, been there a few times when I've been to Oxford.

Barnaby Rudge: Ah, well I went there with two mates.

Joey: You have a good time?

Barnaby Rudge: Yeah, it was good.

Joey: You're sounding very coy!

Barnaby Rudge: Am I? Don't mean to be, soz.

It was like agony. I didn't know what else to say to her; I sure as hell didn't want to tell her about Nic, though.

Joey: Which means you must have copped off with someone LOL.

I didn't know how to answer that, so instead I just wrote:

Barnaby Rudge: What about you? Did you have a good night?

Joey didn't reply for ages. I was just about to message her again when she suddenly said:

Joey: It was…a night. Listen, Imms, I think I'm gonna go.

Barnaby Rudge: Oh, okay.

Joey: I thought I'd be fine talking to you, feeling the way I do about you, but I don't think I can.

Barnaby Rudge: Have I done something wrong?

Joey: No.

Barnaby Rudge: Then stay. Please!

Joey: I don't think I want to hear about you going out and copping off with people. It hurts, Imms, you know? I'm jealous. I've tried not to be, but I can't stop it.

I read her message and felt my throat tighten. I wasn't sure what to write, but I knew I'd have to write something soon or she'd be off, and I couldn't risk her disappearing away from me. Before I could type anything out to her, she wrote:

Joey: And I know I said it wouldn't affect our friendship, but I don't know how it can't. I'm always gonna like you, Imms, and knowing you don't feel the same way, well, it's hard, and I don't think I can cope with it anymore.

Barnaby Rudge: Wait, Joey!

I immediately thought about Willow.

Barnaby Rudge: I thought you'd moved on?

Joey: No. I can't seem to.

Barnaby Rudge: No, I mean, I saw you talking to someone on the board on Friday night and thought you'd moved on.

Joey: Someone on the board? Who?

Barnaby Rudge: Willow.

Joey: Willow? LMAO!!

Barnaby Rudge: It's not funny! LOL.

Joey: I chatted to Willow for a few hours on the board, yeah, but that was all.

Barnaby Rudge: Oh. I kinda thought you and her might
   be…you know?

Joey: Imms, Willow is a guy. A gay guy who lives in
   London with his boyfriend called Jeff.

I put my head in my hands and groaned to myself. I felt soooo
stupid.

I peeked through my fingers at Joey's message and groaned
again, while at the same time fighting the urge to grin. Willow was
a guy?

Barnaby Rudge: Strange name for a guy.

Joey: Something to do with Buffy the Vampire Whatsit. I
   have no idea!

There was a brief silence, then:

Joey: Anyway, why'd you wanna know about Willow?

I took a deep breath. My fingers kept heading towards my
keyboard, then away again.

Joey: Imms?

Barnaby Rudge: Because I was jealous.

Joey: Jealous of Willow??

Barnaby Rudge: Yuh-huh.

Joey: Oh.

Barnaby Rudge: Because I've been thinking about you,
   Joe.

Joey: Me?

Barnaby Rudge: Yuh-huh. You.

Joey: But, but…

Barnaby Rudge: And I did kiss a girl last night, and I know
   you don't wanna hear that, and I'm sorry, but all I've
   been able to think about lately is you.

Joey: Even when you were kissing this girl? LOL.

Barnaby Rudge: Probably, yeah. And I don't know where

it's come from, or how long it's been there, but it's there. Last night just confirmed that to me.

Joey: Maybe it'll pass?

Barnaby Rudge: I don't want it to pass, Joey.

Joey: But…what about all that stuff about me being more like your sister and it'd be too weird, and all that?

Barnaby Rudge: I dunno…I really wish I hadn't said that, 'cos none of this feels weird now. I just realised you were always on my mind, no matter what I was doing, who I was with, or where I was. Every thought I had just came back to you.

Joey: And you're not just saying this because I told you I liked you?

Barnaby Rudge: No, I'm not.

Joey: And you're not just saying this because, I dunno, because of Fickle and you wanna get back at her?

Barnaby Rudge: That doesn't even deserve an answer, Joe! Fickle can't even begin to hold a candle to you— that's bloody clear to me now!

Joey: Wow! That's a really lovely thing to say.

Barnaby Rudge: It's how I feel, Joe. It's kinda crept up me without me even knowing.

Joey: But you do feel something?

Barnaby Rudge: Yeah, I do.

Joey: You'll understand me being a bit cautious here, won't you Imms? I don't really understand how you can think of me as just a friend one minute, then realise you think of me as more.

Barnaby Rudge: I dunno either, but it has.

Joey: OK…

Barnaby Rudge: But, I dunno, the whole night I was there, and with this girl, and all I was just thinking about was you. She said I spent the night talking about you as well.

Joey: LMAO! Bet that was a passion-killer.

Barnaby Rudge: I was talking about you 'cos I couldn't stop thinking about you, and I couldn't stop thinking about you 'cos, well, 'cos I like you. You're really important to me, Joe.

Joey: You're important to me, Imms. You have no idea.

Barnaby Rudge: When I saw your messages to Willow as well, I thought I'd lost you. And that thought scared the hell out of me.

We both paused, evidently taking in everything that had just been written. I suddenly had a thought:

Barnaby Rudge: You do still feel the same way about me, don't you?

Joey: You're kidding me? You're the last thing I think about when I go to sleep and the first thing I think about when I wake up, Imms.

Barnaby Rudge: I'm sorry if I hurt you in the past, Joe.

Joey: You didn't hurt me, chickeroo. Well, not really.

I clenched my jaw tight.

Barnaby Rudge: Well, I'm sorry. I mean it.

Joey: Let's talk about something else, hey? You wanna get together? Meet in town?

Barnaby Rudge: Of course! At least if we meet in the flesh, so to speak, we'll know for sure where this is heading. If it's heading anywhere, I mean.

Joey: I hope it is, Imms…

Barnaby Rudge: Me too, Joe.

Joey: And at least we're only a ten-minute train ride away from each other. Better than that hour and a half you had to do with Fickle, hey?

Barnaby Rudge: Everything's better than Fickle, Joey. Everything!

❖

Joey and I chatted on for the next few hours, making arrangements to meet, discussing what we'd do and where we'd go. I felt so happy I thought I might burst. It was how I felt when me and Fickle first hooked up, but it felt, I dunno, different somehow. Better. There were no nerves with Joey, no feelings of insecurity now that everything was out in the open.

We arranged to meet that coming weekend, with Joey coming to meet me down in town, and then we agreed that I'd get the train over to Abingdon and see her the next time. I loved that we were both looking past our first date, both us of in no doubt that we would get on like a house on fire; confident enough to be already talking about future dates. It made it real, somehow.

We rang each other just before bed and said our good nights to each other, doing that cheesy thing that you see in the movies when neither of you wants to put the phone down first, finally saying a final good night and going. I texted her again just before I went to bed, telling her again not to be paranoid, that I meant every word I said to her, and that I couldn't wait to finally meet her on Saturday. It felt like I'd known Joey all my life; meeting her would now be the icing on the cake.

❖

The next morning, I woke up early and, for the briefest moment, forgot everything that had happened the previous day. When it eventually came back to me, dripping bit by bit through my foggy, sleepy head, I couldn't help but lie in bed, just grinning away to myself. It was Monday. Five days until I'd get to meet Joey.

I practically bounced all the way to college, convinced that everyone who saw me would know why I was so happy. It was like, you know how sometimes you think everyone can tell you're in love just by looking at you? Like you have an aura around you or something—a love aura. They can't, of course, but you're so loved up that you're sure everyone can tell? That was how I felt walking to college that morning.

I went into the canteen as soon as I arrived, getting myself a coffee before heading back up the staircase to the library, where I wanted to quickly grab a book for one of my afternoon lessons. To my dismay, as I turned into the library, I spotted Beth sitting with Matt, the pair of them deep in conversation about something, an array of books spread out around them. I hoped they wouldn't spot me and kinda sidled myself along to one of the other tables further over, but it was too late. With a wave and a loudly hissed "Immeeee!" Beth frantically beckoned me over to her.

I stood at their table, coffee in one hand, files in the other and felt, well, pretty uncomfortable. I smiled tightly at Matt.

"All right?" He jerked his chin.

"Not bad, yeah," I said. "You?"

"Yeah, good," he replied.

So, not too awkward, then!

Beth whispered something to him, briefly kissing him on the cheek, and rose from her table, linking her arm with mine and taking me over to another table where she sat down and nodded her head towards the chair opposite me, indicating I was to sit down too.

"I didn't want to talk in front of Matt," she said by way of explanation.

"About?" I asked, raising my eyebrows.

"You know what about!" Beth grinned. "About Saturday! About you and that girl!"

"Oh, Nic, you mean?" I said, looking at Beth with amusement.

"Well, who else, silly?" Beth pulled a face.

I sipped at my coffee and looked at Beth, who was practically wriggling in her seat with excitement.

"So?" she asked. "Did you call her?"

"Why are you so interested?" I licked my spoon.

"Because you're my friend!" Beth looked hurt. "And I'm excited for you!"

"You were never this excited when I started going out with Matt," I said, raising my eyebrow at her.

"That was different!" Beth hissed.

"How?" I was being obtuse, I knew. I didn't care; it was fun for now.

"Oh, shut up." Beth waved a dismissive hand. "So? Did you call her? You're looking coy, so something must have happened."

"I'm not looking coy!" I laughed. "I'm just drinking my bloody coffee!"

I looked at her mischievously over my cup.

"Come on, spill!" Beth made a show of looking at her watch. "I don't have all day here, you know."

"Well, I didn't call her," I said. "That's the first thing."

Beth sat back in her chair, looking like I'd just slapped her.

"You didn't call her?" she said. "Why not?"

"Because I didn't want to!" I said.

"I thought you were well into her?" Beth asked. "Sure looked like it from where me and Em were sitting."

"She was nice, yeah," I said. "But then I realised I was more into someone else."

"Not this Gemma girl?" Beth grimaced. "I thought you were over her?"

"I am," I said. "No, not Gemma. Someone else."

Beth waved her hand as if to prompt me.

"Joey," I said, simply.

"Joey?" Beth raised an eyebrow. "Joey's a girl, right?"

I rolled my eyes at Beth.

"Yes, Joey's a girl!"

"Consistency. I like it."

"So, anyway, we're gonna meet up this Saturday," I carried on, "And I have a feeling it's gonna go really well."

"Well, I'm really happy for you," Beth said, reaching over and rubbing my hands excitedly.

"Thanks. I'm really happy for me too."

"I'm chuffed that you finally know exactly who you are and what you want," Beth went on. "Not having to live life pretending to be someone you're not, being unhappy and confused."

"It's been tough, I won't lie," I said. "And there have been times when I've thought I was going mad, but I think," I touched the wood of the table, "I think I've come out of it the other end okay, you know?"

I thought for a second and laughed.

"Ha, ha! Come out. No pun intended."

"And Matt seems to have as well," Beth said, turning to look back over towards Matt, his head bowed over a book, furiously scribbling something down.

"He's probably writing a song when he should be doing college work." I followed Beth's gaze.

"Probably." Beth rolled her eyes.

"And now, it feels like the missing piece of the jigsaw is waiting to meet me on Saturday," I said, thinking about Joey. "Then I'll be complete."

CHAPTER TWENTY-FOUR

The rest of that week absolutely limped by, each day just making Saturday feel further away rather than nearer. Joey and I had texted each other and spoken on the phone every single day, talking about everything we'd spoken about on our confessions night, talking about where to meet, and what time, both of us practically giddy with excitement about meeting up that weekend.

But Saturday did actually finally arrive. There had been times when I'd seriously thought we'd never get there, but now here I was, wide awake with butterflies inside me, butterflies that didn't want to go away even when I pulled back the curtains to be greeted by a grey, damp, miserable day. Nothing, not even a bit of rain, was going to spoil my day. I was sure of it. I sent Joey a text, making some joke about her not being able to recognise me because I'd be covered up from head to foot in rain gear, and grinned happily when she sent me one back saying she'd just be wearing galoshes and a smile.

I just about managed to eat some breakfast, but my nerves were by now starting to kick in, nerves which I knew were ridiculous and would probably disappear the second I saw her. I sat at the kitchen table, lost in my own thoughts, wondering what she'd be wearing, what the first thing she'd say to me would be, and jumped, startled, when my phone suddenly rang. It was Joey.

I watched her name flashing on and off, a sudden, horrible thought that she'd had second thoughts briefly entering my head then leaving it again just as quickly, then kinda nervously answered the phone.

"Anything wrong?" I asked, sounding more startled than I probably should have done.

"I'm fine." Joey's familiar, soft voice sounded at the other end. "Are you up?"

"Yeah, course!" I got up and closed the kitchen door so that Mum and Dad, in the lounge watching some Saturday-morning live cookery show, couldn't hear me.

"I wanna come over and see you now," Joey said excitedly. "I know we said eleven-ish but I can't wait till then. Can I come now? I'm pacing the house, dying to see you."

I laughed, her infectious enthusiasm making me feel happy. I looked at my watch: 9.35.

"You sound like a kid at Christmas," I said, lowering my voice.

"I feel like it!" Joey breathed. "So can I? There's a train at nine fifty, gets me to you just gone ten."

I looked at my watch again. Twenty-five minutes. Twenty-five minutes to get dressed, look half-decent, and get myself into town for ten a.m. Could I do it?

For Joey, I'd do it.

"Sounds good to me," I said, getting up from the table and heading back upstairs. "I'll see you at the station in half an hour."

We said our hasty good-byes as I flung my wardrobe doors open, chucking various items of clothing onto the bed, rifling through tops and jeans that I thought would be suitable. I opted for this neat sorta patterned tunic-type top that I'd hardly worn before and a pair of black skinny jeans that I paired up with my tidiest Airwalks. After quickly putting a bit of makeup on to brighten up my face, I cleaned my teeth, flung on a jacket, wrapped a multicoloured silk scarf round my neck, grabbed my bag and, hollering a good-bye to anyone within earshot, left the house, practically running down to the railway station.

The train had arrived by the time I got down there. I yanked the entrance door to the station open and practically fell in through it, gasping for breath from my route-march down the hill to the station, and that's when I saw her. She was sitting on a bench by the ticket machine, long legs stretched out in front of her, hands stuffed deep inside her jacket, watching in amusement as I stumbled into the station foyer, probably looking a bit like I'd been dragged through a hedge backwards.

"Now that's what I call making an entrance," she said, getting to her feet and walking towards me, wrapping her arms tight around me when we finally reached each other.

I hugged her back, any feelings of anxiety or apprehension I may have had rapidly disappearing as I felt her warm, soft body against mine.

"Good job you recognised me," I whispered into her hair, "or else you'd be hugging a very frightened stranger!"

Joey pulled away and gazed at me.

"I knew it was you the second you came in—sorry, fell in—here," she said.

She looked at me, suddenly serious.

"And I've imagined your face from your photos and all our Skype convos over the last few weeks enough times to be able to recognise you too," she added, lowering her voice.

I smiled nervously, taking in every tiny detail of her face. She was taller than I imagined she'd be—a good couple of inches taller than me—and thinner than her photos or Skype had ever indicated to me.

"I like your Vans," I said, nodding in approval down at her feet.

"I like your Airwalks," Joey countered, looping her arm in mine and making for the exit. "We have good taste, huh? Now, where are you taking me, missy?"

We headed for a neat little café I knew, just off the main shopping centre, down one of the little side streets that Oxford has, and managed to dive inside just as the heavens opened and the rain came teeming down. As Joey went to the counter to buy us a cappuccino each, I sat myself down in the corner of the café and watched her.

I'd seen her face so many times before this, but in the flesh she was a hundred times more stunning than her photos and the webcam had ever hinted. I couldn't take my eyes off her as I watched her order us our coffees, then saunter back over to our table, a lazy grin on her face.

"What're you looking at?" She laughed as she sat down opposite me, handing me my cappuccino.

"You," I said quietly, looking down to the table, suddenly embarrassed.

She looked at me carefully as she drank her cappuccino.

"You have lovely eyes," she said, still watching me. "You don't see how nice they are on the computer!"

I picked up my cappuccino.

"I was thinking the same thing about you," I said. "I mean, that you're far lovelier in the flesh than you are on the webcam…" I suddenly stopped myself.

"Thanks!" Joey laughed. "I think."

"You know what I mean," I mumbled sheepishly, playfully flicking my hand towards her arm.

"I do, yeah." Joey's face flushed slightly and I felt my tummy flip over. I liked the feeling of butterflies fluttering again inside me, and this time I particularly loved that it was Joey making them do it.

We talked solidly for over an hour, just in that one café, buying another coffee each, listening to the rain pouring down outside, neither of us wanting to leave the safe, warm, and more importantly, dry café. We talked about everything: the message board, the people on it, Joey's course at college, my course at college, our families and friends. We even briefly talked about Fickle and Claire, but only for the briefest of moments. This wasn't a time to talk about exes.

I looked out of the café window.

"Rain's stopped," I said. "Wanna go somewhere quieter?"

"You betcha!"

Joey drained her coffee and got to her feet, waiting for me to do the same. We walked through town a while, stopping occasionally to look in shop windows, but mainly just chatting and joking with each other, happy in one another's company. We headed up to a park at the far end of the town centre and perched on the edge of a soggy, graffiti-covered bench, to eat the sandwiches we'd hastily bought in a busy Subway on the way up. The rain had eased at long last, allowing the sunshine to finally break through.

"I don't want today to end," Joey said, chucking her bread crusts down onto the grass for the scrawny park pigeons to come and peck.

"Me neither," I said, watching as the pigeons hopped over towards us to gobble up the crumbs. "I wish we could stay here forever."

I looked at her and felt like I'd gone full circle, like everything that had happened over the last few months had been for a reason. We sat in the sunshine together, feeding the birds our scraps and laughing at the silliness of them, both of us just happy and comfortable in one another's company. Our first date was everything I'd hoped it would be—and more. I felt so at ease in her company, as I instinctively knew I would. There were no awkward silences, no moments of self-consciousness, no hints of shyness; there was just ease and this wonderful sense of us each feeling complete.

"You have no idea how nuts I am about you, Imms," Joey sighed, squinting up into the late afternoon sunshine. "No idea. One day you were just this Barnaby Rudge person on my MSN, okay for a laugh and a joke with, and then the next day…POW…you were Imogen Summers, and I knew I'd fallen head over heels for you."

"You do believe me now when I tell you I feel exactly the same, don't you?" I asked Joey earnestly.

"I think so," she started.

Instinctively, I reached out and took her hands, suddenly wanting to feel her skin on mine, loving the feeling of her hands, so warm and soft and comfortable in mine.

Kinda like they belonged there, you know?

"You should," I said, gazing over at her. "I can't believe I could so easily have let you go. The perfect girl was right there under my nose all the time and I just couldn't see it." I shook my head. "I'm such a dumbass sometimes…"

"Well, I'm not going anywhere." Joey grinned, playfully bumping her shoulder against mine. "Even if you are a dumbass!"

"You know, it's almost like we were both meant to go through all that shit, you with Claire and me with Fickle," I said, stroking the palm of her hand with my thumb, "just so that we could get to this point. It's kinda like we were meant for each other. Does that make sense?"

"I think so," Joey said, reaching down to tighten one of her trainer laces. She stared at her feet. "I s'pose it's like, I dunno, always thinking you never found shoes comfortable and assuming it was 'cos you've got funny feet, and that's why the shoes aren't comfortable, you know? And then you find a pair of shoes that feel comfortable and nice, and that fit exactly as they should do, and you realise that it hasn't been your funny feet, it's been the wrong shoes all along."

"You're saying I'm like a pair of shoes?" I looked at her and laughed. "You better mean really *hot* shoes!"

"I'm saying you feel comfortable to me, like you belong with me." Joey looked back at me. "You mean everything to me, Imms."

"And you mean the world to me too, Joe," I said. "It just took a while for me to realise it."

We sat there on that park bench for pretty much the rest of the afternoon, our hands entwined, just lost in each other, each occasionally looking at the other, kinda like we wanted to take in every last detail, knowing that it would be another week until we could see each other again. When it was finally time for Joey to catch her train back home, neither of us could bear to part.

We walked back to the station together, both of us lost in our own thoughts, and headed up to the platform. Her train was on time, much to my annoyance, a part of me desperately hoping it would be delayed so that I could spend a few precious extra moments with her.

"You'll come over to me next week, won't you?" Joey asked earnestly.

I paused.

"I could come over tomorrow?" I said in a rush, then added, "I mean, if you want?"

Joey wrapped her arms round herself. "I want, Imms," she said. "Very much."

"We can talk about it on MSN later."

Joey glanced over her shoulder as we heard the rumble of her train approaching. "I don't want to go," she said, her face beginning to crumple.

"I know," I said, just as the train pulled into the station with a shrill whistle of brakes.

We stood waiting and looking at each other a while longer as the train doors opened with a clatter and passengers got on and off, both of us desperate to hold on until the very last moment. When the train finally looked like it was ready to leave again, Joey leaned in and briefly kissed my cheek.

"You're everything to me, Imms," she whispered into my hair.

"And you to me too," I whispered back.

"No one else matters, you know." Joey linked her fingers briefly in mine and turned to go. "No one."

She started to disappear into the throng of people on the train, then turned back and looked at me, a wide grin on her face. "From now on, kiddo, it's just me and you."

About the Author

KE Payne was born in Bath, the English city, not the tub, and after leaving school she worked for the British government for fifteen years, which probably sounds a lot more exciting than it really was.

Fed up with spending her days moving paperwork around her desk and making models of the Taj Mahal out of paperclips, she packed it all in to go to university in Bristol and graduated as a mature student in 2006 with a degree in linguistics and history.

After graduating, she worked at a university in the Midlands for a while, again moving all that paperwork around, before finally leaving to embark on her dream career as a writer.

She moved to the idyllic English countryside in 2007 where she now lives and works happily surrounded by dogs and guinea pigs.

Soliloquy Titles From Bold Strokes Books

me@you.com by KE Payne. Is it possible to fall in love with someone you've never met? Imogen Summers thinks so because it's happened to her. (978-1-60282-592-5)

Swimming to Chicago by David-Matthew Barnes. As the lives of the adults around them unravel, high school students Alex and Robby form an unbreakable bond, vowing to do anything to stay together—even if it means leaving everything behind. (978-1-60282-572-7)

Speaking Out edited by Steve Berman. Inspiring stories written for and about LGBT and Q teens of overcoming adversity (against intolerance and homophobia) and experiencing life after "coming out." (978-1-60282-566-6)

365 Days by K.E. Payne. Life sucks when you're seventeen years old and confused about your sexuality, and the girl of your dreams doesn't even know you exist. Then in walks sexy new emo girl, Hannah Harrison. Clemmie Atkins has exactly 365 days to discover herself, and she's going to have a blast doing it! (978-1-60282-540-6)

Cursebusters! by Julie Smith. Budding-psychic Reeno is the most accomplished teenage burglar in California, but one tiny screw-up and poof!—she's sentenced to Bad Girl School. And that isn't even her worst problem. Her sister Haley's dying of an illness no one can diagnose, and now she can't even help. (978-1-60282-559-8)

Who I Am by M.L. Rice. Devin Kelly's senior year is a disaster. She's in a new school in a new town, and the school bully is making her life miserable—but then she meets his sister Melanie and realizes her feelings for her are more than platonic. (978-1-60282-231-3)

Sleeping Angel by Greg Herren. Eric Matthews survives a terrible car accident only to find out everyone in town thinks he's a murderer—and he has to clear his name even though he has no memories of what happened. (978-1-60282-214-6)

Mesmerized by David-Matthew Barnes. Through her close friendship with Brodie and Lance, Serena Albright learns about the many forms of love and finds comfort for the grief and guilt she feels over the brutal death of her older brother, the victim of a hate crime. (978-1-60282-191-0)

The Perfect Family by Kathryn Shay. A mother and her gay son stand hand in hand as the storms of change engulf their perfect family and the life they knew. (978-1-60282-181-1)

Father Knows Best by Lynda Sandoval. High school juniors and best friends Lila Moreno, Meryl Morganstern, and Caressa Thibodoux plan to make the most of the summer before senior year. What they discover that amazing summer about girl power, growing up, and trusting friends and family more than prepares them to tackle that all-important senior year! (978-1-60282-147-7)